太平記英勇傳

根來小水茶

紀伊國海部郡根來寺の僧なり意和山の樵篭ともいふ徒らふ怪力ありて長さ二丈八角に削へる鐵る棒を得り物とし群敵を打挫ぐさる漢土の呂布和朝義秀の有様と少しも更ふ佐藤家の勇臣志村政蔵稲上九郎おと根討の中に取筆篭息をもつつ戦ふに政蔵を馬より落いざ討と政蔵志村を小水茶馬上ふくとしける入刃ふ志村を小水茶れて落んとかるを政蔵手早く引上り

お前ふ見がど春永家の隊將ね毎度其動を心敵と打挫ぐさる漢土の呂布和朝義秀の有様と

無雙力政蔵が為ふ討死うさ—グ
無雙力小水茶れと競ふ
の馬の
無双の勇士

一勇齋

一家暑傳史
柳下亭種員記

TALES OF THE
SAMURAI

ILLUSTRATED EDITION

TALES OF THE
SAMURAI

A.B. MITFORD

FALL RIVER PRESS

FALL RIVER PRESS

New York

An Imprint of Sterling Publishing Co., Inc.
1166 Avenue of the Americas
New York, NY 10036

Originally published in 1871 as *Tales of Old Japan*

ISBN 978-1-4351-6678-3

Distributed in Canada by Sterling Publishing Co., Inc.
c/o Canadian Manda Group, 664 Annette Street
Toronto, Ontario M6S 2C8, Canada
Distributed in the United Kingdom by
GMC Distribution Services
Castle Place, 166 High Street, Lewes,
East Sussex BN7 1XU, England
Distributed in Australia by NewSouth Books
45 Beach Street, Coogee NSW 2034, Australia

For information about custom editions, special sales, and premium and corporate purchases, please contact Sterling Special Sales at 800-805-5489 or specialsales@sterlingpublishing.com.

Manufactured in China

4 6 8 10 9 7 5 3

sterlingpublishing.com

Book design by Scott Russo
Cover design by Scott Russo and David Ter-Avanesyan

Cover(Jacket) Illustration(s): Samurai illustrations courtesy Dover Publications, wooden sign © flas100/depositphotos.com, blood by nicemonkey/Shutterstock.com

Endpaper Illustration(s): courtesy Dover Publications

CONTENTS

Preface

n the Introduction to the story of the Forty-seven Rōnin, I have said almost as much as is needful by way of preface to my stories.

Those of my readers who are most capable of pointing out the many shortcomings and faults of my work, will also be the most indulgent towards me; for any one who has been in Japan, and studied Japanese, knows the great difficulties by which the learner is beset.

For the illustrations, at least, I feel that I need make no apology. Drawn, in the first instance, by one Ōdaké, an artist in my employ, they were cut on wood by a famous wood-engraver at Yedo, and are therefore genuine specimens of Japanese art. Messrs Dalziel, on examining the wood blocks, pointed out to me, as an interesting fact, that the lines are cut with the grain of the wood, after the manner of Albert Dürer and some of the old German masters—a process which has been abandoned by modern European wood-engravers.

It will be noticed that very little allusion is made in these Tales to the Emperor and his Court. Although I searched diligently, I was able to find no story in which they played a conspicuous part.

Another class to which no allusion is made is that of the Gōshi. The Gōshi are a kind of yeomen, or bonnet-lairds, as they would be called over the border, living on their own land, and owning no allegiance to any feudal lord. Their rank is inferior to that of the Samurai, or men of the military class, between whom and the peasantry they hold a middle place. Like the Samurai, they wear two swords, and are in many cases prosperous and wealthy men claiming a descent more ancient than that of many of the feudal Princes. A large number of them are enrolled among the Emperor's bodyguard;

and these have played a conspicuous part in the recent political changes in Japan, as the most conservative and anti-foreign element in the nation.

With these exceptions, I think that all classes are fairly represented in my stories.

The feudal system has passed away like a dissolving view before the eyes of those who have lived in Japan during the last few years. But when they arrived there it was in full force, and there is not an incident narrated in the following pages, however strange it may appear to Europeans, for the possibility and probability of which those most competent to judge will not vouch. Nor, as many a recent event can prove, have heroism, chivalry, and devotion gone out of the land altogether. We may deplore and inveigh against the Yamato Damashi, or Spirit of Old Japan, which still breathes in the soul of the Samurai, but we cannot withhold our admiration from the self-sacrifices which men will still make for the love of their country.

The first two of the Tales have already appeared in the *Fortnightly Review*, and two of the sermons, with a portion of the appendix on the subject of the *hara-kiri*, in the pages of the *Cornhill Magazine*. I have to thank the editors of those periodicals for permission to reprint them here.

LONDON
7 January 1871

The 47 Rōnin

The books which have been written of late years about Japan, have either been compiled from official records, or have contained the sketchy impressions of passing travellers. Of the inner life of the Japanese, the world at large knows but little: their religion, their superstitions, their ways of thought, the hidden springs by which they move—all these are as yet mysteries. Nor is this to be wondered at. The first Western men who came in contact with Japan—I am speaking not of the old Dutch and Portuguese traders and priests, but of the diplomatists and merchants of eleven years ago—met with a cold reception. Above all things, the native Government threw obstacles in the way of any inquiry into their language, literature, and history. The fact was that the Tycoon's Government—with whom alone, so long as the Mikado remained in seclusion in his sacred capital at Kioto, any relations were maintained—knew that the Imperial purple with which they sought to invest their chief must quickly fade before the strong sunlight which would be brought upon it so soon as there should be European linguists capable of examining their books and records. No opportunity was lost of throwing dust in the eyes of the new-comers, whom, even in the most trifling details, it was the official policy to lead astray. Now, however, there is no cause for concealment; the *Roi Fainéant* has shaken off his sloth, and his *Maire du Palais*, together, and an intelligible Government, which need not fear scrutiny from abroad, is the result: the records of the country being but so many proofs of the Mikado's title to power, there is no reason for keeping up any show of mystery. The path of inquiry is open to all; and although there is yet much to be learnt, some knowledge has been attained, in which it may interest those who stay at home to share.

The recent revolution in Japan has wrought changes social as well as political; and it may be that when, in addition to the advance which has already been made, railways and telegraphs shall have connected the principal points of the Land of Sunrise, the old Japanese, such as he was and had been for centuries when we found him eleven short years ago, will have become extinct. It has appeared to me that no better means could be chosen of preserving a record of a curious and fast disappearing civilisation, than the translation of some of the most interesting national legends and histories, together with other specimens of literature bearing upon the same subject. Thus the Japanese may tell their own tale, their translator only adding here and there a few words of heading or tag to a chapter, where an explanation or amplification may seem necessary. I fear that the long and hard names will often make my tales tedious reading, but I believe that those who will bear with the difficulty will learn more of the character of the Japanese people than by skimming over descriptions of travel and adventure, however brilliant. The lord and his retainer, the warrior and the priest, the humble artisan and the despised Eta or pariah, each in his turn will become a leading character in my budget of stories; and it is out of the mouths of these personages that I hope to show forth a tolerably complete picture of Japanese society.

Having said so much by way of preface, I beg my readers to fancy themselves wafted away to the shores of the Bay of Yedo—a fair, smiling landscape: gentle slopes, crested by a dark fringe of pines and firs, lead down to the sea; the quaint eaves of many a temple and holy shrine peep out here and there from the groves; the bay itself is studded with picturesque fisher-craft, the torches of which shine by night like glow-worms among the outlying forts; far away to the west loom the goblin-haunted heights of Oyama, and beyond the twin hills of the Hakoné Pass—Fuji-Yama, the Peerless Mountain, solitary and grand, stands in the centre of the plain, from which it sprang vomiting flames twenty-one centuries ago.[1] For a hundred and sixty years the huge mountain has been at peace, but the frequent earthquakes still tell of hidden fires, and none can say when the red-hot stones and ashes may once more fall like rain over five provinces.

In the midst of a nest of venerable trees in Takanawa, a suburb of Yedo, is hidden Sengakuji, or the Spring-hill Temple, renowned throughout the length and breadth of the land for its cemetery, which contains the graves of the Forty-seven Rōnins,[2] famous in Japanese history, heroes of Japanese drama, the tale of whose deeds I am about to transcribe.

On the left-hand side of the main court of the temple is a chapel, in which, surmounted by a gilt figure of Kwanyin, the goddess of mercy, are enshrined the images of the forty-seven men, and of the master whom they loved so well. The statues are carved in wood, the faces coloured, and the dresses richly lacquered; as works of art they have great merit—the action of the heroes, each armed with his favourite weapon, being wonderfully life-like and spirited. Some are venerable men, with thin, grey hair (one is seventy-seven years old); others are mere boys of sixteen. Close by the chapel, at the side of a path leading up the hill, is a little well of pure water, fenced in and adorned with a tiny fernery, over which is an inscription, setting forth that 'This is the well in which the head was washed; you must not wash your hands or your feet here.' A little further on is a stall, at which a poor old man earns a pittance by selling books, pictures, and medals, commemorating the loyalty of the Forty-seven; and higher up yet, shaded by a grove of stately trees, is a neat inclosure, kept up, as a signboard announces, by voluntary contributions, round which are ranged forty-eight little tombstones, each decked with evergreens, each with its tribute of water and incense for the comfort of the departed spirit. There were forty-seven Rōnin; there are forty-eight tombstones, and the story of the forty-eighth is truly characteristic of Japanese ideas of honour. Almost touching the rail of the graveyard is a more imposing monument under which lies buried the lord, whose death his followers piously avenged.

And now for the story.

At the beginning of the eighteenth century there lived a daimio, called Asano Takumi no Kami, the Lord of the castle of Akō, in the province of Harima. Now it happened that an Imperial ambassador from the Court of the Mikado having been sent to the Shogun³ at Yedo, Takumi no Kami and another noble called Kamei Sama were appointed to receive and feast the envoy; and a high official, named Kira Kōtsuké no Suké, was named to teach them the proper ceremonies to be observed upon the occasion. The two nobles were accordingly forced to go daily to the castle to listen to the instructions of Kōtsuké no Suké. But this Kōtsuké no Suké was a man greedy of money; and as he deemed that the presents which the two daimios, according to time-honoured custom, had brought him in return for his instruction, were mean and unworthy, he conceived a great hatred against them, and took no pains in teaching them, but on the contrary rather sought to make laughing-stocks of them. Takumi no Kami, restrained by a stern sense of duty, bore his insults with patience; but Kamei Sama, who had less control over his temper, was violently incensed, and determined to kill Kōtsuké no Suké.

One night when his duties at the castle were ended, Kamei Sama returned to his own palace, and having summoned his councillors[4] to a secret conference, said to them: 'Kōtsuké no Suké has insulted Takumi no Kami and myself during our service in attendance on the Imperial envoy. This is against all decency, and I was minded to kill him on the spot; but I bethought me that if I did such a deed within the precincts of the castle, not only would my own life be forfeit, but my family and vassals would be ruined: so I stayed my hand. Still the life of such a wretch is a sorrow to the people, and tomorrow when I go to Court I will slay him: my mind is made up, and I will listen to no remonstrance.' And as he spoke his face became livid with rage.

Now one of Kamei Sama's councillors was a man of great judgment, and when he saw from his lord's manner that remonstrance would be useless, he said: 'Your lordship's words are law; your servant will make all preparations accordingly; and tomorrow, when your lordship goes to Court, if this Kōtsuké no Suké should again be insolent, let him die the death.' And his lord was pleased at this speech, and waited with impatience for the day to break, that he might return to Court and kill his enemy.

The well in which the head was washed
....

But the councillor went home, and was sorely troubled, and thought anxiously about what his prince had said. And as he reflected, it occurred to him that since Kōtsuké no Suké had the reputation of being a miser he would certainly be open to a bribe, and that it was better to pay any sum, no matter how great, than that his lord and his house should be ruined. So he collected all the money he could, and, giving it to his servants to carry, rode off in the night to Kōtsuké no Suké's palace, and said to his retainers: 'My master, who is now in attendance upon the Imperial envoy, owes much thanks to my Lord Kōtsuké no Suké, who has been at so great pains to teach him the proper ceremonies to be observed during the reception of the Imperial envoy. This is but a shabby present which he has sent by me, but he hopes that his lordship will condescend to accept it, and commends himself to his lord-ship's favour.' And, with these words, he produced a thousand ounces of silver for Kōtsuké no Suké, and a hundred ounces to be distributed among his retainers.

When the latter saw the money, their eyes sparkled with pleasure, and they were profuse in their thanks; and begging the councillor to wait a little, they went and told their master of the lordly present which had arrived with a polite message from Kamei Sama. Kōtsuké no Suké in eager delight sent for the councillor into an inner chamber, and, after thanking him, promised on the morrow to instruct his master carefully in all the different points of etiquette. So the councillor, seeing the miser's glee, rejoiced at the success of his plan; and having taken his leave returned home in high spirits. But Kamei Sama, little thinking how his vassal had propitiated his enemy, lay brooding over his vengeance, and on the following morning at daybreak went to Court in solemn procession.

When Kōtsuké no Suké met him, his manner had completely changed, and nothing could exceed his courtesy. 'You have come early to Court this morning, my Lord Kamei,' said he. 'I cannot sufficiently admire your zeal. I shall have the honour to call your attention to several points of etiquette today. I must beg your lordship to excuse my previous conduct, which must have seemed very rude; but I am naturally of a cross-grained disposition, so I pray you to forgive me.' And as he kept on humbling himself and making fair speeches, the heart of Kamei Sama was gradually softened, and he renounced his intention of killing him. Thus by the cleverness of his councillor was Kamei Sama, with all his house, saved from ruin.

Shortly after this, Takumi no Kami, who had sent no present, arrived at the castle, and Kōtsuké no Suké turned him into ridicule even more than before, provoking him with sneers and covert insults; but Takumi no Kami affected to ignore all this, and submitted himself patiently to Kōtsuké no Suké's orders.

This conduct, so far from producing a good effect, only made Kōtsuké no Suké despise him the more, until at last he said hastily: 'Here, my Lord of Takumi, the ribbon of my sock has come untied; be so good as to tie it up for me.'

Takumi no Kami, although burning with rage at the affront, still thought that as he was on duty he was bound to obey, and tied up the ribbon of the sock. Then Kōtsuké no Suké, turning from him, petulantly exclaimed: 'Why, how clumsy you are! You cannot so much as tie up the ribbon of a sock properly! Any one can see that you are a boor from the country, and know nothing of the manners of Yedo.' And with a scornful laugh he moved towards an inner room.

But the patience of Takumi no Kami was exhausted; this last insult was more than he could bear.

'Stop a moment, my lord,' cried he.

'Well, what is it?' replied the other. And, as he turned round, Takumi no Kami drew his dirk, and aimed a blow at his head; but Kōtsuké no Suké, being protected by the Court cap which he wore, the wound was but a scratch, so he ran away; and Takumi no Kami, pursuing him, tried a second time to cut him down, but, missing his aim, struck his dirk into a pillar. At this moment an officer, named Kajikawa Yosobei, seeing the affray, rushed up, and holding back the infuriated noble, gave Kōtsuké no Suké time to make good his escape.

Then there arose a great uproar and confusion, and Takumi no Kami was arrested and disarmed, and confined in one of the apartments of the palace under the care of the censors. A council was held, and the prisoner was given over to the safeguard of a daimio, called Tamura Ukiyō no Daibu, who kept him in close custody in his own house, to the great grief of his wife and of his retainers; and when the deliberations of the council were completed, it was decided that, as he had committed an outrage and attacked another man within the precincts of the palace, he must perform *hara-kiri*—that is, commit suicide by disembowelling; his goods must be confiscated, and his family ruined. Such was the law. So Takumi no Kami performed *hara-kiri*, his castle of Akō was confiscated, and his retainers having become Rōnins, some of them took service with other daimios, and others became merchants.

Now amongst these retainers was his principal councillor, a man called Oishi Kuranosuké, who, with forty-six other faithful dependants, formed a league to avenge their master's death by killing Kōtsuké no Suké. This Oishi Kuranosuké was absent at the castle of Ako at the time of the affray, which, had he been with his prince, would never have occurred; for, being a wise man, he would not have failed to propitiate Kōtsuké no Suké by sending him suitable presents; while the councillor who was in attendance on the prince at Yedo was a dullard, who neglected this precaution, and so caused the death of his master and the ruin of his house.

So Oishi Kuranosuké and his forty-six companions began to lay their plans of vengeance against Kōtsuké no Suké; but the latter was so well guarded by a body of men lent to him by a daimio called Uyésugi Sama, whose daughter he had married, that they saw that the only way of attaining their end would be to throw their enemy off his guard. With this object they separated and disguised themselves, some as carpenters or craftsmen, others as merchants; and their chief, Kuranosuké, went to Kiōto, and built a house in the quarter called Yamashina, where he took to frequenting

houses of the worst repute, and gave himself up to drunkenness and debauchery, as if nothing were further from his mind than revenge. Kōtsuké no Suké, in the meanwhile, suspecting that Takumi no Kami's former retainers would be scheming against his life, secretly sent spies to Kiōto, and caused a faithful account to be kept of all that Kuranosuké did. The latter, however, determined thoroughly to delude the enemy into a false security, went on leading a dissolute life with harlots and winebibbers. One day, as he was returning home drunk from some low haunt, he fell down in the street and went to sleep, and all the passers-by laughed him to scorn. It happened that a Satsuma man saw this, and said: 'Is not this Oishi Kuranosuké, who was a councillor of Asano Takumi no Kami, and who, not having the heart to avenge his lord, gives himself up to women and wine? See how he lies drunk in the public street! Faithless beast! Fool and craven! Unworthy the name of a Samurai!'[5]

The Satsuma man insults Oishi Kuranosuké

And he trod on Kuranosuké's face as he slept, and spat upon him; but when Kōtsuké no Suké's spies reported all this at Yedo, he was greatly relieved at the news, and felt secure from danger.

One day Kuranosuké's wife, who was bitterly grieved to see her husband lead this abandoned life, went to him and said: 'My lord, you told me at first that your debauchery was but a trick to make your enemy relax in watchfulness. But indeed, indeed, this has gone too far. I pray and beseech you to put some restraint upon yourself.'

'Trouble me not,' replied Kuranosuké, 'for I will not listen to your whining. Since my way of life is displeasing to you, I will divorce you, and you may go about your business; and I will buy some pretty young girl from one of the public-houses, and marry her for my pleasure. I am sick of the sight of an old woman like you about the house, so get you gone—the sooner the better.'

So saying, he flew into a violent rage, and his wife, terror-stricken, pleaded piteously for mercy.

'Oh, my lord! unsay those terrible words! I have been your faithful wife for twenty years, and have borne you three children; in sickness and in sorrow I have been with you; you cannot be so cruel as to turn me out of doors now. Have pity! have pity!'

'Cease this useless wailing. My mind is made up, and you must go; and as the children are in my way also, you are welcome to take them with you.'

When she heard her husband speak thus, in her grief she sought her eldest son, Oishi Chikara, and begged him to plead for her, and pray that she might be pardoned. But nothing would turn Kuranosuké from his purpose, so his wife was sent away, with the two younger children, and went back to her native place. But Oishi Chikara remained with his father.

The spies communicated all this without fail to Kōtsuké no Suké, and he, when he heard how Kuranosuké, having turned his wife and children out of doors and bought a concubine, was grovelling in a life of drunkenness and lust, began to think that he had no longer anything to fear from the retainers of Takumi no Kami, who must be cowards, without the courage to avenge their lord. So by degrees he began to keep a less strict watch, and sent back half of the guard which had been lent to him by his father-in-law, Uyésugi Sama. Little did he think how he was falling into the trap laid for him by Kuranosuké, who, in his zeal to slay his lord's enemy, thought nothing of divorcing his wife and sending away his children! Admirable and faithful man!

In this way Kuranosuké continued to throw dust in the eyes of his foe, by persisting in his apparently shameless conduct; but his associates all went to Yedo, and, having in their several capacities as workmen and pedlars contrived to gain access to Kōtsuké no Suké's house, made themselves familiar with the plan of the building and the arrangement of the different rooms, and ascertained the character of the inmates, who were brave and loyal men, and who were cowards; upon all of which matters they sent regular reports to Kuranosuké. And when at last it became evident from the letters which arrived from Yedo that Kōtsuké no Suké was thoroughly off his guard, Kuranosuké rejoiced that the day of vengeance was at hand; and, having appointed a trysting-place at Yedo, he fled secretly from Kiōto, eluding the vigilance of his enemy's spies. Then the forty-seven men, having laid all their plans, bided their time patiently.

It was now mid-winter, the twelfth month of the year, and the cold was bitter. One night, during a heavy fall of snow, when the whole world was hushed, and peaceful men were stretched in sleep upon the mats, the Rōnins determined that no more favourable opportunity could occur for carrying out their purpose. So they took counsel together, and, having divided their band into two parties, assigned to each man his post. One band, led by Oishi Kuranosuké, was to attack the front gate, and the other, under his son Oishi Chikara, was to attack the postern of Kōtsuké no Suké's house; but as Chikara was only sixteen years of age, Yoshida Chiuzayémon was appointed to act as his guardian. Further it was arranged that a drum, beaten at the order of Kuranosuké, should be the signal for the simultaneous attack; and that if any one slew Kōtsuké no Suké and cut off his head he should blow a shrill whistle, as a signal to his comrades, who would hurry to the spot, and, having identified the head, carry it off to the temple called Sengakuji, and lay it as an offering before the tomb of their dead lord. Then they must report their deed to the Government, and await the sentence of death which would surely be passed upon them. To this the Rōnins one and all pledged themselves. Midnight was fixed upon as the hour, and the forty-seven comrades, having made all ready for the attack, partook of a last farewell feast together, for on the morrow they must die. Then Oishi Kuranosuké addressed the band, and said:

'Tonight we shall attack our enemy in his palace; his retainers will certainly resist us, and we shall be obliged to kill them. But to slay old men and women and children is a pitiful thing; therefore, I pray you each one to take great heed lest you kill a single helpless person.' His comrades all applauded this speech, and so they remained, waiting for the hour of midnight to arrive.

When the appointed hour came, the Rōnins set forth. The wind howled furiously, and the driving snow beat in their faces; but little cared they for wind or snow as they hurried on their road, eager for revenge. At last they reached Kōtsuké no Suké's house, and divided themselves into two bands; and Chikara, with twenty-three men, went round to the back gate. Then four men, by means of a ladder of ropes which they hung on to the roof of the porch, effected an entry into the court-yard; and, as they saw signs that all the inmates of the house were asleep, they went into the porter's lodge where the guard slept, and, before the latter had time to recover from their astonishment, bound them. The terrified guard prayed hard for mercy, that their lives might be spared; and to this the Rōnins agreed on condition that the keys of the gate should be given up; but the others tremblingly said that the keys were kept in the house of one of their officers, and that they had no means of obtaining them. Then the Rōnins lost patience, and with a hammer dashed in pieces the big wooden bolt which secured the gate, and the doors flew open to the right and to the left. At the same time Chikara and his party broke in by the back gate.

Then Oishi Kuranosuké sent a messenger to the neighbouring houses, bearing the following message: 'We, the Rōnins who were formerly in the service of Asano Takumi no Kami, are this night about to break into the palace of Kōtsuké no Suké, to avenge our lord. As we are neither night robbers nor ruffians, no hurt will be done to the neighbouring houses.

We pray you to set your minds at rest.' And as Kōtsuké no Suké was hated by his neighbours for his covetousness, they did not unite their forces to assist him. Another precaution was yet taken. Lest any of the people inside should run out to call the relations of the family to the rescue, and these coming in force should interfere with the plans of the Rōnins, Kuranosuké stationed ten of his men armed with bows on the roof of the four sides of the courtyard, with orders to shoot any retainers who might attempt to leave the place. Having thus laid all his plans and posted his men, Kuranosuké with his own hand beat the drum and gave the signal for attack.

Ten of Kōtsuké no Suké's retainers, hearing the noise, woke up; and, drawing their swords, rushed into the front room to defend their master. At this moment the Rōnins, who had burst open the door of the front hall, entered the same room. Then arose a furious fight between the two parties, in the midst of which Chikara, leading his men through the garden, broke into the back of the house; and Kōtsuké no Suké, in terror of his life, took refuge, with his wife and female servants, in a closet in the verandah; while the rest of his retainers, who slept in the barrack outside the house, made ready to go to the rescue. But the Rōnins who had come in by the front door, and were fighting with the ten retainers, ended by overpowering and slaying the latter without losing one of their own number; after which, forcing their way bravely towards the back rooms, they were joined by Chikara and his men, and the two bands were united in one.

By this time the remainder of Kōtsuké no Suké's men had come in, and the fight became general; and

Kuranosuké, sitting on a camp-stool, gave his orders and directed the Rōnins. Soon the inmates of the house perceived that they were no match for their enemy, so they tried to send out intelligence of their plight to Uyésugi Sama, their lord's father-in-law, begging him to come to the rescue with all the force at his command. But the messengers were shot down by the archers whom Kuranosuké had posted on the roof. So no help coming, they fought on in despair. Then Kuranosuké cried out with a loud voice: 'Kōtsuké no Suké alone is our enemy; let some one go inside and bring him forth dead or alive!'

Now in front of Kōtsuké no Suké's private room stood three brave retainers with drawn swords. The first was Kobayashi Héhachi, the second was Waku Handaiyu, and the third was Shimidzu Ikkaku, all good men and true, and expert swordsmen. So stoutly did these men lay about them that for a while they kept the whole of the Rōnins at bay, and at one moment even forced them back. When Oishi Kuranosuké saw this, he ground his teeth with rage, and shouted to his men: 'What! did not every man of you swear to lay down his life in avenging his lord, and now are you driven back by three men? Cowards, not fit to be spoken to! To die fighting in a master's cause should be the noblest ambition of a retainer!' Then turning to his own son Chikara, he said, 'Here, boy! engage those men, and if they are too strong for you, die!'

Spurred by these words, Chikara seized a spear and gave battle to Waku Handaiyu, but could not hold his ground, and backing by degrees, was driven out into the garden, where he missed his footing and slipped into a pond; but as Handaiyu, thinking to kill him, looked down into the pond, Chikara cut his enemy in the leg and caused him to fall, and then crawling out of the water dispatched him. In the meanwhile Kobayashi Héhachi and Shimidzu Ikkaku had been killed by the other Rōnins, and of all Kōtsuké no Suké's retainers not one fighting man remained. Chikara, seeing this, went with his bloody sword in his hand into a back room to search for Kōtsuké no Suké, but he only found the son of the latter, a young lord named Kira Sahioyé, who, carrying a halberd, attacked him, but was soon wounded and fled. Thus the whole of Kōtsuké no Suké's men having been killed, there was an end of the fighting; but as yet there was no trace of Kōtsuké no Suké to be found.

Then Kuranosuké divided his men into several parties and searched the whole house, but all in vain; women and children weeping were alone to be seen. At this the forty-seven men began to lose heart in regret, that after all their toil they had allowed their enemy to escape them, and there was a moment when in their despair they agreed to commit suicide together upon the spot; but they determined to make one more effort. So Kuranosuké went into Kōtsuké no Suké's sleeping-room, and touching the quilt with his hands, exclaimed, 'I have just felt the bed-clothes and they are yet warm, and so methinks that our enemy is not far off. He must certainly be hidden somewhere in the house.' Greatly excited by this, the Rōnins renewed their search. Now in the raised part of the room, near the place of honour, there was a picture hanging; taking down this picture, they saw that there was a large hole in the plastered wall, and on thrusting a spear in they could feel nothing beyond it. So one of the Rōnins, called Yazama Jiutarō, got into the hole, and found that on the other side there was a little courtyard, in which there stood an outhouse for holding charcoal and firewood. Looking into the outhouse, he spied something white at the further end, at which he struck with his spear, when two armed men sprang out upon him and tried to cut him down, but he kept them back until one of his comrades came up and killed one of the two men and engaged the other, while Jiutarō entered the outhouse and felt about with his spear. Again seeing something white, he struck it with his lance, when a cry of pain betrayed that it was a man; so he rushed up, and the man in white clothes, who had been wounded in the thigh, drew a dirk and aimed a blow at him. But Jiutarō wrested the dirk from him, and clutching him by the collar, dragged him out of the outhouse. Then the other Rōnin came up, and they examined the prisoner attentively, and saw that he was a noble-looking man, some sixty years of age, dressed in a white satin sleeping-robe, which was stained by the blood from the thigh-wound which, Jiutarō had inflicted. The two men felt convinced that this was no other than Kōtsuké no Suké, and they asked him his name, but he gave no answer, so they gave the signal whistle, and all their comrades collected together at the call; then Oishi Kuranosuké, bringing a lantern, scanned the old man's features, and it was indeed Kōtsuké no Suké; and if further proof were wanting, he still bore a scar on his forehead where their master, Asano Takumi no Kami, had wounded him during the affray in the castle. There being no possibility of mistake, therefore, Oishi Kuranosuké went down on his knees, and addressing the old man very respectfully, said:

'My lord, we are the retainers of Asano Takumi no Kami. Last year your lordship and our master quarrelled in the palace, and our master was sentenced to *hara-kiri*, and his family was ruined. We have come tonight to avenge him,

The Ronins invite Kotsuké no Suké to perform hara-kiri

as is the duty of faithful and loyal men. I pray your lordship to acknowledge the justice of our purpose. And now, my lord, we beseech you to perform *hara-kiri*. I myself shall have the honour to act as your second, and when, with all humility, I shall have received your lordship's head, it is my intention to lay it as an offering upon the grave of Asano Takumi no Kami.'

Thus, in consideration of the high rank of Kōtsuké no Suké, the Rōnins treated him with the greatest courtesy, and over and over again entreated him to perform *hara-kiri*. But he crouched speechless and trembling. At last Kuranosuké, seeing that it was vain to urge him to die the death of a nobleman, forced him down, and cut off his head with the same dirk with which Asano Takumi no Kami had killed himself. Then the forty-seven comrades, elated at having accomplished their design, placed the head in a bucket, and prepared to depart; but before leaving the house they carefully extinguished all the lights and fires in the place, lest by any accident a fire should break out and the neighbours suffer.

As they were on their way to Takanawa, the suburb in which the temple called Sengakuji stands, the day broke; and the people flocked out to see the forty-seven men, who, with their clothes and arms all blood-stained, presented a terrible appearance; and every one praised them, wondering at their valour and faithfulness. But they expected every moment that Kōtsuké no Suké's father-in-law would attack them and carry off the head, and made ready to die bravely sword in hand. However, they reached Takanawa in safety, for Matsudaira Aki no Kami, one of the eighteen chief daimios of Japan, of whose house Asano Takumi no Kami had been a cadet, had been highly pleased when he heard of the last night's work, and he had made ready to assist the Rōnins in case they were attacked. So Kōtsuké no Suké's father-in-law dared not pursue them.

At about seven in the morning they came opposite to the palace of Matsudaira Mutsu no Kami, the Prince of Sendai, and the Prince, hearing of it, sent for one of his councillors and said: 'The retainers of Takumi no Kami have slain their lord's enemy, and are passing this way; I cannot sufficiently admire their devotion, so, as they must be tired and hungry after their night's work, do you go and invite them to come in here, and set some gruel and a cup of wine before them.'

So the councillor went out and said to Oishi Kuranosuké: 'Sir, I am a councillor of the Prince of Sendai, and my master bids me beg you, as you must be worn out after all you have undergone, to come in and partake of such poor refreshment as we can offer you. This is my message to you from my lord.'

'I thank you, sir,' replied Kuranosuké. 'It is very good of his lordship to trouble himself to think of us. We shall accept his kindness gratefully.'

So the forty-seven Rōnins went into the palace, and were feasted with gruel and wine, and all the retainers of the Prince of Sendai came and praised them.

Then Kuranosuké turned to the councillor and said, 'Sir, we are truly indebted to you for this kind hospitality; but as we have still to hurry to Sengakuji, we must needs humbly take our leave.' And, after returning many thanks to their hosts, they left the palace of the Prince of Sendai and hastened to Sengakuji, where they were met by the abbot of the monastery, who went to the front gate to receive them, and led them to the tomb of Takumi no Kami.

And when they came to their lord's grave, they took the head of Kōtsuké no Suké, and having washed it clean in a well hard by, laid it as an offering before the tomb. When they had done this, they engaged the priests of the temple to come and read prayers while they burnt incense: first Oishi Kuranosuké burnt incense, and then his son Oishi Chikara, and after them the other forty-five men performed the same ceremony. Then Kuranosuké, having given all the money that he had by him to the abbot, said:

'When we forty-seven men shall have performed *hara-kiri*, I beg you to bury us decently. I rely upon your kindness. This is but a trifle that I have to offer; such as it is, let it be spent in masses for our souls!'

And the abbot, marvelling at the faithful courage of the men, with tears in his eyes pledged himself to fulfil their wishes. So the forty-seven Rōnins, with their minds at rest, waited patiently until they should receive the orders of the Government.

At last they were summoned to the Supreme Court, here the governors of Yedo and the public censors had assembled;

and the sentence passed upon them was as follows: 'Whereas, neither respecting the dignity of the city nor fearing the Government, having leagued yourselves together to slay your enemy, you violently broke into the house of Kira Kôtsuké no Suké by night and murdered him, the sentence of the Court is, that, for this audacious conduct, you perform *hara-kiri*.' When the sentence had been read, the forty-seven Rônins were divided into four parties, and handed over to the safe keeping of four different daimios; and sheriffs were sent to the palaces of those daimios in whose presence the Rônins were made to perform *hara-kiri*. But, as from the very beginning they had all made up their minds that to this end they must come, they met their death nobly; and their corpses were carried to Sengakuji, and buried in front of the tomb of their master, Asano Takumi no Kami. And when the fame of this became noised abroad, the people flocked to pray at the graves of these faithful men.

Among those who came to pray was a Satsuma man, who, prostrating himself before the grave of Oishi Kuranosuké, said: 'When I saw you lying drunk by the roadside at Yamashina, in Kiôto, I knew not that you were plotting to avenge your lord; and, thinking you to be a faithless man, I trampled on you and spat in your face as I passed. And now I have come to ask pardon and offer atonement for the insult of last year.' With those words he prostrated himself again before the grave, and, drawing a dirk from his girdle, stabbed himself in the belly and died. And the chief priest of the temple, taking pity upon him, buried him by the side of the Rônins; and his tomb still remains to be seen with those of the forty-seven comrades. This is the end of the story of the forty-seven Rōnins.

A terrible picture of fierce heroism which it is impossible not to admire. In the Japanese mind this feeling of admiration is unmixed, and hence it is that the forty-seven Rōnins receive almost divine honours. Pious hands still deck their graves with green boughs and burn incense upon them; the clothes and arms which they wore are preserved carefully in a fire-proof store-house attached to the temple, and exhibited yearly to admiring crowds, who behold them probably with little less veneration than is accorded to the relics of Aix-la-Chapelle or Trèves; and once in sixty years the monks of Sengakuji reap quite a harvest for the good of their temple by holding a commemorative fair or festival, to which the people flock during nearly two months.

The tombs of the Rōnins

A silver key once admitted me to a private inspection of the relics. We were ushered, my friend and myself, into a back apartment of the spacious temple, overlooking one of those marvellous miniature gardens, cunningly adorned with rockeries and dwarf trees, in which the Japanese delight. One by one, carefully labelled and indexed boxes containing the precious articles were brought out and opened by the chief priest. Such a curious medley of old rags and scraps of metal and wood! Home-made chain armour, composed of wads of leather secured together by pieces of iron, bear witness to the secrecy with which the Rōnins made ready for the fight. To have bought armour would have attracted attention, so they made it with their own hands. Old moth-eaten surcoats, bits of helmets, three flutes, a writing-box that must have been any age at the time of the tragedy, and is now tumbling to pieces; tattered trousers of what once was rich silk brocade, now all unravelled and befringed; scraps of leather, part of an old gauntlet, crests and badges, bits of sword handles, spear-heads and dirks, the latter all red with rust, but with certain patches more deeply stained as if the fatal clots of blood were never to be blotted out: all these were reverently shown to us. Among the confusion and litter were a number of documents, yellow with age and much worn at the folds. One was a plan of Kōtsuké no Suké's house, which one of the Rōnins obtained by marrying the daughter of the builder who designed it. Three of the manuscripts appeared to me so curious that I obtained leave to have copies taken of them.

The first is the receipt given by the retainers of Kōtsuké no Suké's son in return for the head of their lord's father, which the priests restored to the family, and runs as follows:

MEMORANDUM

Item. One head.

Item. One Paper Parcel.

The above articles are acknowledged to have been received.

> Signed, SAYADA MAGOBEI (*Loc. sigill.*)
>
> SAITŌ KUNAI (*Loc. sigill.*)

To the priests deputed from the Temple Sengakuji,

His Reverence SEKISHI,

His Reverence ICHIDON

The second paper is a document explanatory of their conduct, a copy of which was found on the person of each of the forty-seven men:

> *Last year, in the third month, Asano Takumi no Kami, upon the occasion of the entertainment of the Imperial ambassador, was driven, by the force of circumstances, to attack and wound my Lord Kōtsuké no Suké in the castle, in order to avenge an insult offered to him. Having done this without considering the dignity of the place, and having thus disregarded all rules of propriety, he was condemned to hara-kiri, and his property and castle of Ako were forfeited to the State, and were delivered up by his retainers to the officers deputed by the Shogun to receive them. After this his followers were all dispersed. At the time of the quarrel the high officials present prevented Asano Takumi no Kami from carrying out his intention of killing his enemy, my Lord Kōtsuké no Suké. So Asano Takumi no Kami died without having avenged himself, and this was more than his retainers could endure. It is impossible to remain under the same heaven with the enemy of lord or father; for this reason we have dared*

to declare enmity against a personage of so exalted rank. This day we shall attack Kira Kōtsuké no Suké, in order to finish the deed of vengeance which was begun by our dead lord. If any honourable person should find our bodies after death, he is respectfully requested to open and read this document.

15th year of Genroku. 12th month.

Signed, OISHI KURANOSUKÉ

Retainer of Asano Takumi no Kami,

and forty-six others[6]

The third manuscript is a paper which the Forty-seven Rōnins laid upon the tomb of their master, together with the head of Kira Kōtsuké no Suké:

The 15th year of Genroku, the 12th month, and 15th day. We have come this day to do homage here, forty-seven men in all, from Oishi Kuranosuké down to the foot-soldier, Terasaka Kichiyémon, all cheerfully about to lay down our lives on your behalf. We reverently announce this to the honoured spirit of our dead master. On the 14th day of the third month of last year our honoured master was pleased to attack Kira Kōtsuké no Suké, for what reason we know not. Our honoured master put an end to his own life, but Kira Kōtsuké no Suké lived. Although we fear that after the decree issued by the Government this plot of ours will be displeasing to our honoured master, still we, who have eaten of your food, could not without blushing repeat the verse, 'Thou shalt not live under the same heaven nor tread the same earth with the enemy of thy father or lord,' nor could we have dared to leave hell and present ourselves before you in paradise, unless we had carried out the vengeance which you began. Every day that we waited seemed as three autumns to us. Verily, we have trodden the snow for one day, nay, for two days, and have tasted food but once. The old and decrepit, the sick and ailing, have come forth gladly to lay down their lives. Men might laugh at us, as at grasshoppers trusting in the strength of their arms, and thus shame our honoured lord; but we could not halt in our deed of vengeance. Having taken counsel together last night, we have escorted my Lord Kōtsuké no Suké hither to your tomb. This dirk,[7] by which our honoured lord set great store last year, and entrusted to our care, we now bring back. If your noble spirit be now present before this tomb, we pray you, as a sign, to take the dirk, and, striking the head of your enemy with it a second time, to dispel your hatred for ever. This is the respectful statement of forty-seven men._

The text, 'Thou shalt not live under the same heaven with the enemy of thy father,' is based upon the Confucian books. Dr. Legge, in his *Life and Teachings of Confucius*, p. 113, has an interesting paragraph summing up the doctrine of the sage upon the subject of revenge.

In the second book of the 'Le Ke' there is the following passage:

'With the slayer of his father a man may not live under the same heaven; against the slayer of his brother a man must never have to go home to fetch a weapon; with the slayer of his friend a man may not live in the same State.' The lex talionis is here laid down in its fullest extent. The 'Chow Le' tells us of a provision made against *the evil consequences of the principle by the appointment of a minister called 'The Reconciler.' The provision is very inferior to the cities of refuge which were set apart by Moses for the manslayer to flee to from the fury of the avenger. Such as it was, however, it existed, and it is remarkable that Confucius, when consulted on the subject, took no notice of it, but affirmed the duty of blood-revenge in the strongest and most unrestricted terms. His disciple, Tsze Hea, asked him, 'What course is to be pursued in the murder of a father or mother?' He replied, 'The son must sleep upon a matting of grass with his shield for his pillow; he must decline to take office; he must not live under the same heaven with the slayer. When he meets him in the market-place or the court, he must have his weapon ready to strike him.' 'And what is the course in the murder of a brother?' 'The surviving brother must not take office in the same State with the slayer; yet, if he go on his prince's service to the State where the slayer is, though he meet him, he must not fight with him.' 'And what is the course in the murder of an uncle or cousin?' 'In this case the nephew or cousin is not the principal. If the principal, on whom the revenge devolves, can take it, he has only to stand behind with his weapon in his hand, and support him."*

I will add one anecdote to show the sanctity which is attached to the graves of the Forty-seven. In the month of September 1868, a certain man came to pray before the grave of Oishi Chikara. Having finished his prayers, he deliberately performed *hara-kiri*,[8] and, the belly wound not being mortal, dispatched himself by cutting his throat. Upon his person were found papers setting forth that, being a Rōnin and without means of earning a living, he had petitioned to be allowed to enter the clan of the Prince of Chōshiu, which he looked upon as the noblest clan in the realm; his petition having been refused, nothing remained for him but to die, for to be a Rōnin was hateful to him, and he would serve no other master than the Prince of Chōshiu: what more fitting place could he find in which to put an end to his life than the graveyard of these Braves? This happened at about two hundred yards' distance from my house, and when I saw the spot an hour or two later, the ground was all bespattered with blood, and disturbed by the death-struggles of the man.

Notes:

1. According to Japanese tradition, in the fifth year of the Emperor Kōrei (286 BC), the earth opened in the province of Omi, near Kioto, and Lake Biwa, sixty miles long by about eighteen broad, was formed in the shape of a *Biwa*, or four-stringed lute, from which it takes its name. At the same time, to compensate for the depression of the earth, but at a distance of over three hundred miles from the lake, rose Fuji-Yama, the last eruption of which was in the year 1707. The last great earthquake at Yedo took place about fifteen years ago. Twenty thousand souls are said to have perished in it, and the dead were carried away and buried by cart loads; many persons, trying to escape from their falling and burning houses, were caught in great clefts, which yawned suddenly in the earth, and as suddenly closed upon the victims, crushing them to death. For several days heavy shocks continued to be felt, and the people camped out, not daring to return to such houses as had been spared, nor to build up those which lay in ruins.

2. The word *Rōnin* means, literally, a 'wave-man'; one who is tossed about hither and thither, as a wave of the sea. It is used to designate persons of gentle blood, entitled to bear arms, who, having become separated from their feudal lords by their own act, or by dismissal, or by fate, wander about about the country in the capacity of somewhat disreputable knights-errant, without ostensible means of living, in some cases offering themselves themselves for hire to new masters, in others supporting themselves by pillage; or who, falling a grade in the social scale, go into trade and, become

become simple wardsmen. Sometimes it happens that for political reasons a man will become Rōnin, in order that his lord may not be implicated in some deed of blood in which he is about to engage. Sometimes, also men become Rōnins, and leave their native place for a while, until some scrape in which they have become entangled shall have blown over; after which they return to their former allegiance. Now-a-days it is not unusual for men to become Rōnins for a time, and engage themselves in the service of foreigners at the open ports, even in menial capacities, in the hope that they may pick up something of the language and lore of Western folks. I know instances of men of considerable position who have adopted this course in their zeal for education.

3. The full title of the Tycoon was Sei-i-tai-Shogun, 'Barbarian-repressing Commander-in-chief.' The style Tai Kun, Great Prince, was borrowed, in order to convey the idea of sovereignty to foreigners, at the time of the conclusion of the Treaties. The envoys sent by the Mikado from Kiōto to communicate to the Shogun the will of his sovereign, were received with Imperial honours, and the duty of entertaining them was confided to nobles of rank. The title Sei-i-tai-Shogun was first borne by Minamoto no Yoritomo, in the seventh month of the year 1192 AD.

4. Councillor, lit. 'elder'. The councillors of daimios were of two classes: the *Karō*, or 'elder,' an hereditary office, held by cadets of the Prince's family, and the *Yōnin*, or 'man of business,' who was selected on account of his merits. These 'councillors' play no mean part in Japanese history.

5. *Samurai*, a man belonging to the *Buké* or military class, entitled to bear arms.

6. It is usual for a Japanese, when bent upon some deed of violence, the end of which, in his belief, justifies the means, to carry about with him a document, such as that translated above, in which he sets forth his motives, that his character may be cleared after death.

7. The dirk with which Asano Takumi no Kumi disembowelled himself and with which Oishi Kuranosuké cut off Kōtsuké no Suké's head.

8. A purist in Japanese matters may object to the use of the words *hara-kiri* instead of the more elegant expression *Seppuku*. I retain the more vulgar form as being better known, and therefore more convenient.

Kazuma's Revenge

I t is a law that he who lives by the sword shall die by the sword. In Japan, where there exists a large armed class over whom there is practically little or no control, party and clan broils, and single quarrels ending in bloodshed and death, are matters of daily occurrence; and it has been observed that Edinburgh in the olden time, when the clansmen, roistering through the streets at night, would pass from high words to deadly blows, is perhaps the best European parallel of modern Yedo or Kiōto.

It follows that of all his possessions the Samurai sets most store by his sword, his constant companion, his ally, defensive and offensive. The price of a sword by a famous maker reaches a high sum: a Japanese noble will sometimes be found girding on a sword, the blade of which unmounted is worth from six hundred to a thousand riyos, say from £200 to £300, and the mounting, rich in cunning metal work, will be of proportionate value. These swords are handed down as heirlooms from father to son, and become almost a part of the wearer's own self. Iyéyasu, the founder of the last dynasty of Shoguns, wrote in his Legacy,[1] a code of rules drawn up for the guidance of his successors and their advisers in the government, 'The girded sword is the living soul of the Samurai. In the case of a Samurai forgetting his sword, act as is appointed: it may not be overlooked.'

The occupation of a swordsmith is an honourable profession, the members of which are men of gentle blood. In a country where trade is looked down upon as degrading, it is strange to find this single exception to the general rule. The traditions of the craft are many and curious. During the most critical moment of the forging of the sword, when the steel edge is being welded into the body of the iron blade, it is a custom which still obtains among old-fashioned armourers to put on the cap and robes worn by the Kugé, or nobles of the Mikado's court, and, closing the doors of the workshop, to labour in secrecy and freedom from interruption, the half gloom adding to the mystery of the operation. Sometimes the occasion is even invested with a certain sanctity, a tasselled cord of straw, such as is hung before the shrines of the Kami, or native gods of Japan, being suspended between two bamboo poles in the forge, which for the nonce is converted into a holy altar.

forging the sword

At Osaka, I lived opposite to one Kusano Yoshiaki, a swordsmith, a most intelligent and amiable gentleman, who was famous throughout his neighbourhood for his good and charitable deeds. His idea was that, having been bred up to a calling which trades in life and death, he was bound, so far as in him lay, to atone for this by seeking to alleviate the suffering which is in the world; and he carried out his principle to the extent of impoverishing himself. No neighbour ever appealed to him in vain for help in tending the sick or burying the dead. No beggar or lazar was ever turned from his door without receiving some mark of his bounty, whether in money or in kind. Nor was his scrupulous honesty less remarkable than his charity. While other smiths are in the habit of earning large sums of money by counterfeiting the marks of the famous makers of old, he was able to boast that he had never turned out a weapon which bore any other mark than his own. From his father and his forefathers he inherited his trade, which, in his turn, he will hand over to his son—a hard-working, honest, and sturdy man, the clank of whose hammer and anvil may be heard from daybreak to sundown.

The trenchant edge of the Japanese sword is notorious. It is said that the best blades will in the hands of an expert swordsman cut through the dead bodies of three men, laid one upon the other, at a blow. The swords of the Shogun used to be tried upon the corpses of executed criminals; the public headsman was entrusted with the duty, and for a 'nose medicine,' or bribe of two bus (about three shillings), would substitute the weapon of a private individual for that of his Lord. Dogs and beggars, lying helpless by the roadside, not unfrequently serve to test a ruffian's sword; but the executioner earns many a fee from those who wish to see how their blades will cut off a head.

The statesman who shall enact a law forbidding the carrying of this deadly weapon will indeed have deserved well of his country; but it will be a difficult task to undertake, and a dangerous one. I would not give much for that man's life. The hand of every swashbuckler in the empire would be against him. One day as we were talking over this and other kindred subjects, a friend of mine, a man of advanced and liberal views, wrote down his opinion, more Japonico, in a verse of poetry which ran as follows: 'I would that all the swords and dirks in the country might be collected in one place and molten down, and that, from the metal so produced, one huge sword might be forged, which, being the only blade left, should be the girded sword of Great Japan.'

The following history is in more senses than one a 'Tale of a Sword.'

About two hundred and fifty years ago Ikéda Kunaishōyu was Lord of the Province of Inaba. Among his retainers were two gentlemen, named Watanabé Yukiyé and Kawai Matazayémon, who were bound together by strong ties of friendship, and were in the habit of frequently visiting at one another's houses. One day Yukiyé was sitting conversing with Matazayémon in the house of the latter, when, on a sudden, a sword that was lying in the raised part of the room caught his eye. As he saw it, he started and said:

'Pray tell me, how came you by that sword?'

'Well, as you know, when my Lord Ikéda followed my Lord Tokugawa Iyéyasu to fight at Nagakudé, my father went in his train; and it was at the battle of Nagakudé that he picked up this sword.'

'My father went too, and was killed in the fight, and this sword, which was an heirloom in our family for many generations, was lost at that time. As it is of great value in my eyes, I do wish that, if you set no special store by it, you would have the great kindness to return it to me.'

'That is a very easy matter, and no more than what one friend should do by another. Pray take it.'

Upon this Yukiyé gratefully took the sword and carried it home put it carefully away.

At the beginning of the ensuing year Matagorō fell sick and died, and Yukiyé, mourning bitterly for the loss of his good friend, and anxious to requite the favour which he had received in the matter of his father's sword, did many acts of kindness to the dead man's son—a young man twenty-two years of age, named Matagorō.

Now this Matagorō was a base-hearted cur, who had begrudged the sword that his father had given to Yukiyé, and complained publicly and often that Yukiyé had never made any present in return; and in this way Yukiyé got a bad name in my Lord's palace as a stingy and illiberal man.

But Yukiyé had a son, called Kazuma, a youth sixteen years of age, who served as one of the Prince's pages of honour. One evening, as he and one of his brother pages were talking together, the latter said:

'Matagorō is telling everybody that your father accepted a handsome sword from him and never made him any present in return, and people are beginning to gossip about it.'

'Indeed,' replied the other, 'my father received that sword from Matagorō's father as a mark of friendship and goodwill, and, considering that it would be an insult to send a present of money in return, thought to return the favour by acts of kindness towards Matagorō. I suppose it is money he wants.'

When Kazuma's service was over, he returned home, and went to his father's room to tell him the report that was being spread in the palace, and begged him to send an ample present of money to Matagorō. Yukiyé reflected for a while, and said:

'You are too young to understand the right line of conduct in such matters. Matagorō's father and myself were very close friends; so, seeing that he had ungrudgingly given me back the sword of my ancestors, I, thinking to requite his kindness at his death, rendered important services to Matagorō. It would be easy to finish the matter by sending a present of money; but I had rather take the sword and return it than be under an obligation to this mean churl, who knows not the laws which regulate the intercourse and dealings of men of gentle blood.'

So Yukiyé, in his anger, took the sword to Matagorō's house, and said to him:

'I have come to your house this night for no other purpose than to restore to you the sword which your father gave me;' and with this he placed the sword before Matagorō.

'Indeed,' replied the other, 'I trust that you will not pain me by returning a present which my father made you.'

'Amongst men of gentle birth,' said Yukiyé, laughing scornfully, 'it is the custom to requite presents, in the first place by kindness, and afterwards by a suitable gift offered with a free heart. But it is no use talking to such as you, who are ignorant of the first principles of good breeding; so I have the honour to give you back the sword.'

As Yukiyé went on bitterly to reprove Matagorō, the latter waxed very wroth, and, being a ruffian, would have killed Yukiyé on the spot; but he, old man as he was, was a skilful swordsman, so Matagorō, craven-like, determined to wait until he could attack him unawares. Little suspecting any treachery, Yukiyé started to return home, and Matagorō, under the pretence of attending him to the door, came behind him with his sword drawn and cut him in the shoulder.

The older man, turning round, drew and defended himself; but having received a severe wound in the first instance, he fainted away from loss of blood, and Matagorō slew him.

The mother of Matagorō, startled by the noise, came out; and when she saw what had been done, she was afraid, and said:

'Passionate man! what have you done? You are a murderer; and now your life will be forfeit. What terrible deed is this!'

Matagorō kills Yukiyé
· ·

'I have killed him now, and there's nothing to be done. Come, mother, before the matter becomes known, let us fly together from this house.'

'I will follow you; do you go and seek out my Lord Abé Shirogorō, a chief among the Hatamotos,[2] who was my foster-child. You had better fly to him for protection, and remain in hiding.'

So the old woman persuaded her son to make his escape, and sent him to the palace of Shirogorō.

Now it happened that at this time the Hatamotos had formed themselves into a league against the powerful Daimios; and Abé Shirogorō, with two other noblemen, named Kondō

Noborinosuké and Midzuno Jiurozayémon, was at the head of the league. It followed, as a matter of course, that his forces were frequently recruited by vicious men, who had no means of gaining their living, and whom he received and entreated kindly without asking any questions as to their antecedents; how much the more then, on being applied to for an asylum by the son of his own foster-mother, did he willingly extend his patronage to him, and guarantee him against all danger. So he called a meeting of the principal Hatamotos, and introduced Matagorō to them, saying:

'This man is a retainer of Ikéda Kunaishōyu, who, having cause of hatred against a man named Watanabé Yukiyé, has slain him, and has fled to me for protection; this man's mother suckled me when I was an infant, and, right or wrong, I will befriend him. If, therefore, Ikéda Kunaishōyu should send to require me to deliver him up, I trust that you will one and all put forth your strength and help me to defend him.'

'Ay! that will we, with pleasure!' replied Kondō Noborinosuké. 'We have for some time had cause to complain of the scorn with which the Daimios have treated us. Let Ikéda Kunaishōyu send to claim this man, and we will show him the power of the Hatamotos.'

All the other Hatamotos, with one accord, applauded this determination, and made ready their force for an armed resistance, should my Lord Kunaishōyu send to demand the surrender of Matugorō. But the latter remained as a welcome guest in the house of Abé Shirogorō.

Now when Watanabé Kazuma saw that, as the night advanced, his father Yukiyé did not return home, he became anxious, and went to the house of Matagorō to seek for him, and finding to his horror that he was murdered, fell upon the corpse and, embraced it, weeping. On a sudden, it flashed across him that this must assuredly be the handiwork of Matagorō; so he rushed furiously into the house, determined to kill his father's murderer upon the spot. But Matagorō had already fled, and he found only the mother, who was making her preparations for following her son to the house of Abé Shirogorō: so he bound the old woman, and searched all over the house for her son; but, seeing that his search was fruitless, he carried off the mother, and handed her over to one of the elders of the clan, at the same time laying information against Matagorō as his father's murderer. When the affair was reported to the Prince, he was very angry, and ordered that the old woman should remain bound and be cast into prison until the whereabouts of her son should be discovered. Then Kazuma buried his father's corpse with great pomp, and the widow and the orphan mourned over their loss.

It soon became known amongst the people of Abé Shirogorō that the mother of Matagorō had been imprisoned for her son's crime, and they immediately set about planning her rescue; so they sent to the palace of my Lord Kunaishōyu a messenger, who, when he was introduced to the councillor of the Prince, said:

'We have heard that, in consequence of the murder of Yukiyé, my lord has been pleased to imprison the mother of Matagorō. Our master Shirogorō has arrested the criminal, and will deliver him up to you. But the mother has committed no crime, so we pray that she may be released from a cruel imprisonment: she was the foster-mother of our master, and he would fain intercede to save her life. Should you consent to this, we, on our side, will give up the murderer, and hand him over to you in front of our master's gate tomorrow.'

The councillor repeated this message to the Prince, who, in his pleasure at being able to give Kazuma his revenge on the morrow, immediately agreed to the proposal, and the messenger returned triumphant at the success of the scheme. On the following day, the Prince ordered the mother of Matagorō to be placed in a litter and carried to the Hatamoto's dwelling, in charge of a retainer named Sasawo Danyémon, who, when he arrived at the door of Abé Shirogorō's house, said:

'I am charged to hand over to you the mother of Matagorō, and, in exchange, I am authorized to receive her son at your hands.'

'We will immediately give him up to you; but, as the mother and son are now about to bid an eternal farewell to one another, we beg you to be so kind as to tarry a little.'

With this the retainers of Shirogorō led the old woman inside their master's house, and Sasawo Danyémon remained waiting outside, until at last he grew impatient, and ventured to hurry on the people within.

'We return you many thanks,' replied they, 'for your kindness in bringing us the mother; but, as the son cannot go with you at present, you had better return home as quickly as possible. We are afraid we have put you to much trouble.' And so they mocked him.

When Danyémon saw that he had not only been cheated into giving up the old woman, but was being made a laughing-stock of into the bargain, he flew into a great rage, and thought to break into the house and seize Matagorō and his mother by force; but, peeping into the courtyard, he saw that it was filled with Hatamotos, carrying guns and naked swords. Not caring then to die fighting a hopeless battle, and at the same time feeling that, after having been so cheated, he would be put to shame before his lord, Sasawo Danyémon went to the burial-place of his ancestors, and disembowelled himself in front of their graves.

The death of Danyémon

When the Prince heard how his messenger had been treated, he was indignant, and summoning his councillors resolved, although he was suffering from sickness, to collect his retainers and attack Abé Shirogorō; and the other chief Daimios, when the matter became publicly known, took up the cause, and determined that the Hatamotos must be chastised for their insolence. On their side, the Hatamotos put forth all their efforts to resist the Daimios. So Yedo became disturbed, and the riotous state of the city caused great anxiety to the Government, who took counsel together how they might restore peace. As the Hatamotos were directly under the orders of the Shogun, it was no difficult matter to put them down: the hard question to solve was how to put a restraint upon the great

Daimios. However, one of the Gorōjiu,[3] named Matsudaira Idzu no Kami, a man of great intelligence, hit upon a plan by which he might secure this end.

There was at this time in the service of the Shogun a physician, named Nakarai Tsusen, who was in the habit of frequenting the palace of my Lord Kunaishōyu, and who for some time past had been treating him for the disease from which he was suffering. Idzu no Kami sent secretly for this physician, and, summoning him to his private room, engaged him in conversation, in the midst of which he suddenly dropped his voice and said to him in a whisper:

'Listen, Tsusen. You have received great favours at the hands of the Shogun. The Government is now sorely straitened: are you willing to carry your loyalty so far as to lay down your life on its behalf?'

'Ay, my lord; for generations my forefathers have held their property by the grace of the Shogun. I am willing this night to lay down my life for my Prince, as a faithful vassal should.' 'Well, then, I will tell you. The great Daimios and the Hatamotos have fallen out about this affair of Matagorō, and lately it has seemed as if they meant to come to blows. The country will be agitated, and the farmers and townsfolk suffer great misery, if we cannot quell the tumult. The Hatamotos will be easily kept under, but it will be no light task to pacify the great Daimios. If you are willing to lay down your life in carrying out a stratagem of mine, peace will be restored to the country; but your loyalty will be your death.' 'I am ready to sacrifice my life in this service.'

'This is my plan. You have been attending my Lord

Kunaishōyu in his sickness; tomorrow you must go to see him, and put poison in his physic. If we can kill him, the agitation will cease. This is the service which I ask of you.'

Tsusen agreed to undertake the deed; and on the following day, when he went to see Kunaishōyu, he carried with him poisoned drugs. Half the draught he drank himself,[4] and thus put the Prince off his guard, so that he swallowed the remainder fearlessly. Tsusen, seeing this, hurried away, and as he was carried home in his litter the death-agony seized him, and he died, vomiting blood.

My Lord Kunaishōyu died in the same way in great torture, and in the confusion attending upon his death and funeral ceremonies the struggle which was impending with the Hatamotos was delayed.

In the meanwhile the Gorōjiu Idzu no Kami summoned the three leaders of the Hatamotos and addressed them as follows:

'The secret plottings and treasonable, turbulent conduct of you three men, so unbecoming your position as Hatamotos, have enraged my lord the Shogun to such a degree, that he has been pleased to order that you be imprisoned in a temple, and that your patrimony be given over to your next heirs.'

Accordingly the three Hatamotos, after having been severely admonished, were confined in a temple called Kanyeiji; and the remaining Hatamotos, scared by this example, dispersed in peace. As for the great Daimios, inasmuch as after the death of my Lord Kunaishōyu the Hatamotos were all dispersed, there was no enemy left for them to fight with; so the tumult was quelled, and peace was restored.

Thus it happened that Matagorō lost his patron; so, taking his mother with him, he went and placed himself under the protection of an old man named Sakurai Jiuzayémon. This old man was a famous teacher of lance exercise, and enjoyed both wealth and honour; so he took in Matagorō, and having engaged as a guard thirty Rōnins, all resolute fellows and well skilled in the arts of war, they all fled together to a distant place called Sagara.

All this time Watanabé Kazuma had been brooding over his father's death, and thinking how he should be revenged upon the murderer; so when my Lord Kunaishōyu suddenly died, he went to the young Prince who succeeded him and obtained leave of absence to go and seek out his father's enemy. Now Kazuma's elder sister was married to a man named Araki Matayémon, who at that time was famous as the first swords-man in Japan. As Kazuma was but sixteen years of age, this Matayémon, taking into consideration his near relationship as son-in-law to the murdered man, determined to go forth with the lad, as his guardian, and help him to seek out Matagorō; and two of Matayémon's retainers, named Ishidomé Busuké and Ikezoyé Magohachi, made up their minds, at all hazards, to follow their master. The latter, when he heard their intention, thanked them, but refused the offer, saying that as he was now about to engage in a vendetta in which his life would be con-tinually in jeopardy, and as it would be a lasting grief to him should either of them receive a wound in such a service, he must beg them to renounce their intention; but they answered:

'Master, this is a cruel speech of yours. All these years have we received nought but kindness and favours at your hands; and now that you are engaged in the pursuit of this murderer, we desire to follow you, and, if needs must, to lay down our lives in your service. Furthermore, we have heard that the friends of this Matagorō are no fewer than thirty-six men; so, however bravely you may fight, you will be in peril from the superior numbers of your enemy. However, if you are pleased to persist in your refusal to take us, we have made up our minds that there is no resource for us but to disembowel ourselves on the spot.'

When Matayémon and Kazuma heard these words, they wondered at these faithful and brave men, and were moved to tears. Then Matayémon said:

'The kindness of you two brave fellows is without precedent. Well, then, I will accept your services gratefully.'

Then the two men, having obtained their wish, cheerfully followed their master; and the four set out together upon their journey to seek out Matagorō, of whose whereabouts they were completely ignorant.

Matagorō in the meanwhile had made his way, with the old man Sakurai Jiuzayémon and his thirty Rōnins, to Osaka. But, strong as they were in numbers, they travelled in great secrecy. The reason for this was that the old man's younger brother, Sakurai Jinsuké, a fencing-master by profession, had once had a fencing-match with Matayémon, Kazuma's brother-in-law, and had been shamefully beaten; so that the party were greatly afraid of Matayémon, and felt that, since he was taking up Kazuma's cause and acting as his guardian, they might be worsted in spite of their numbers: so they went on their way with great caution, and, having reached Osaka, put

up at an inn in a quarter called Ikutama, and hid from Kazuma and Matayémon.

The latter also in good time reached Osaka, and spared no pains to seek out Matagorō. One evening towards dusk, as Matayémon was walking in the quarter where the enemy were staying, he saw a man, dressed as a gentleman's servant, enter a cook-shop and order some buckwheat porridge for thirty-six men, and looking attentively at the man, he recognised him as the servant of Sakurai Jiuzayémon; so he hid himself in a dark place and watched, and heard the fellow say:

'My master, Sakurai Jiuzayémon, is about to start for Sagara tomorrow morning, to return thanks to the gods for his recovery from a sickness from which he has been suffering; so I am in a great hurry.'

With these words the servant hastened away; and Matayémon, entering the shop, called for some porridge, and as he ate it, made some inquiries as to the man who had just given so large an order for buckwheat porridge. The master of the shop answered that he was the attendant of a party of thirty-six gentlemen who were staying at such and such an inn. Then Matayémon, having found out all that he wanted to know, went home and told Kazuma, who was delighted at the prospect of carrying his revenge into execution on the morrow. That same evening Matayémon sent one of his two faithful retainers as a spy to the inn, to find out at what hour Matagorō was to set out on the following morning; and he ascertained from the servants of the inn, that the party was to start at daybreak for Sagara, stopping at Isé to worship at the shrine of Tershō Daijin.[5]

Matayémon made his preparations accordingly, and, with Kazuma and his two retainers, started before dawn.

Beyond Uyéno, in the province of Iga, the castle-town of the Daimio Tōdō Idzumi no Kami, there is a wide and lonely moor; and this was the place upon which they fixed for the attack upon the enemy. When they had arrived at the spot, Matayémon went into a tea-house by the roadside, and wrote a petition to the governor of the Daimio's castle town for permission to carry out the vendetta within its precincts;[6] then he addressed Kazuma, and said:

'When we fall in with Matagorō and begin the fight, do you engage and slay your father's murderer; attack him and him only, and I will keep off his guard of Rōnins;' then turning to his two retainers, 'As for you, keep close to Kazuma; and should the Rōnins attempt to rescue Matagorō, it will be your duty to prevent them, and succour Kazuma.' And having further laid down each man's duties with great minuteness, they lay in wait for the arrival of the enemy. Whilst they were resting in the tea-house, the governor of the castle-town arrived, and, asking for Matayémou, said:

'I have the honour to be the governor of the castle-town of Tōdō Idzumi no Kami. My lord, having learnt your intention of slaying your enemy within the precincts of his citadel, gives his consent; and as a proof of his admiration of your fidelity and valour, he has further sent you a detachment of infantry, one hundred strong, to guard the place; so that should any of the thirty-six men attempt to escape, you may set your mind at ease, for flight will be impossible.'

When Matayémon and Kazuma had expressed their thanks for his lordship's gracious kindness, the governor took his leave and returned home. At last the enemy's train was seen in the distance. First came Sakurai Jiuzayémon and his younger brother Jinsuké; and next to them followed Kawai

Matagorō and Takénouchi Gentan. These four men, who were the bravest and the foremost of the band of Rōnins, were riding on pack-horses, and the remainder were marching on foot, keeping close together.

As they drew near, Kazuma, who was impatient to avenge his father, stepped boldly forward and shouted in a loud voice:

'Here stand I, Kazuma, the son of Yukiyé, whom you, Matagorō, treacherously slew, determined to avenge my father's death. Come forth, then, and do battle with me, and let us see which of us twain is the better man.'

And before the Rōnins had recovered from their astonishment, Matayémon said:

'I, Araké Matayémon, the son-in-law of Yukiyé, have come to second Kazuma in his deed of vengeance. Win or lose, you must give us battle.'

When the thirty-six men heard the name of Matayémon, they were greatly afraid; but Sakurai Jiuzayémon urged them to be upon their guard, and leaped from his horse; and Matayémon, springing forward with his drawn sword, cleft him from the shoulder to the nipple of his breast, so that he fell dead. Sakurai Jinsuké, seeing his brother killed before his eyes, grew furious, and shot an arrow at Matayémon, who deftly cut the shaft in two with his dirk as it flew; and Jinsuké, amazed at this feat, threw away his bow and attacked Matayémon, who, with his sword in his right hand and his dirk in his left, fought with desperation. The other Rōnins attempted to rescue Jinsuké, and, in the struggle, Kazuma, who had engaged Matagorō, became separated from Matayémon, whose two retainers, Busuké and Magohachi, bearing in mind their master's orders, killed five Rōnins who had attacked Kazuma, but were themselves badly wounded. In the meantime, Matayémon, who had killed seven of the Rōnins, and who the harder he was pressed the more bravely he fought, soon cut down three more, and the remainder dared not approach him. At this moment there came up one Kanō Tozayémon, a retainer of the lord of the castle town, and an old friend of Matayémon, who, when he heard that Matayémon was this day about to avenge his father-in-law, had seized his spear and set out, for the sake of the goodwill between them, to help him, and act as his second, and said:

'Sir Matayémon, hearing of the perilous adventure in which you have engaged, I have come out to offer myself as your second.'

Matayémon, hearing this, was rejoiced, and fought with renewed vigour. Then one of the Rōnins, named Takénouchi Gentan, a very brave man, leaving his companions to do battle with Matayémon, came to the rescue of Matagorō, who was being hotly pressed by Kazuma, and, in attempting to prevent this, Busuké fell covered with wounds. His companion Magohachi, seeing him fall, was in great anxiety; for should any harm happen to Kazuma, what excuse could he make to Matayémon? So, wounded as he was, he too engaged Takénouchi Gentan, and, being crippled by the gashes he had received, was in deadly peril. Then the man who had come up from the castle-town to act as Matayémon's second cried out:

'See there, Sir Matayémon, your follower who is fighting with Gentan is in great danger. Do you go to his rescue, and second Sir Kazuma: I will give an account of the others!'

'Great thanks to you, sir. I will go and second Kazuma.'

So Matayémon went to help Kazuma, whilst his second and the infantry soldiers kept back the surviving Rōnins, who, already wearied by their fight with Matayémon, were unfit for any further exertion. Kazuma meanwhile was still fighting with Matagorō, and the issue of the conflict was doubtful; and Takénouchi Gentan, in his attempt to rescue Matagorō, was being kept at bay by Magohachi, who, weakened by his wounds, and blinded by the blood which was streaming into his eyes from a cut in the forehead, had given himself up for lost when Matayémon came and cried:

'Be of good cheer, Magohachi; it is I, Matayémon, who have come to the rescue. You are badly hurt; get out of harm's way, and rest yourself.'

Then Magohachi, who until then had been kept up by his anxiety for Kazuma's safety, gave in, and fell fainting from loss of blood; and Matayémon worsted and slew Gentan; and even then, although he had received two wounds, he was not exhausted, but drew near to Kazuma and said:

'Courage, Kazuma! The Rōnins are all killed, and there now remains only Matagorō, your father's murderer. Fight and win!'

The youth, thus encouraged, redoubled his efforts; but Matagorō, losing heart, quailed and fell. So Kazuma's vengeance was fulfilled, and the desire of his heart was accomplished.

The two faithful retainers, who had died in their loyalty, were buried with great ceremony, and Kazuma carried the head of Matagorō and piously laid it upon his father's tomb.

So ends the tale of Kazuma's revenge.

fear that stories of which killing and bloodshed form the principal features can hardly enlist much sympathy in these peaceful days. Still, when such tales are based upon history, they are interesting to students of social phenomena. The story of Kazuma's revenge is mixed up with events which at the present time are peculiarly significant: I mean the feud between the great Daimios and the Hatamotos. Those who have followed the modern history of Japan will see that the recent struggle, which has ended in the ruin of the Tycoon's power and the abolition of his office, was the outburst of a hidden fire which had been smouldering for centuries. But the repressive might had been gradually weakened, and contact with Westernpowers had rendered still more odious a feudality which men felt to be out of date. The revolution which has ended in the triumph of the Daimios over the Tycoon, is also the triumph of the vassal over his feudal lord, and is the harbinger of political life to the people at large. In the time of Iyéyasu the burden might be hateful, but it had to be borne; and so it would have been to this day, had not circumstances from without broken the spell. The Japanese Daimio, in advocating the isolation of his country, was hugging the very yoke which he hated. Strange to say, however, there are still men who, while they embrace the new political creed, yet praise the past, and look back withregret upon the day when Japan stood alone, without part or share in the great family of nations.

Note:—HATAMOTO. This word means 'under the flag.' The Hatamotos were men who, as their name implied, rallied round the standard of the Shogun, or Tycoon, in war-time. They were eighty thousand in number. When Iyéyasu left the Province of Mikawa and became Shogun, the retainers whom he ennobled, and who received from him grants of land yielding revenue to the amount of ten thousand kokus of rice a year, and from that down to one hundred kokus, were called *Hatamoto*. In return for these grants of land, the Hatamotos had in war-time to furnish a contingent of soldiers in proportion to their revenue. For every thousand kokus of rice five men were required. Those Hatamotos whose revenue fell short of a thousand kokus substituted a quota of money. In time of peace most of the minor offices of the Tycoon's government were filled by Hatamotos, the more important places being held by the Fudai, or vassal Daimios of the Shogun. Seven years ago, in imitation of the customs of foreign nations, a standing army was founded; and then the Hatamotos hadto contribute their quota of men or of money, whether the country were at peace or at war. When the Shogun wasreduced in 1868 to the rank of a simple Daimio, his revenue of eight million kokus reverted to the Government, with the exception of seven hundred thousand kokus. The title of Hatamoto exists no more, and those who until a few months ago held the rank are for the most part ruined or dispersed. From having been perhaps the proudest and most overbearing class in Japan, they are driven to the utmost straits of poverty. Some have gone into trade, with the heirlooms of their families as their stock; others are wandering through the country as Rōnins; while a small minority have been allowed to follow the fallen fortunes of their master's family, the present chief of which is known as the Prince of Tokugawa. Thus are the eighty thousand dispersed.

The koku of rice, in which all revenue is calculated, is of varying value. At the cheapest it is worth rather more than a pound sterling, and sometimes almost three times as much. The salaries of officials being paid in rice, it follows that there is a large and influential class throughout the country who are interested in keeping up the price of the staple article of food. Hence the opposition with which a free trade in rice has met, even in famine times. Hence also the frequent so-called 'Rice Riots'.

The amounts at which the lands formerly held by the chief Daimios, but now patriotically given up by them to the Mikado, were assessed, sound fabulous. The Prince of Kaga alone had an income of more than one million two hundred thousand kokus. Yet these great proprietors were, latterly at least, embarrassed men. They had many thousand mouths to feed, and were mulcted of their dues right and left; while their mania for buying foreign ships and munitions of war, often at exorbitant prices, had plunged them heavily in debt.

Notes:

1. *The Legacy of Iyéyasu*, translated by F. Lowder. Yokohama, 1868. (Printed for private circulation.)

2. *Hatamotos*. The Hatamotos were the feudatory nobles of the Shogun or Tycoon. The office of Taikun having been abolished, the Hatamotos no longer exist. For further information respecting them, see the note at the end of the story.

3. The first Council of the Shogun's ministers; literally, 'assembly of imperial elders.'

4. A physician attending a personage of exalted rank has always to drink half the potion he prescribes as a test of his good faith.

5. Goddess of the sun, and ancestress of the Mikados.

6. 'In respect to revenging injury done to master or father, it is granted by the wise and virtuous (Confucius) that you and the injurer cannot live together under the canopy of heaven.

'A person harbouring such vengeance shall notify the same in writing to the Criminal Court; and although no check or hindrance may be offered to his carrying out his desire within the period allowed for that purpose, it is forbidden that the chastisement of an enemy be attended with riot.

'Fellows who neglect to give notice of their intended revenge are like wolves of pretext, and their punishment or pardon should depend upon the circumstances of the case.'—*Legacy of Iyéyasu, ut supra.*

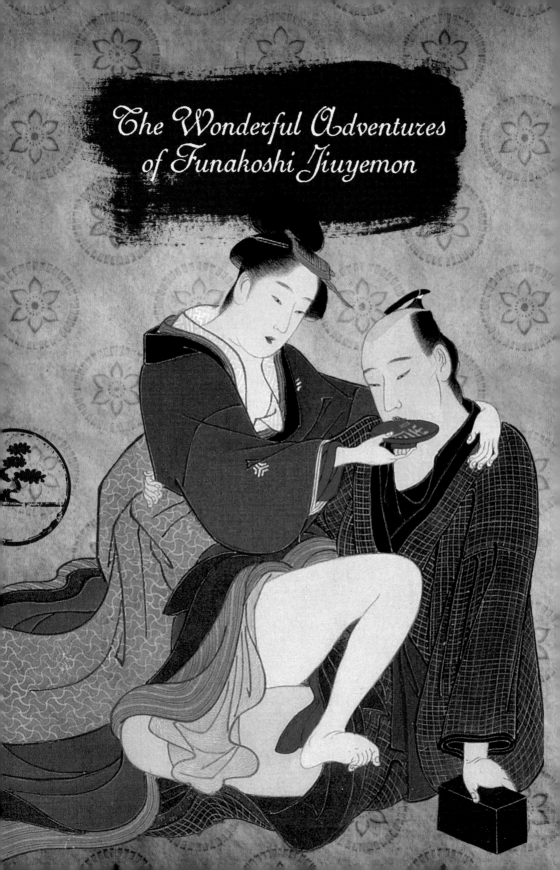

The Wonderful Adventures of Funakoshi Jiuyemon

The doughty deeds and marvellous experiences of Funakoshi Jiuyémon are perhaps, like those of Robin Hood and his Merry Men, rather traditional than historical; but even if all or part of the deeds which popular belief ascribes to him be false, his story conveys a true picture of manners and customs. Above all, the manner of the vengeance which he wreaked upon the wife who had dishonoured him, and upon her lover, shows the high importance which the Japanese attach to the sanctity of the marriage tie.

The 50th and 51st chapters of the 'Legacy of Iyéyasu,' already quoted, say: 'If a married woman of the agricultural, artisan, or commercial class shall secretly have intercourse with another man, it is not necessary for the husband to enter a complaint against the persons thus confusing the great relation of mankind, but he may put them both to death. Nevertheless, should he slay one of them and spare the other, his guilt is the same as that of the unrighteous persons.

'In the event, however, of advice being sought, the parties not having been slain, accede to the wishes of the complainant with regard to putting them to death or not.

'Mankind, in whose bodies the male and female elements induce a natural desire towards the same object, do not look upon such practices with aversion; and the adjudication of such cases is a matter of special deliberation and consultation.

'Men and women of the military class are expected to know better than to occasion disturbance by violating existing regulations; and such an one breaking the regulations by lewd, trifling, or illicit intercourse shall at once be punished, without deliberation or consultation. It is not the same in this case as in that of agriculturists, artisans, and traders.'

As a criminal offence, adultery was, according to the ancient laws of Japan, punished by crucifixion. In more modern times it has been punished by decapitation and the disgraceful exposure of the head after death; but if the murder of the injured husband accompany the crime of adultery, then the guilty parties are crucified to this day. At the present time the husband is no longer allowed to take the law into his own hands: he must report the matter to the Government, and trust to the State to avenge his honour.

Sacred as the marriage tie is so long as it lasts, the law which cuts it is curiously facile, or rather there is no law: a man may turn his wife out of doors, as it may suit his fancy. An example of this practice was shown in the story of 'The Forty-seven Rōnins.' A husband has but to report the matter to his lord, and the ceremony of divorce is completed. Thus, in the days of the Shoguns' power, a Hatamoto who had divorced his wife reported the matter to the Shogun. A Daimio's retainer reports the matter to his Prince.

The facility of divorce, however, seems to be but rarely taken advantage of: this is probably owing to the practice of keeping concubines. It has often been asked, Are the Japanese polygamists? The answer is, Yes and no. They marry but one wife; but a man may, according to his station and means, have one or more concubines in addition. The Emperor has twelve concubines, called Kisaki; and Iyéyasu, alluding forcibly to excess in this respect as *teterrima belli causa*, laid down that the princes might have eight, high officers five, and ordinary Samurai two handmaids. 'In the olden times,' he writes, 'the downfall of castles and the overthrow of kingdoms all proceeded from this alone. Why is not the indulgence of passions guarded against?'

The difference between the position of the wife and that of the concubine is marked. The legitimate wife is to the handmaid as a lord is to his vassal. Concubinage being a legitimate institution, the son of a handmaid is no bastard, nor is he in any way the child of shame; and yet, as a general rule, the son of the bondwoman is not heir with the son of the free, for the son of the wife inherits before the son of a concubine, even where the latter be the elder; and it frequently happens that a noble, having children by his concubines but none by his wife, selects a younger brother of his own, or even adopts the son of some relative, to succeed him in the family honours. The family line is considered to be thus more purely preserved. The law of succession is, however, extremely lax. Excellent personal merits will sometimes secure to the left-handed son the inheritance of his ancestors; and it often occurs that the son of a concubine, who is debarred from succeeding to his own father, is adopted as the heir of a relation or friend of even higher rank. When the wife of a noble has a daughter but no son, the practice is to adopt a youth of suitable family and age, who marries the girl and inherits as a son.

The principle of adoption is universal among all classes, from the Emperor down to his meanest subject; nor is the family line considered to have been broken because an adopted son has succeeded to the estates. Indeed, should a noble die without heir male, either begotten or adopted, his lands are forfeited to the State. It is a matter of care that the person adopted should be himself sprung from a stock of rank suited to that of the family into which he is to be received.

Sixteen and upwards being considered the marriageable age for a man, it is not usual for persons below that age to adopt an heir; yet an infant at the point of death may adopt a person older than himself, that the family line may not become extinct.

In the olden time, in the island of Shikoku[1] there lived one Funakoshi Jiuyémon, a brave Samurai and accomplished man, who was in great favour with the prince, his master. One day, at a drinking-bout, a quarrel sprung up between him and a brother-officer, which resulted in a duel upon the spot, in which Jiuyémon killed his adversary. When Jiuyémon awoke to a sense of what he had done, he was struck with remorse, and he thought to disembowel himself; but, receiving a private summons from his lord, he went to the castle, and the prince said to him:

'So it seems that you have been getting drunk and quarrelling, and that you have killed one of your friends; and now I suppose you will have determined to perform hara-kiri. It is a great pity, and in the face of the laws I can do nothing for you openly. Still, if you will escape and fly from this part of the country for a while, in two years' time the affair will have blown over, and I will allow you to return.'

And with these words the prince presented him with a fine sword, made by Sukésada,[2] and a hundred ounces of silver, and, having bade him farewell, entered his private apartments; and Jiuyémon, prostrating himself, wept tears of gratitude; then, taking the sword and the money, he went home and prepared to fly from the province, and secretly took

leave of his relations, each of whom made him some parting present. These gifts, together with his own money, and what he had received from the prince, made up a sum of two hundred and fifty ounces of silver, with which and his Sukésada sword he escaped under cover of darkness, and went to a seaport called Marugamé, in the province of Sanuki, where he proposed to wait for an opportunity of setting sail for Osaka. As ill luck would have it, the wind being contrary, he had to remain three days idle; but at last the wind changed; so he went down to the beach, thinking that he should certainly find a junk about to sail; and as he was looking about him, a sailor came up, and said:

'If your honour is minded to take a trip to Osaka, my ship is bound thither, and I should be glad to take you with me as passenger.'

'That's exactly what I wanted. I will gladly take a passage,' replied Jiuyémon, who was delighted at the chance.

'Well, then, we must set sail at once, so please come on board without delay.'

So Jiuyémon went with him and embarked; and as they left the harbour and struck into the open sea, the moon was just rising above the eastern hills, illumining the dark night like a noonday sun; and Jiuyémon, taking his place in the bows of the ship, stood wrapt in contemplation of the beauty of the scene.

funakoshi Jiuyémon on board the pirate ship
....

Now it happened that the captain of the ship, whose name was Akagōshi Kuroyémon, was a fierce pirate who, attracted by Jiuyémon's well-to-do appearance, had determined to decoy him on board, that he might murder and rob him; and while Jiuyémon was looking at the moon, the pirate and his companions were collected in the stern of the ship, taking counsel together in whispers as to how they might slay him. He, on the other hand, having for some time past fancied their conduct somewhat strange, bethought him that it was not prudent to lay aside his sword, so he went towards the place where he had been sitting, and had left his weapon lying, to fetch it, when he was stopped by three of the pirates, who blocked up the gangway, saying:

'Stop, Sir Samurai! Unluckily for you, this ship in which you have taken a passage belongs to the pirate Akagōshi Kuroyémon. Come, sir! whatever money you may chance to have about you is our prize.'

When Jiuyémon heard this he was greatly startled at first, but soon recovered himself, and being an expert wrestler, kicked over two of the pirates, and made for his sword; but in the meanwhile Shichirohei, the younger brother of the pirate captain, had drawn the sword, and brought it towards him, saying:

'If you want your sword, here it is!' and with that he cut at him; but Jiuyémon avoided the blow, and closing with the ruffian, got back his sword. Ten of the pirates then attacked him with spear and sword; but he, putting his back against the bows of the ship, showed such good fight that he killed three of his assailants, and the others stood off, not daring to approach him. Then the pirate captain, Akagōshi Kuroyémon, who had been watching the fighting from the stern, seeing that his men stood no chance against Jiuyémon's dexterity, and that he was only losing them to no purpose, thought to shoot him with a matchlock. Even Jiuyémon, brave as he was, lost heart when he saw the captain's gun pointed at him, and tried to jump into the sea; but one of the pirates made a dash at him with a boat-hook, and caught him by the sleeve; then Jiuyémon, in despair, took the fine Sukésada sword which he had received from his prince, and throwing it at his captor, pierced him through the breast so that he fell dead, and himself plunging into the sea swam for his life. The pirate captain shot at him and missed him, and the rest of the crew made every endeavour to seize him with their boat-hooks, that they might avenge the death of their mates; but it was all in vain, and Jiuyémon, having shaken off his clothes that he might swim the better, made good his escape. So the pirates threw the bodies of their dead comrades into the sea, and the captain was partly consoled for their loss by the possession of the Sukésada sword with which one of them had been transfixed.

As soon as Jiuyémon jumped over the ship's side, being a good swimmer, he took a long dive, which carried him well out of danger, and struck out vigorously; and although he was tired and distressed by his exertions, he braced himself up to greater energy, and faced the waves boldly. At last, in the far distance, to his great joy, he spied a light, for which he made, and found that it was a ship carrying lanterns marked with the badge of the governor of Osaka; so he hailed her, saying:

'I have fallen into great trouble among pirates: pray rescue me.'

'Who and what are you?' shouted an officer, some forty years of age.

'My name is Funakoshi Jiuyémon, and I have unwittingly fallen in with pirates this night. I have escaped so far: I pray you save me, lest I die.'

'Hold on to this, and come up,' replied the other, holding out the butt end of a spear to him, which he caught hold of and clambered up the ship's side. When the officer saw before him a handsome gentleman, naked all but his loin-cloth, and with his hair all in disorder, he called to his servants to bring some of his own clothes, and, having dressed him in them, said:

'What clan do you belong to, sir?'

'Sir, I am a Rōnin, and was on my way to Osaka; but the sailors of the ship on which I had embarked were pirates;' and so he told the whole story of the fight and of his escape.

'Well done, sir!' replied the other, astonished at his prowess. 'My name is Kajiki Tozayémon, at your service. I am an officer attached to the the governor of Osaka. Pray, have you any friends in that city?'

'No, sir, I have no friends there; but as in two years I shall be able to return to my own country, and re-enter my lord's service, I thought during that time to engage in trade and live as a common wardsman.'

'Indeed, that's a poor prospect! However, if you will allow me, I will do all that is in my power to assist you. Pray excuse the liberty I am taking in making such a proposal.'

Jiuyémon warmly thanked Kajiki Tozayémon for his kindness; and so they reached Osaka without further adventures.

Jiuyémon, who had secreted in his girdle the two hundred and fifty ounces which he had brought with him from home, bought a small house, and started in trade as a vendor of perfumes, tooth-powder, combs, and other toilet articles; and Kajiki Tozayémon, who treated him with great kindness, and rendered him many services, prompted him, as he was a single man, to take to himself a wife. Acting upon this advice, he married a singing-girl, called O Hiyaku.[3]

Now this O Hiyaku, although at first she seemed very affectionately disposed towards Jiuyémon, had been, during the time that she was a singer, a woman of bad and profligate character; and at this time there was in Osaka a certain wrestler, named Takaségawa Kurobei, a very handsome man, with whom O Hiyaku fell desperately in love; so that at last, being by nature a passionate woman, she became unfaithful to Jiuyémon. The latter, little suspecting that anything was amiss, was in the habit of spending his evenings at the house of his patron Kajiki Tozayémon, whose son, a youth of eighteen, named Tōnoshin, conceived a great friendship for Jiuyémon, and used constantly to invite him to play a game at checkers; and it was on these occasions that O Hiyaku, profiting by her husband's absence, used to arrange her meetings with the wrestler Takaségawa.

One evening, when Jiuyémon, as was his wont, had gone out to play at checkers with Kajiki Tōnoshin, O Hiyaku took advantage of the occasion to go and fetch the wrestler, and invite him to a little feast; and as they were enjoying themselves over their wine, O Hiyaku said to him:

'Ah! Master Takaségawa, how wonderfully chance favours us! and how pleasant these stolen interviews are! How much nicer still it would be if we could only be married. But, as long as Jiuyémon is in the way, it is impossible; and that is my one cause of distress.'

'It's no use being in such a hurry. If you only have patience, we shall be able to marry, sure enough. What you have got to look out for now is, that Jiuyémon does not find out what we are about. I suppose there is no chance of his coming home tonight, is there?'

'Oh dear, no! You need not be afraid. He is gone to Kajiki's house to play checkers; so he is sure to spend the night there.'

And so the guilty couple went on gossiping, with their minds at ease, until at last they dropped off asleep.

In the meanwhile Jiuyémon, in the middle of his game at checkers, was seized with a sudden pain in his stomach, and said to Kajiki Tōnoshin, 'Young sir, I feel an unaccountable pain in my stomach. I think I had better go home, before it gets worse.'

'That is a bad job. Wait a little, and I will give you some physic; but, at any rate, you had better spend the night here.'

'Many thanks for your kindness,' replied Jiuyémon; 'but I had rather go home.'

So he took his leave, and went off to his own house, bearing the pain as best he might. When he arrived in front of his own door, he tried to open it; but the lock was fastened, and he could not get in, so he rapped violently at the shutters to try and awaken his wife. When O Hiyaku heard the noise, she woke with a start, and roused the wrestler, saying to him in a whisper:

'Get up! get up! Jiuyémon has come back. You must hide as fast as possible.'

'Oh dear! oh dear!' said the wrestler, in a great fright; 'here's a pretty mess! Where on earth shall I hide myself?' and he stumbled about in every direction looking for a hiding-place, but found none.

Jiuyémon, seeing that his wife did not come to open the door, got impatient at last, and forced it open by unfixing the sliding shutter and, entering the house, found himself face to face with his wife and her lover, who were both in such confusion that they did not know what to do. Jiuyémon, however, took no notice of them, but lit his pipe and sat smoking and watching them in silence. At last the wrestler, Takaségawa, broke the silence by saying:

'I thought, sir, that I should be sure to have the pleasure of finding you at home this evening, so I came out to call upon you. When I got here, the Lady O Hiyaku was so kind as to offer me some wine; and I drank a little more than was good for me, so that it got into my head, and I fell asleep. I must really apologize for having taken such a liberty in your absence; but, indeed, although appearances are against us, there has been nothing wrong.'

'Certainly,' said O Hiyaku, coming to her lover's support, 'Master Takaségawa is not at all to blame. It was I who invited him to drink wine; so I hope you will excuse him.'

Jiuyémon sat pondering the matter over in his mind for a moment, and then said to the wrestler, 'You say that you are innocent; but, of course, that is a lie. It's no use trying to conceal your fault. However, next year I shall, in all probability, return to my own country, and then you may take O Hiyaku and do what you will with her: far be it from me to care what becomes of a woman with such a stinking heart.'

When the wrestler and O Hiyaku heard Jiuyémon say this quite quietly, they could not speak, but held their peace for very shame.

'Here, you Takaségawa,' pursued he; 'you may stop here tonight, if you like it, and go home tomorrow.'

'Thank you, sir,' replied the wrestler, 'I am much obliged to you; but the fact is, that I have some pressing business in another part of the town, so, with your permission, I will take my leave;' and so he went out, covered with confusion.

As for the faithless wife, O Hiyaku, she was in great agitation, expecting to be severely reprimanded at least; but Jiuyémon took no notice of her, and showed no anger; only from that day forth, although she remained in his house as his wife, he separated himself from her entirely.

Matters went on in this way for some time, until at last, one fine day, O Hiyaku, looking out of doors, saw the wrestler Takaségawa passing in the street, so she called out to him:

'Dear me, Master Takaségawa, can that be you! What a long time it is since we have met! Pray come in, and have a chat.'

'Thank you, I am much obliged to you; but as I do not like the sort of scene we had the other day, I think I had rather not accept your invitation.'

'Pray do not talk in such a cowardly manner. Next year, when Jiuyémon goes back to his own country, he is sure to give me this house, and then you and I can marry and live as happily as possible.'

'I don't like being in too great a hurry to accept fair offers.'[4]

'Nonsense! There's no need for showing such delicacy about accepting what is given you.'

And as she spoke, she caught the wrestler by the hand and led him into the house. After they had talked together for some time, she said:

'Listen to me, Master Takaségawa. I have been thinking over all this for some time, and I see no help for it but to kill Jiuyémon and make an end of him.'

'What do you want to do that for?'

'As long as he is alive, we cannot be married. What I propose is that you should buy some poison, and I will put it secretly into his food. When he is dead, we can be happy to our hearts' content.'

At first Takaségawa was startled and bewildered by the audacity of their scheme; but forgetting the gratitude which he owed to Jiuyémon for sparing his life on the previous occasion, he replied:

'Well, I think it can be managed. I have a friend who is a physician, so I will get him to compound some poison for me, and will send it to you. You must look out for a moment when your husband is not on his guard, and get him to take it.'

Having agreed upon this, Takaségawa went away, and, having employed a physician to make up the poison, sent it to O Hiyaku in a letter, suggesting that the poison should be mixed up with a sort of macaroni, of which Jiuyémon was very fond. Having read the letter, she put it carefully away in a drawer of her cupboard, and waited until Jiuyémon should express a wish to eat some macaroni.

One day, towards the time of the New Year, when O Hiyaku had gone out to a party with a few of her friends, it happened that Jiuyémon, being alone in the house, was in want of some little thing, and, failing to find it anywhere, at last bethought himself to look for it in O Hiyaku's cupboard; and as he was searching amongst the odds and ends which it contained, he came upon the fatal letter. When he read the scheme for putting poison in his macaroni, he was taken aback, and said to himself, 'When I caught those two beasts in their wickedness I spared them, because their blood would have defiled my sword; and now they are not even grateful for my mercy. Their crime is beyond all power of language to express, and I will kill them together.'

So he put back the letter in its place, and waited for his wife to come home. So soon as she made her appearance he said:

'You have come home early, O Hiyaku. I feel very dull and lonely this evening; let us have a little wine.'

And as he spoke without any semblance of anger, it never entered O Hiyaku's mind that he had seen the letter; so she went about her household duties with a quiet mind.

The following evening, as Jiuyémon was sitting in his shop casting up his accounts, with his counting-board[5] in his hand, Takaségawa passed by, and Jiuyémon called out to him, saying:

'Well met, Takaségawa! I was just thinking of drinking a cup of wine tonight; but I have no one to keep me company, and it is dull work drinking alone. Pray come in, and drink a bout with me.'

'Thank you, sir, I shall have much pleasure,' replied the wrestler, who little expected what the other was aiming at; and so he went in, and they began to drink and feast.

'It's very cold tonight,' said Jiuyémon, after a while; 'suppose we warm up a little macaroni, and eat it nice and hot. Perhaps, however, you do not like it?'

'Indeed, I am very fond of it, on the contrary.'

'That is well. O Hiyaku, please go and buy a little for us.'

'Directly,' replied his wife, who hurried off to buy the paste, delighted at the opportunity for carrying out her murderous design upon her husband. As soon she had prepared it, she poured it into bowls and set it before the two men; but into her husband's bowl only she put poison.

Jiuyémon, who well knew what she had done, did not eat the mess at once, but remained talking about this, that, and the other; and the wrestler, out of politeness, was obliged to wait also. All of a sudden, Jiuyémon cried out:

'Dear me! whilst we have been gossiping, the macaroni has been getting cold. Let us put it all together and warm it up again. As no one has put his lips to his bowl yet, it will all be clean; so none need be wasted.' And with these words he took the macaroni that was in the three bowls, and, pouring it altogether into an iron pot, boiled it up again. This time Jiuyémon served out the food himself, and, setting it before his wife and the wrestler, said:

'There! make haste and eat it up before it gets cold.'

Jiuyémon, of course, did not eat any of the mess; and the would-be murderers, knowing that sufficient poison had been originally put into Jiuyémon's bowl to kill them all three, and that now the macaroni, having been well mixed up, would all be poisoned, were quite taken aback, and did not know what to do.

'Come! make haste, or it will be quite cold. You said you liked it, so I sent to buy it on purpose. O Hiyaku! come and make a hearty meal. I will eat some presently.'

At this the pair looked very foolish, and knew not what to answer; at last the wrestler got up and said:

'I do not feel quite well. I must beg to take my leave; and, if you will allow me, I will come and accept your hospitality tomorrow instead.'

'Dear me! I am sorry to hear you are not well. However, O Hiyaku, there will be all the more macaroni for you.'

As for O Hiyaku, she put a bold face upon

the matter, and replied that she had supped already, and had no appetite for any more.

Then Jiuyémon, looking at them both with a scornful smile, said:

'It seems that you, neither of you, care to eat this maca- roni; however, as you, Takaségawa, are unwell, I will give you some excellent medicine;' and going to the cupboard, he drew out the letter, and laid it before the wrestler. When O Hiyaku and the wrestler saw that their wicked schemes had been brought to light, they were struck dumb with shame.

Takaségawa, seeing that denial was useless, drew his dirk and cut at Jiuyémon; but he, being nimble and quick, dived under the wrestler's arm, and seizing his right hand from behind, tightened his grasp upon it until it became numbed, and the dirk fell to the ground; for, powerful man as the wrestler was, he was no match for Jiuyémon, who held him in so fast a grip that he could not move. Then Jiuyémon took the dirk which had fallen to the ground, and said:

'Oh! I thought that you, being a wrestler, would at least be a strong man, and that there would be some pleasure in fighting you; but I see that you are but a poor feckless creature, after all. It would have defiled my sword to have killed such an ungrateful hound with it; but luckily here is your own dirk, and I will slay you with that.'

Takaségawa struggled to escape, but in vain; and O Hiyaku, seizing a large kitchen knife, attacked Jiuyémon; but he, furious, kicked her in the loins so violently that she fell powerless, then brandishing the dirk, he cleft the wrestler from the shoulder down to the nipple of his breast, and the big man fell in his agony. O Hiyaku, seeing this, tried to fly; but Jiuyémon,

funakoshi Jiuyémon punishes his wife and the wrestler

seizing her by the hair of the head, stabbed her in the bosom, and, placing her by her lover's side, gave her the death-blow.

On the following day, he sent in a report of what he had done to the governor of Osaka, and buried the corpses; and from that time forth he remained a single man, and pursued his trade as a seller of perfumery and such-like wares; and his leisure hours he continued to spend as before, at the house of his patron, Kajiki Tozayémon.

One day, when Jiuyémon went to call upon Kajiki Tozayémon, he was told by the servant-maid, who met him at the door, that her master was out, but that her young master, Tōnoshin, was at home; so, saying that he would go in and pay his respects to the young gentleman, he entered the house; and as he suddenly pushed open the sliding-door of the room in which Tōnoshin was sitting, the latter gave a great start, and his face turned pale and ghastly.

'How now, young sir!' said Jiuyémon, laughing at him, 'surely you are not such a coward as to be afraid because the sliding-doors are opened? That is not the way in which a brave Samurai should behave.'

'Really I am quite ashamed of myself,' replied the other, blushing at the reproof; 'but the fact is that I had some reason for being startled. Listen to me, Sir Jiuyémon, and I will tell you all about it. Today, when I went to the academy to study, there were a great number of my fellow-students gathered together, and one of them said that a ruinous old shrine, about two miles and a half to the east of this place, was the nightly resort of all sorts of hobgoblins, who have been playing pranks and bewitching the people for some time past; and he proposed that we should all draw lots, and that the one upon whom the lot fell should go tonight and exorcise those evil beings; and further that, as a proof of his having gone, he should write his name upon a pillar in the shrine. All the rest agreed that this would be very good sport; so I, not liking to appear a coward, consented to take my chance with the rest; and, as ill luck would have it, the lot fell upon me. I was thinking over this as you came in, and so it was that when you suddenly opened the door, I could not help giving a start.'

'If you only think for a moment,' said Jiuyémon, 'you will see that there is nothing to fear. How can beasts[6] and hobgoblins exercise any power over men? However, do not let the matter trouble you. I will go in your place tonight, and see if I cannot get the better of these goblins, if any there be, having done which, I will write your name upon the pillar, so that everybody may think that you have been there.'

'Oh! thank you: that will indeed be a service. You can dress yourself up in my clothes, and nobody will be the wiser. I shall be truly grateful to you.'

So Jiuyémon having gladly undertaken the job, as soon as the night set in made his preparations, and went to the place indicated—an uncanny-looking, tumble-down, lonely old shrine, all overgrown with moss and rank vegetation. However, Jiuyémon, who was afraid of nothing, cared little for the appearance of the place, and having made himself as comfortable as he could in so dreary a spot, sat down on the floor, lit his pipe, and kept a sharp look-out for the goblins. He had not been waiting long before he saw a movement among the bushes; and presently he was surrounded by a host of elfish-looking creatures, of all shapes and kinds, who came and made hideous faces at him. Jiuyémon quietly knocked the ashes out of his pipe, and then, jumping up, kicked over first one and then another of the elves, until several of them lay sprawling in the grass; and the rest made off, greatly astonished at this unexpected reception. When Jiuyémon took his lantern and examined the fallen goblins attentively, he saw that they were all Tōnoshin's fellow-students, who had painted their faces,

funakoshi Jiuyémon and the goblins

and made themselves hideous, to frighten their companion, whom they knew to be a coward: all they got for their pains, however, was a good kicking from Jiuyémon, who left them groaning over their sore bones, and went home chuckling to himself at the result of the adventure.

The fame of this exploit soon became noised about Osaka, so that all men praised Jiuyémon's courage; and shortly after this he was elected chief of the Otokodaté,[7] or friendly society of the wardsmen, and busied himself no longer with his trade, but lived on the contributions of his numerous apprentices.

Now Kajiki Tōnoshin was in love with a singing-girl named Kashiku, upon whom he was in the habit of spending a great deal of money. She, however, cared nothing for him, for she had a sweetheart named Hichirobei, whom she used to contrive to meet secretly, although, in order to support her parents, she was forced to become the mistress of Tōnoshin. One evening, when the latter was on guard at the office of his chief, the Governor of Osaka, Kashiku sent word privately to Hichirobei, summoning him to go to her house, as the coast would be clear.

While the two were making merry over a little feast, Tōnoshin, who had persuaded a friend to take his duty for him on the plea of urgent business, knocked at the door, and Kashiku, in a great fright, hid her lover in a long clothes-box, and went to let in Tōnoshin, who, on entering the room and seeing the litter of the supper lying about, looked more closely, and perceived a man's sandals, on which, by the light of a candle, he saw the figure seven.[8] Tōnoshin had heard some ugly reports of Kashiku's proceedings with this man Hichirobei, and when he saw this proof before his eyes he grew very angry;

but he suppressed his feelings, and, pointing to the wine-cups and bowls, said:

'Whom have you been feasting with tonight?'

'Oh!' replied Kashiku, who, notwithstanding her distress, was obliged to invent an answer, 'I felt so dull all alone here, that I asked an old woman from next door to come in and drink a cup of wine with me, and have a chat.'

All this while Tōnoshin was looking for the hidden lover; but, as he could not see him, he made up his mind that Kashiku must have let him out by the back door; so he secreted one of the sandals in his sleeve as evidence, and, without seeming to suspect anything, said:

'Well, I shall be very busy this evening, so I must go home.'

'Oh! won't you stay a little while? It is very dull here, when I am all alone without you. Pray stop and keep me company.'

But Tōnoshin made no reply, and went home. Then Kashiku saw that one of the sandals was missing, and felt certain that he must have carried it off as proof; so she went in great trouble to open the lid of the box, and let out Hichirobei. When the two lovers talked over the matter, they agreed that, as they both were really in love, let Tōnoshin kill them if he would, they would gladly die together: they would enjoy the present; let the future take care of itself.

The following morning Kashiku sent a messenger to Tōnoshin to implore his pardon; and he, being infatuated by the girl's charms, forgave her, and sent a present of thirty ounces of silver to her lover, Hichirobei, on the condition that he was never to see her again; but, in spite of this, Kashiku and Hichirobei still continued their secret meetings.

It happened that Hichirobei, who was a gambler by profession, had an elder brother called Chōbei, who kept a wineshop in the Ajikawa-Street, at Osaka; so Tōnoshin thought that he could not do better than depute Jiuyémon to go and seek out this man Chōbei, and urge him to persuade his younger brother to give up his relations with Kashiku; acting upon this resolution, he went to call upon Jiuyémon, and said to him:

'Sir Jiuyémon, I have a favour to ask of you in connection with that girl Kashiku, whom you know all about. You are aware that I paid thirty ounces of silver to her lover Hichirobei to induce him to give up going to her house; but, in spite of this, I cannot help suspecting that they still meet one another. It seems that this Hichirobei has an elder brother—one Chōbei; now, if you would go to this man and tell him to reprove his brother for his conduct, you would be doing me a great service. You have so often stood my friend, that I venture to pray you to oblige me in this matter, although I feel that I am putting you to great inconvenience.'

Jiuyémon, out of gratitude for the kindness which he had received at the hands of Kajiki Tozayémon, was always willing to serve Tōnoshin; so he went at once to find out Chōbei, and said to him:

'My name, sir, is Jiuyémon, at your service; and I have come to beg your assistance in a matter of some delicacy.'

'What can I do to oblige you, sir?' replied Chōbei, who felt bound to be more than usually civil, as his visitor was the chief of the Otokodaté.

'It is a small matter, sir,' said Jiuyémon. 'Your younger brother Hichirobei is intimate with a woman named Kashiku, whom he meets in secret. Now, this Kashiku is the mistress of the son of a gentleman to whom I am under great obligation: he bought her of her parents for a large sum of money, and, besides this, he paid your brother thirty ounces of silver some time since, on condition of his separating himself from the girl; in spite of this, it appears that your brother continues to see her, and I have come to beg that you will remonstrate with your brother on his conduct, and make him give her up.'

'That I certainly will. Pray do not be uneasy; I will soon find means to put a stop to my brother's bad behaviour.'

And so they went on talking of one thing and another, until Jiuyémon, whose eyes had been wandering about the room, spied out a very long dirk lying on a cupboard, and all at once it occurred to him that this was the very sword which had been a parting gift to him from his lord: the hilt, the mountings, and the tip of the scabbard were all the same, only the blade had been shortened and made into a long dirk. Then he looked more attentively at Chōbei's features, and saw that he was no other than Akagōshi Kuroyémon, the pirate chief. Two years had passed by, but he could not forget that face.

Jiuyémon would have liked to have arrested him at once; but thinking that it would be a pity to give so vile a robber a chance of escape, he constrained himself, and, taking his leave, went straightway and reported the matter to the Governor of Osaka. When the officers of justice heard of the prey that awaited them, they made their preparations forthwith. Three men of the secret police went to Chōbei's wine-shop, and, having called for wine, pretended to get up a drunken brawl; and as Chōbei went up to them and tried to pacify them, one of the policemen seized hold of him, and another tried to pinion him. It at once flashed across Chōbei's mind that his old misdeeds had come to light at last, so with a desperate effort he shook off the two police-men and knocked them down, and, rushing into the inner room, seized the famous Sukésada sword and sprang upstairs. The three policemen, never thinking that he could escape, mounted the stairs close after him; but Chōbei with a terrible cut cleft the front man's head in sunder, and the other two fell back appalled at their comrade's fate. Then Chōbei climbed on to the roof, and, looking out, perceived that the house was sur-rounded on all sides by armed men. Seeing this, he made up his mind that his last moment was come, but, at any rate, he determined to sell his life dearly, and to die fighting; so he stood up bravely, when one of the officers, coming up from the roof of a neighbouring house, attacked him with a spear; and at the same time several other soldiers clambered up. Chōbei, seeing that he was overmatched, jumped down, and before the soldiers below had recovered from their surprise he had dashed through their ranks, laying about him right and left, and cut-ting down three men. At top speed he fled, with his pursuers close behind him; and, seeing the broad river ahead of him, jumped into a small boat that lay moored there, of which the boatmen, frightened at the sight of his bloody sword, left him in undisputed possession. Chōbei pushed off, and sculled vigorously into the middle of the river; and the officers—there being no other boat near—were for a moment baffled. One of them, however, rushing down the river bank, hid him-self on a bridge, armed with a spear, and lay in wait for Chōbei to pass in his boat; but when the little boat came up, he missed his aim, and only scratched Chōbei's elbow; and he, seizing the spear, dragged down his adversary into the river, and killed him as he was struggling in the water; then, sculling for his life, he gradually drew near to the sea. The other officers in the mean time had secured ten boats, and, having come up with Chōbei, surrounded him; but he, having formerly been a pirate, was far better skilled in the management of a boat than his pursuers, and had no great difficulty in eluding them; so at last he pushed out to sea, to the great annoyance of the officers, who followed him closely.

Then Jiuyémon, who had come up, said to one of the officers on the shore:

'Have you caught him yet?'

'No; the fellow is so brave and so cunning that our men can do nothing with him.'

'He's a determined ruffian, certainly. However, as the fellow has got my sword, I mean to get it back by fair means or foul: will you allow me to undertake the job of seizing him?'

'Well, you may try; and you will have officers to assist you, if you are in peril.'

Jiuyémon, having received this permission, stripped off his clothes and jumped into the sea, carrying with him a policeman's mace, to the great astonishment of all the bystanders. When he got near Chōbei's boat, he dived and came up alongside, without the pirate perceiving him until he had clambered into the boat. Chōbei had the good Sukésada sword, and Jiuyémon was armed with nothing but a mace; but Chōbei, on the other hand, was exhausted with his previous exertions, and was taken by surprise at a moment when he was thinking of nothing but how he should scull away from the pursuing boats; so it was not long before Jiuyémon mastered and secured him.

For this feat, besides recovering his Sukésada sword, Jiuyémon received many rewards and great praise from the Governor of Osaka. But the pirate Chōbei was cast into prison.

Hichirobei, when he heard of his brother's capture, was away from home; but seeing that he too would be sought for, he determined to escape to Yedo at once, and travelled along the Tōkaidō, the great highroad, as far as Kuana. But the secret police had got wind of his movements, and one of them was at his heels disguised as a beggar, and waiting for an opportunity to seize him.

Hichirobei in the meanwhile was congratulating himself on his escape; and, little suspecting that he would be in danger so far away from Osaka, he went to a house of pleasure, intending to divert himself at his ease. The policeman, seeing this, went to the master of the house and said:

'The guest who has just come in is a notorious thief, and I am on his track, waiting to arrest him. Do you watch for the moment when he falls asleep, and let me know. Should he escape, the blame will fall upon you.'

The master of the house, who was greatly taken aback, consented of course; so he told the woman of the house to hide Hichirobei's dirk, and as soon as the latter, wearied with his journey, had fallen asleep, he reported it to the policeman, who went upstairs, and having bound Hichirobei as he lay wrapped up in his quilt, led him back to Osaka to be imprisoned with his brother.

When Kashiku became aware of her lover's arrest, she felt certain that it was the handiwork of Jiuyémon; so she determined to kill him, were it only that she might die with Hichirobei. So hiding a kitchen knife in the bosom of her dress, she went at midnight to Jiuyémon's house, and looked all round to see if there were no hole or cranny by which she might slip in unobserved; but every door was carefully closed, so she was obliged to knock at the door and feign an excuse.

'Let me in! let me in! I am a servant-maid in the house of Kajiki Tozayémon, and am charged with a letter on most pressing business to Sir Jiuyémon.'

Hearing this, one of Jiuyémon's servants, thinking her tale was true, rose and opened the door; and Kashiku, stabbing him in the face, ran past him into the house. Inside she met another apprentice, who had got up, aroused by the noise; him too she stabbed in the belly, but as he fell he cried out to Jiuyémon, saying:

'Father, father!⁹ take care! Some murderous villain has broken into the house.'

'Gokumon'

And Kashiku, desperate, stopped his further utterance by cutting his throat. Jiuyémon, hearing his apprentice cry out, jumped up, and, lighting his night-lamp, looked about him in the half-gloom, and saw Kashiku with the bloody knife, hunting for him that she might kill him. Springing upon her before she saw him, he clutched her right hand, and, having secured her, bound her with cords so that she could not move. As soon as he had recovered from his surprise, he looked about him, and searched the house, when, to his horror, he found one of his apprentices dead, and the other lying bleeding from a frightful gash across the face. With the first dawn of day, he reported the affair to the proper authorities, and gave Kashiku in custody. So, after due examination, the two pirate brothers and the girl Kashiku were executed, and their heads were exposed together.[10]

Now the fame of all the valiant deeds of Jiuyémon having reached his own country, his lord ordered that he should be pardoned for his former offence, and return to his allegiance; so, after thanking Kajiki Tozuyémon for the manifold favours which he had received at his hands, he went home, and became a Samurai as before.

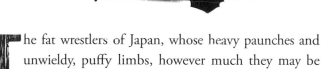

The fat wrestlers of Japan, whose heavy paunches and unwieldy, puffy limbs, however much they may be admired by their own country-people, form a striking contrast to our Western notions of training, have attracted some attention from travellers;

and those who are interested in athletic sports may care to learn something about them.

The first historical record of wrestling occurs in the sixth year of the Emperor Suinin (24 BC), when one Taima no Kéhaya, a noble of great stature and strength, boasting that there was not his match under heaven, begged the Emperor that his strength might be put to the test. The Emperor accordingly caused the challenge to be proclaimed; and one Nomi no Shikuné answered it, and having wrestled with Kéhaya, kicked him in the ribs and broke his bones, so that he died. After this Shikuné was promoted to high office, and became further famous in Japanese history as having substituted earthen images for the living men who, before his time, used to be buried with the coffin of the Mikado.

In the year AD 858 the throne of Japan was wrestled for. The Emperor Buntoku had two sons, called Koréshito and Korétaka, both of whom aspired to the throne. Their claims were decided in a wrestling match, in which one Yoshirō was the champion of Koréshito, and Natora the champion of Korétaka. Natora having been defeated, Koréshito ascended his father's throne under the style of Seiwa.

In the eighth century, when Nara was the capital of Japan, the Emperor Shōmu instituted wrestling as part of the ceremonies of the autumn festival of the Five Grains, or Harvest Home; and as the year proved a fruitful one, the custom was continued as auspicious. The strong men of the various provinces were collected, and one Kiyobayashi was proclaimed the champion of Japan. Many a brave and stout man tried a throw with him, but none could master him. Rules of the ring were now drawn up; and in order to prevent disputes, Kiyobayashi was appointed by the Emperor to be the judge of wrestling-matches, and was presented, as a badge of his office, with a fan, upon which were inscribed the words the 'Prince of Lions.'

The wrestlers were divided into wrestlers of the eastern and of the western provinces, Omi being taken as the centre province. The eastern wrestlers wore in their hair the badge of the hollyhock; the western wrestlers took for their sign the gourd-flower. Hence the passage leading up to the wrestling-stage was called the 'Flower Path.' Forty-eight various falls were fixed upon as fair—twelve throws, twelve lifts, twelve twists, and twelve throws over the back. All other throws not included in these were foul, and it was the duty of the umpire to see that no unlawful tricks were resorted to. It was decided that the covered stage should be composed of sixteen rice-bales, in the shape of one huge bale, supported by four pillars at the four points of the compass, each pillar being painted a different colour, thus, together with certain paper pendants, making up five colours, to symbolize the Five Grains.

The civil wars by which the country was disturbed for a while put a stop to the practice of wrestling; but when peace

A wrestling match

was restored it was proposed to re-establish the athletic games, and the umpire Kiyobayashi, the 'Prince of Lions,' was sought for; but he had died or disappeared, and could not be found, and there was no umpire forthcoming. The various provinces were searched for a man who might fill his place, and one Yoshida Iyétsugu, a Rōnin of the province of Echizen, being reported to be well versed in the noble science, was sent for to the capital, and proved to be a pupil of Kiyobayashi. The Emperor, having approved him, ordered that the fan of the 'Prince of Lions' should be made over to him, and gave him the title of Bungo no Kami, and commanded that his name in the ring should be Oi-Kazé, the 'Driving Wind.' Further, as a sign that there should not be two styles of wrestling, a second fan was given to him bearing the inscription, 'A single flavour is a beautiful custom.' The right of acting as umpire in wrestling-matches was vested in his family, that the 'Driving Wind' might for future generations preside over athletic sports. In ancient days, the prizes for the three champion wrestlers were a bow, a bowstring, and an arrow: these are still brought into the ring, and, at the end of the bout, the successful competitors go through a variety of antics with them.

To the champion wrestlers—to two or three men only in a generation—the family of the 'Driving Wind' awards the privilege of wearing a rope-girdle. In the time of the Shogunate these champions used to wrestle before the Shogun.

At the beginning of the seventeenth century (AD 1606) wrestling-matches, as forming a regular part of a religious ceremony, were

discontinued. They are still held, however, at the shrines of Kamo, at Kiōto, and of Kasuga, in Yamato. They are also held at Kamakura every year, and at the shrines of the patron saints of the various provinces, in imitation of the ancient customs.

In the year 1623 one Akashi Shiganosuké obtained leave from the Government to hold public wrestling matches in the streets of Yedo. In the year 1644 was held the first wrestling match for the purpose of raising a collection for building a temple. This was done by the priests of Kofukuji, in Yamashiro. In the year 1660 the same expedient was resorted to in Yedo, and the custom of getting up wrestling matches for the benefit of temple funds holds good to this day.

The following graphic description of a Japanese wrestling-match is translated from the 'Yedo Hanjōki'.

> From daybreak till eight in the morning a drum is beaten to announce that there will be wrestling. The spectators rise early for the sight. The adversaries having been settled, the wrestlers enter the ring from the east and from the west. Tall stalwart men are they, with sinews and bones of iron. Like the Gods Niō,[11] they stand with their arms akimbo, and, facing one another, they crouch in their strength. The umpire watches until the two men draw their breath at the same time, and with his fan gives the signal. They jump up and close with one another, like tigers springing on their prey, or dragons playing with a ball. Each is bent on throwing the other by twisting or by lifting him. It is no mere trial of brute strength;

it is a tussle of skill against skill. Each of the forty-eight throws is tried in turn. From left to right, and from right to left, the umpire hovers about, watching for the victory to declare itself. Some of the spectators back the east, others back the west. The patrons of the ring are so excited that they feel the strength tingling within them; they clench their fists, and watch their men, without so much as blinking their eyes. At last one man, east or west, gains the advantage, and the umpire lifts his fan in token of victory. The plaudits of the bystanders shake the neighbourhood, and they throw their clothes or valuables into the ring, to be redeemed afterwards in money; nay, in his excitement, a man will even tear off his neighbour's jacket and throw it in.

Before beginning their tussle, the wrestlers work up their strength by stamping their feet and slapping their huge thighs. This custom is derived from the following tale of the heroic or mythological age:

Champion Wrestler

After the seven ages of the heavenly gods came the reign of Tensho Daijin, the Sun Goddess, and first Empress of Japan. Her younger brother, Sosanöö no Mikoto, was a mighty and a brave hero, but turbulent, and delighted in hunting the deer and the boar. After killing these beasts, he would throw their dead bodies into the sacred hall of his sister, and otherwise defile her dwelling.

When he had done this several times, his sister was angry, and hid in the cave called the Rock Gate of Heaven; and when her face was not seen, there was no difference between the night and the day. The heroes who served her, mourning over this, went to seek her; but she placed a huge stone in front of the cave, and would not come forth. The heroes, seeing this, consulted together, and danced and played antics before the cave to lure her out. Tempted by curiosity to see the sight, she opened the gate a little and peeped out. Then the hero Tajikaraō, or 'Great Strength,' clapping his hands and stamping his feet, with a great effort grasped and threw down the stone door, and the heroes fetched back the Sun Goddess.[12] As Tajikaraō is the patron god of Strength, wrestlers, on entering the ring, still commemorate his deed by clapping their hands and stamping their feet as a preparation for putting forth their strength.

The great Daimios are in the habit of attaching wrestlers to their persons, and assigning to them a yearly portion of rice. It is usual for these athletes to take part in funeral or wedding processions, and to escort the princes on journeys. The rich wardsmen or merchants give money to their favourite wrestlers, and invite them to their houses to drink wine and feast. Though low, vulgar fellows, they are allowed something of the same familiarity which is accorded to prize-fighters, jockeys, and the like, by their patrons in our own country.

The Japanese wrestlers appear to have no regular system of training; they harden their naturally powerful limbs by much beating, and by butting at wooden posts with their shoulders. Their diet is stronger than that of the ordinary Japanese, who rarely touch meat.

Notes:

1. *Shikoku*, one of the southern islands separated from the chief island of Japan by the beautiful 'Inland Sea'; it is called *Shikoku*, or the 'Four Provinces', because it is divided into the four provinces, *Awa, Sanuki, Iyo*, and *Tosa*.

2. *Sukésada*, a famous family of swordsmiths, belonging to the Bizen clan. The Bizen men are notoriously good armourers, and their blades fetch high prices. The sword of Jiuyémon is said to have been made by one of the Sukésada who lived about two hundred years ago.

3. The O before women's names signifies '*Imperial*,' and is simply an honorific.

4. The original is a proverbial expression like 'Timeo Danaos et dona ferentes.'

5. The abacus, or counting-board, is the means of calculation in use throughout the Continent from St. Petersburg to Peking, in Corea, Japan, and the Liukiu Islands.

6. Foxes, badgers, and cats. See the stories respecting their tricks.

7. See the Introduction to the Story of Chōbei of Bandzuin.

8. *Hichi*, the first half of *Hichirobei*, signifies seven.

9. The apprentice addresses his patron as 'father.'

10. The exposure of the head, called *Gokumon*, is a disgraceful addition to the punishment of beheading. A document, placed on the execution-ground, sets forth the crime which has called forth the punishment.

11. The Japanese Gog and Magog.

12. The author of the history called 'Kokushi Riyaku' explains this fable as being an account of the first eclipse.

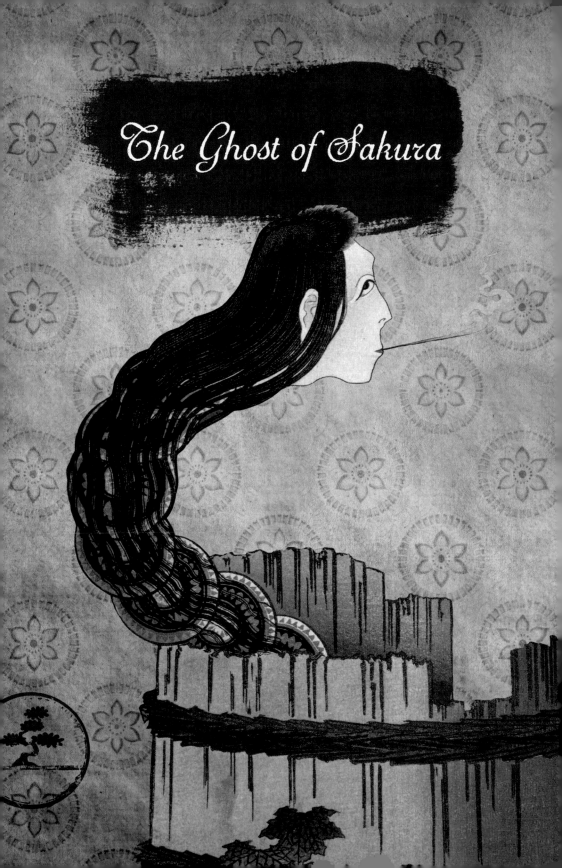

The Ghost of Sakura

The misfortunes and death of the farmer Sōgorō, which, although the preternatural appearances by which they are said to have been followed may raise a smile, are matters of historic notoriety with which every Japanese is familiar, furnish a forcible illustration of the relations which exist between the tenant and the lord of the soil, and of the boundless power for good or for evil exercised by the latter. It is rather remarkable that in a country where the peasant—placed as he is next to the soldier, and before the artisan and merchant, in the four classes into which the people are divided—enjoys no small consideration, and where agriculture is protected by law from the inroads of wild vegetation, even to the lopping of overshadowing branches and the cutting down of hedgerow timber, the lord of the manor should be left practically without control in his dealings with his people.

The land-tax, or rather the yearly rent paid by the tenant, is usually assessed at forty per cent of the produce; but there is no principle clearly defining it, and frequently the landowner and the cultivator divide the proceeds of the harvest in equal shapes. Rice land is divided into three classes; and, according to these classes, it is computed that one *tan* (1,800 square feet) of the best land should yield to the owner a revenue of five bags of rice per annum; each of these bags holds four *tō* (a *tō* is rather less than half an imperial bushel), and is worth at present (1868) three riyos, or about sixteen shillings; land of the middle class should yield a revenue of three or four bags. The rent is paid either in rice or in money, according to the actual price of the grain, which varies considerably. It is due in the eleventh month of the year, when the crops have all been gathered, and their market value fixed.

The rent of land bearing crops other than rice, such

as cotton, beans, roots, and so forth, is payable in money during the twelfth month. The choice of the nature of the crops to be grown appears to be left to the tenant.

The Japanese landlord, when pressed by poverty, does not confine himself to the raising of his legitimate rents: he can always enforce from his needy tenantry the advancement of a year's rent, or the loan of so much money as may be required to meet his immediate necessities. Should the lord be just, the peasant is repaid by instalments, with interest, extending over ten or twenty years. But it too often happens that unjust and merciless lords do not repay such loans, but, on the contrary, press for further advances. Then it is that the farmers, dressed in their grass rain-coats, and carrying sickles and bamboo poles in their hands, assemble before the gate of their lord's palace at the capital, and represent their grievances, imploring the intercession of the retainers, and even of the womankind who may chance to go forth. Sometimes they pay for their temerity by their lives; but, at any rate, they

The deputation of the peasants at their lord's gate

have the satisfaction of bringing shame upon their persecutor, in the eyes of his neighbours and of the populace.

The official reports of recent travels in the interior of Japan have fully proved the hard lot with which the peasantry had to put up during the government of the Tycoons, and especially under the Hatamotos, the created nobility of the dynasty. In one province, where the village mayors appear to have seconded the extortions of their lord, they have had to flee before an exasperated population, who, taking advantage of the revolution, laid waste and pillaged their houses, loudly praying for a new and just assessment of the land; while, throughout the country, the farmers have hailed with acclamations the resumption of the sovereign power by the Mikado, and the abolition of the petty nobility who exalted themselves upon the misery of their dependants. Warming themselves in the sunshine of the court at Yedo, the Hatamotos waxed fat and held high revel, and little cared they who groaned or who starved. Money must be found, and it was found.

It is necessary here to add a word respecting the position of the village mayors, who play so important a part in the tale.

The peasants of Japan are ruled by three classes of officials: the Nanushi, or mayor; the Kumigashira, or chiefs of companies; and the Hiyakushōdai, or farmers' representatives. The village, which is governed by the Nanushi, or mayor, is divided into companies, which, consisting of five families each, are directed by a Kumigashira; these companies, again, are subdivided into groups of five men each, who choose one of their number to represent them in case of their having any petition to present, or any affairs to settle with their superiors. This functionary is the Hiyakushōdai. The mayor, the chief of the company, and the representative keep registers of the families and people under their control, and are responsible for their good and orderly behaviour. They pay taxes like the other farmers, but receive a salary, the amount of which depends upon the size and wealth of the village. Five per cent of the yearly land tax forms the salary of the mayor, and the other officials each receive five per cent of the tax paid by the little bodies over which they respectively rule.

The average amount of land for one family to cultivate is about one chō, or 9,000 square yards; but there are farmers who have inherited as much as five or even six chō from their ancestors. There is also a class of farmers called, from their poverty, 'water-drinking farmers,' who have no land of their own, but hire that of those who have more than they can keep in their own hands. The rent so paid varies; but good rice land will bring in as high a rent as from £1 18s. to £2 6s. per tan (1,800 square feet).

Farm labourers are paid from six or seven riyos a year to as much as thirty riyos (the riyo being worth about 5s. 4d.); besides this, they are clothed and fed, not daintily indeed, but amply. The rice which they cultivate is to them an almost unknown luxury: millet is their staple food, and on high days and holidays they receive messes of barley or buckwheat. Where the mulberry-tree is grown, and the silkworm is 'educated,' there the labourer receives the highest wage.

The rice crop on good land should yield twelve and a half fold, and on ordinary land from six to seven fold only. Ordinary arable land is only half as valuable as rice land, which cannot be purchased for less than forty riyos per tan of 1,800 square feet. Common hill or wood land is cheaper, again, than arable land; but orchards and groves of the Pawlonia are worth from fifty to sixty riyos per tan.

With regard to the punishment of crucifixion, by which Sōgorō was put to death, it is inflicted for the following offences: parricide (including the murder or striking of parents, uncles, aunts, elder brothers, masters, or teachers) coining counterfeit money, and passing the barriers of the Tycoon's territory without a permit.[1] The criminal is attached to an upright post with two cross bars, to which his arms and feet are fastened by ropes. He is then transfixed with spears by men belonging to the Eta or Pariah class. I once passed the execution-ground near Yedo, when a body was attached to the cross. The dead man had murdered his employer, and, having been condemned to death by crucifixion, had died in prison before the sentence could be carried out. He was accordingly packed, in a squatting position, in a huge red earthenware jar, which, having been tightly filled up with salt, was hermetically sealed. On the anniversary of the commission of the crime, the jar was carried down to the execution-ground and broken, and the body was taken out and tied to the cross, the joints of the knees and arms having been cut, to allow of the extension of the stiffened and shrunken limbs; it was then transfixed with spears, and allowed to remain exposed for three days. An open grave, the upturned soil of which seemed almost entirely composed of dead men's remains, waited to receive the dishonoured corpse, over which three or four Etas, squalid and degraded beings, were mounting guard, smoking their pipes by a scanty charcoal fire, and bandying obscene jests. It was a hideous and ghastly warning, had any cared to read the lesson; but the passers-by on the high road took little or no notice of the sight, and a group of chubby and happy children were playing not ten yards from the dead body, as if no strange or uncanny thing were near them.

The Ghost of Sakura[2]

How true is the principle laid down by Confucius, that the benevolence of princes is reflected in their country, while their wickedness causes sedition and confusion!

In the province of Shimōsa, and the district of Sōma, Hotta Kaga no Kami was lord of the castle of Sakura, and chief of a family which had for generations produced famous warriors. When Kaga no Kami, who had served in the Gorōjiu, the cabinet of the Shogun, died at the castle of Sakura, his eldest son Kōtsuké no Suké Masanobu inherited his estates and honours, and was appointed to a seat in the Gorōjiu; but he was a different man from the lords who had preceded him.

He treated the farmers and peasants unjustly, imposing additional and grievous taxes, so that the tenants on his estates were driven to the last extremity of poverty; and although year after year, and month after month, they prayed for mercy, and remonstrated against this injustice, no heed was paid to them, and the people throughout the villages were reduced to the utmost distress. Accordingly, the chiefs of the one hundred and thirty-six villages, producing a total revenue of 40,000 kokus of rice, assembled together in council and determined unanimously to present a petition to the Government, sealed with their seals, stating that their repeated remonstrances had been taken no notice of by their local authorities. Then they assembled in numbers before the house of one of the councillors of their lord, named Ikéura Kazuyé, in order to show the petition to him first, but even then no notice was taken of them; so they returned home, and resolved, after consulting together, to proceed to their lord's yashiki, or palace, at Yedo, on the seventh day of the tenth month. It was determined, with one accord, that one hundred and forty-three village chiefs should go to Yedo; and the chief of the village of Iwahashi, one Sōgorō, a man forty-eight years of age, distinguished for his ability and judgment, ruling a district which produced a thousand kokus, stepped forward, and said:

'This is by no means an easy matter, my masters. It certainly is of great importance that we should forward our complaint to our lord's palace at Yedo; but what are your plans? Have you any fixed intentions?'

'It is, indeed, a most important matter,' rejoined the others; but they had nothing further to say. Then Sōgorō went on to say:

'We have appealed to the public office of our province, but without avail; we have petitioned the Prince's councillors, also in vain. I know that all that remains for us is to lay our case before our lord's palace at Yedo; and if we go there, it is equally certain that we shall not be listened to—on the contrary, we shall be cast into prison. If we are not attended to here, in our own province, how much less will the officials at Yedo care for us. We might hand our petition into the litter of one of the Gorōjiu, in the public streets; but, even in that case, as our lord is a member of the Gorōjiu, none of his peers would care to examine into the rights and wrongs of our complaint, for fear of offending him, and the man who presented the petition in so desperate a manner would lose his life on a bootless errand. If you have made up your minds to this, and are determined, at all hazards, to start, then go to Yedo by all means, and bid a long farewell to parents, children, wives, and relations. This is my opinion.'

The others all agreeing with what Sōgorō said, they determined that, come what might, they would go to Yedo; and they settled to assemble at the village of Funabashi on the thirteenth day of the eleventh month.

On the appointed day all the village officers met at the place agreed upon—Sōgorō, the chief of the village of Iwahashi, alone being missing; and as on the following day Sōgorō had not yet arrived, they deputed one of their number, named Rokurobei, to inquire the reason. Rokurobei arrived at Sōgorō's house towards four in the afternoon, and found him warming himself quietly over his charcoal brazier, as if nothing were the matter. The messenger, seeing this, said rather testily:

'The chiefs of the villages are all assembled at Funabashi according to covenant, and as you, Master Sōgorō, have not arrived, I have come to inquire whether it is sickness or some other cause that prevents you.'

'Indeed,' replied Sōgorō, 'I am sorry that you should have had so much trouble. My intention was to have set out yesterday; but I was taken with a cholic, with which I am often troubled, and, as you may see, I am taking care of myself; so for a day or two I shall not be able to start. Pray be so good as to let the others know this.'

Rokurobei, seeing that there was no help for it, went back to the village of Funabashi and communicated to the others what had occurred. They were all indignant at what they looked upon as the cowardly defection of a man who had spoken so fairly, but resolved that the conduct of one man should not influence the rest, and talked themselves into the belief that the affair which they had in hand would be easily put through; so they agreed with one accord to start and present the petition, and, having arrived at Yedo, put up in the street called Bakurochō. But although they tried to forward their complaint to the various officers of their lord, no one would listen to them; the doors were all shut in their faces, and they had to go back to their inn, crestfallen and without success.

On the following day, being the 18th of the month, they all met together at a tea-house in an avenue, in front of a shrine of Kwannon Sama;[3] and having held a consultation, they determined that, as they could hit upon no good expedient, they would again send for Sōgorō to see whether he could devise no plan. Accordingly, on the 19th, Rokurobei and one Jiuyémon started for the village of Iwahashi at noon, and arrived the same evening.

Now the village chief Sōgorō, who had made up his mind that the presentation of this memorial was not a matter to be lightly treated, summoned his wife and children and his relations, and said to them:

'I am about to undertake a journey to Yedo, for the following reasons: Our present lord of the soil has increased the land-tax, in rice and the other imposts, more than tenfold, so that pen and paper would fail to convey an idea of the poverty to which the people are reduced, and the peasants are undergoing the tortures of hell upon earth. Seeing this, the chiefs of the various villages have presented petitions, but with what result is doubtful. My earnest desire, therefore, is to devise some means of escape from this cruel persecution. If my ambitious scheme does not succeed, then shall I return home no more; and even should I gain my end, it is hard to say how I may be treated by those in power. Let us drink a cup of wine

together, for it may be that you shall see my face no more.
I give my life to allay the misery of the people of this estate.
If I die, mourn not over my fate; weep not for me.'

Having spoken thus, he addressed his wife and his four
children, instructing them carefully as to what he desired to
be done after his death, and minutely stating every wish of his
heart. Then, having drunk a parting cup with them, he cheerfully took leave of all present, and went to a tea-house in the
neighbouring village of Funabashi, where the two messengers,
Rokurobei and Jiuyémon, were anxiously awaiting his arrival,
in order that they might recount to him all that had taken
place at Yedo.

'In short,' said they, 'it appears to us that we have failed
completely; and we have come to meet you in order to hear
what you propose. If you have any plan to suggest, we would
fain be made acquainted with it.'

'We have tried the officers of the district,' replied Sōgorō,
'and we have tried my lord's palace at Yedo. However often we
might assemble before my lord's gate, no heed would be given
to us. There is nothing left for us but to appeal to the Shogun.'

So they sat talking over their plans until the night was far
advanced, and then they went to rest. The winter night as long;
but when the cawing of the crows was about to announce the
morning, the three friends started on their journey for the
tea-house at Asakusa, at which, upon their arrival, they found
the other village elders already assembled.

'Welcome, Master Sōgorō,' said they. 'How is it that you
have come so late? We have petitioned all the officers to no
purpose, and we have broken our bones in vain. We are at our
wits' end, and can think of no other scheme. If there is any plan
which seems good to you, we pray you to act upon it.'

'Sirs,' replied Sōgorō, speaking very quietly, 'although we have met with no better success here than in our own place, there is no use in grieving. In a day or two the Gorōjiu will be going to the castle; we must wait for this opportunity, and following one of the litters, thrust in our memorial. This is my opinion: what think you of it, my masters?'

One and all, the assembled elders were agreed as to the excellence of this advice; and having decided to act upon it, they returned to their inn.

Then Sōgorō held a secret consultation with Jiuyémon, Hanzō, Rokurobei, Chinzō, and Kinshirō, five of the elders, and, with their assistance, drew up the memorial; and having heard that on the 26th of the month, when the Gorōjiu should go to the castle, Kuzé Yamato no Kami would proceed to a palace under the western enclosure of the castle, they kept watch in a place hard by. As soon as they saw the litter of the Gorōjiu approach, they drew near to it, and, having humbly stated their grievances, handed in the petition; and as it was accepted, the six elders were greatly elated, and doubted not that their hearts' desire would be attained; so they went off to a tea-house at Riyōgoku, and Jiuyémon said:

'We may congratulate ourselves on our success. We have handed in our petition to the Gorōjiu, and now we may set our minds at rest; before many days have passed, we shall hear good news from the rulers. To Master Sōgorō is due great praise for his exertions.'

Sōgorō, stepping forward, answered, 'Although we have presented our memorial to the Gorōjiu, the matter will not be so quickly decided; it is therefore useless that so many of us should remain here: let eleven men stay with me, and let the rest return home to their several villages. If we who remain are accused of conspiracy and beheaded, let the others agree to reclaim and bury our corpses. As for the expenses which we shall incur until our suit is concluded, let that be according to our original covenant. For the sake of the hundred and thirty-six villages we will lay down our lives, if needs must, and submit to the disgrace of having our heads exposed as those of common malefactors.'

Then they had a parting feast together, and, after a sad leave-taking, the main body of the elders went home to their own country; while the others, wending their way to their quarters waited patiently to be summoned to the Supreme Court. On the 2nd day of the 12th month, Sōgorō, having received a summons from the residence of the Gorōjiu Kuzé Yamato no Kami, proceeded to obey it, and was ushered to the porch of the house, where two councillors, named Aijima Gidaiyu and Yamaji Yōri, met him, and said:

'Some days since you had the audacity to thrust a memorial into the litter of our lord Yamato no Kami. By an extraordinary exercise of clemency, he is willing to pardon this heinous offence; but should you ever again endeavour to force your petitions; upon him, you will be held guilty of riotous conduct;' and with this they gave back the memorial.

'I humbly admit the justice of his lordship's censure. But oh! my lords, this is no hasty nor ill-considered action. Year after year, affliction upon affliction has been heaped upon us, until at last the people are without even the necessaries of life; and we, seeing no end to the evil, have humbly presented this petition. I pray your lordships of your great mercy to consider our case' and deign to receive our memorial. Vouchsafe to take some measures that the people may live, and our gratitude for your great kindness will know no bounds.'

'Your request is a just one,' replied the two councillors after hearing what he said; 'but your memorial cannot be received: so you must even take it back.'

With this they gave back the document, and wrote down the names of Sōgorō and six of the elders who had accompanied him. There was no help for it: they must take back their petition, and return to their inn. The seven men, dispirited and sorrowful, sat with folded arms considering what was best to be done, what plan should be devised, until at last, when they were at their wits' end, Sōgorō said, in a whisper:

'So our petition, which we gave in after so much pains, has been returned after all! With what face can we return to our villages after such a disgrace? I, for one, do not propose to waste my labour for nothing; accordingly, I shall bide my time until some day, when the Shogun shall go forth from the castle, and, lying in wait by the roadside, I shall make known our grievances to him, who is lord over our lord. This is our last chance.

The others all applauded this speech, and, having with one accord hardened their hearts, waited for their opportunity.

Now it so happened that, on the 20th day of the 12th month, the then Shogun, Prince Iyémitsu, was pleased to worship at the tombs of his ancestors at Uyéno;[4] and Sōgorō and the other elders, hearing this, looked upon it as a special favour from the gods, and felt certain that this time they would not fail. So they drew up a fresh memorial, and at the appointed time Sōgorō hid himself under the Sammayé Bridge, in front of the black gate at Uyéno. When Prince Iyémitsu passed in his litter, Sōgorō clambered up from under the bridge, to the great surprise of the Shogun's attendants, who called out, 'Push the fellow on one side;' but, profiting by the confusion, Sōgorō, raising his voice and crying, 'I wish to humbly present a petition to his

Highness in person,' thrust forward his memorial, which he had tied on to the end of a bamboo stick six feet long, and tried to put it into the litter; and although there were cries to arrest him, and he was buffeted by the escort, he crawled up to the side of the litter, and the Shogun accepted the document. But Sōgorō was arrested by the escort, and thrown into prison. As for the memorial, his Highness ordered that it should be handed in to the Gorōjiu Hotta Kōtsuké no Suké, the lord of the petitioners.

When Hotta Kōtsuké no Suké had returned home and read the memorial, he summoned his councillor, Kojima Shikibu, and said:

'The officials of my estate are mere bunglers. When the peasants assembled and presented a petition, they refused to receive it, and have thus brought this trouble upon me. Their

Sōgorō thrusting the petition into the Shogun's litter

folly has been beyond belief; however, it cannot be helped. We must remit all the new taxes, and you must inquire how much was paid to the former lord of the castle. As for this Sōgorō, he is not the only one who is at the bottom of the conspiracy; however, as this heinous offence of his in going out to lie in wait for the Shogun's procession is unpardonable, we must manage to get him given up to us by the Government, and, as an example for the rest of my people, he shall be crucified—he and his wife and his children; and, after his death, all that he possesses shall be confiscated. The other six men shall be banished; and that will suffice.'

'My lord,' replied Shikibu, prostrating himself, 'your lordship's intentions are just. Sōgorō, indeed, deserves any punishment for his outrageous crime. But I humbly venture to submit that his wife and children cannot be said to be guilty in the same degree: I implore your lordship mercifully to be pleased to absolve them from so severe a punishment.'

'Where the sin of the father is great, the wife and children cannot be spared,' replied Kōtsuké no Suké; and his councillor, seeing that his heart was hardened, was forced to obey his orders without further remonstrance.

So Kōtsuké no Suké, having obtained that Sōgorō should be given up to him by the Government, caused him to be brought to his estate of Sakura as a criminal, in a litter covered with nets, and confined him in prison. When his case had been inquired into, a decree was issued by the Lord Kōtsuké no Suké that he should be punished for a heinous crime; and on the 9th day of the 2nd month of the second year of the period styled Shōhō (AD 1644) he was condemned to be crucified. Accordingly Sōgorō, his wife and children, and the elders of the hundred and thirty-six villages were brought before the

Court-house of Sakura, in which were assembled forty-five chief officers. The elders were then told that, yielding to their petition, their lord was graciously pleased to order that the oppressive taxes should be remitted, and that the dues levied should not exceed those of the olden time. As for Sōgorō and his wife, the following sentence was passed upon them:

'Whereas you have set yourself up as the head of the villagers; whereas, secondly, you have dared to make light of the Government by petitioning his Highness the Shogun directly, thereby offering an insult to your lord; and whereas, thirdly, you have presented a memorial to the Gorōjiu; and, whereas, fourthly, you were privy to a conspiracy: for these four heinous crimes you are sentenced to death by crucifixion. Your wife is sentenced to die in like manner; and your children will be decapitated.

'This sentence is passed upon the following persons:

'Sōgorō, chief of the village of Iwahashi, aged 48.

'His wife, Man, aged 38.

'His son, Gennosuké, aged 13.

'His son, Sōhei, aged 10.

'His son, Kihachi, aged 7.'

The eldest daughter of Sōgorō, named Hatsu, nineteen years of age, was married to a man named Jiuyémon, in the village of Hakamura, in Shitachi, beyond the river, in the territory of Matsudaira Matsu no Kami [the Prince of Sendai]. His second daughter, whose name was Saki, sixteen years of age, was married to one Tōjiurō, chief of a village on the property of my lord Naitō Geki. No punishment was decreed against these two women.

The six elders who had accompanied Sōgorō were told that although by good rights they had merited death, yet by the special clemency of their lord their lives would be spared, but that they were condemned to banishment. Their wives and children would not be attainted, and their property would be spared. The six men were banished to Oshima, in the province of Idzu.

Sōgorō heard his sentence with pure courage.

The six men were banished; but three of them lived to be pardoned on the occasion of the death of the Shogun, Prince Genyuin,[5] and returned to their country.

According to the above decision, the taxes were remitted; and men and women, young and old, rejoiced over the advantage that had been gained for them by Sōgorō and by the six elders, and there was not one that did not mourn for their fate.

When the officers of the several villages left the Courthouse, one Zembei, the chief of the village of Sakato, told the others that he had some important subjects to speak to them upon, andbegged them to meet him in the temple called Fukushōin. Every man having consented, and the hundred and thirty-six men having assembled at the temple, Zembei addressed them as follows:

'The success of our petition, in obtaining the reduction of our taxes to the same amount as was levied by our former lord, is owing to Master Sōgorō, who has thus thrown away his life for us. He and his wife and children are now to suffer as criminals for the sake of the one hundred and thirty-six villages. That such a thing should take place before our very eyes seems to me not to be borne. What say you, my masters?'

'Ay! ay! what you say is just from top to bottom,' replied the others. Then Hanzayémon, the elder of the village of Katsuta, stepped forward and said:

'As Master Zembei has just said, Sōgorō is condemned to die for a matter in which all the village elders are concerned to a man. We cannot look on unconcerned. Full well I know that it is useless our pleading for Sōgorō; but we may, at least, petition that the lives of his wife and children may be spared.'

The assembled elders having all applauded this speech, they determined to draw up a memorial; and they resolved, should their petition not be accepted by the local authorities, to present it at their lord's palace in Yedo, and, should that fail, to appeal to the Government. Accordingly, before noon on the following day, they all affixed their seals to the memorial, which four of them, including Zembei and Hanzayémon, composed, as follows:

With deep fear we humbly venture to present the following petition, which the elders of the one hundred and thirty-six villages of this estate have sealed with their seals. In consequence of the humble petition which we lately offered up, the taxes have graciously been reduced to the rates levied by the former lord of the estate, and new laws have been vouchsafed to us. With reverence and joy the peasants, great and small, have gratefully acknowledged these favours. With regard to Sōgorō, the elder of the village of Iwahashi, who ventured to petition his highness the Shogun in person, thus being guilty of a heinous crime, he has been sentenced to death in the castle-town. With fear and trembling we recognize the justice of his sentence. But in the matter of his wife and children, she is but a woman, and they are so young and innocent that they cannot distinguish the east from the west: we pray that in your great clemency you will remit their sin, and give them up to the representatives of the one hundred and thirty-six villages, for which we shall be ever grateful. We, the elders of the villages, know not to what extent we may be transgressing in presenting this memorial. We were all guilty of affixing our seals to the former petition; but Sōgorō, who was chief of a large district, producing a thousand kokus of revenue, and was therefore a man of experience, acted for the others; and we grieve that he alone should suffer for all. Yet in his case we reverently admit that there can be no reprieve. For his wife and children, however, we humbly implore your gracious mercy and consideration.

Signed by the elders of the villages of the estate, the 2nd year of Shōhō, and the 2nd month.

Having drawn up this memorial, the hundred and thirty-six elders, with Zembei at their head, proceeded to the Court-house to present the petition, and found the various officers seated in solemn conclave. Then the clerk took the petition, and, having opened it, read it aloud; and the councillor, Ikéura Kazuyé, said:

'The petition which you have addressed to us is worthy of all praise. But you must know that this is a matter which is no longer within our control. The affair has been reported to the Government; and although the priests of my lord's ancestral temple have interceded for Sōgorō, my lord is so angry that he will not listen even to them, saying that, had he not been one of the Gorōjiu, he would have been in danger of being ruined by this man: his high station alone saved him. My lord spoke so severely that the priests themselves dare not recur to the subject. You see, therefore, that it will be no use your attempting to take any steps in the matter, for most certainly your petition will not be received. You had better, then, think no more about it.' And with these words he gave back the memorial.

Zembei and the elders, seeing, to their infinite sorrow, that their mission was fruitless, left the Courthouse, and most sorrowfully took counsel together, grinding their teeth in their disappointment when they thought over what the councillor had said as to the futility of their attempt. Out of grief for this, Zembei, with Hanzayémon and Heijiurō, on the 11th day of the 2nd month (the day on which Sōgorō and his wife and children suffered), left Ewaradai, the place of execution, and went to the temple Zenkōji, in the province of Shinshiu, and from thence they ascended Mount Kōya in Kishiu, and, on the 1st day of the 8th month, shaved their heads and became priests; Zembei changed his name to Kakushin, and Hanzayémon changed his to Zenshō: as for Heijiurō, he fell sick at the end of the 7th month, and on the 11th day of the 8th month died, being forty-seven years old that year. These three men, who had loved Sōgorō as the fishes love water, were true to him to the last. Heijiurō was buried on Mount Kōya. Kakushin wandered through the country as a priest, praying for the entry of Sōgorō and his children into the perfection of paradise; and, after visiting all the shrines and temples, came back at last to his own province of Shimōsa, and took up his abode at the temple Riukakuji, in the village of Kano, and in the district of Imban, praying and making offerings on behalf of the souls of Sōgorō, his wife and children. Hanzayémon, now known as the priest Zenshō, remained at Shinagawa, a suburb of Yedo, and, by the charity of good people, collected enough money to erect six bronze Buddhas, which remain standing to this day.

He fell sick and died, at the age of seventy, on the 10th day of the 2nd month of the 13th year of the period styled Kambun. Zembei, who, as a priest, had changed his name to Kakushin, died, at the age of seventy-six, on the 17th day of the 10th month of the 2nd year of the period styled Empō. Thus did those men, for the sake of Sōgorō and his family, give themselves up to works of devotion; and the other villagers also brought food to soothe the spirits of the dead, and prayed for their entry into paradise; and as litanies were repeated without intermission, there can be no doubt that Sōgorō attained salvation.

'In paradise, where the blessings of God are distributed without favour, the soul learns its faults by the measure of the rewards given. The lusts of the flesh are abandoned; and the soul, purified, attains to the glory of Buddha.'[6]

On the 11th day of the 2nd month of the 2nd year of Shōhō, Sōgorō having been convicted of a heinous crime, a scaffold was erected at Ewaradai, and the councillor who resided at Yedo and the councillor who resided on the estate, with the other officers, proceeded to the place in all solemnity. Then the priests of Tōkōji, in the village of Sakénaga, followed by coffin-bearers, took their places in front of the councillors, and said:

'We humbly beg leave to present a petition.'

'What have your reverences to say?'

'We are men who have forsaken the world and entered the priesthood,' answered the monks, respectfully; 'and we would fain, if it be possible, receive the bodies of those who are to die, that we may bury them decently. It will be a great joy to us if our humble petition be graciously heard and granted.'

'Your request shall be granted; but as the crime of Sōgorō was great, his body must be exposed for three days and three nights, after which the corpse shall be given to you.'

At the hour of the snake (10 AM), the hour appointed for the execution, the people from the neighbouring villages and the castle town, old and young, men and women, flocked to see the sight: numbers there were, too, who came to bid a last farewell to Sōgorō, his wife and children, and to put up a prayer for them. When the hour had arrived, the condemned were dragged forth bound, and made to sit upon coarse mats. Sōgorō and his wife closed their eyes, for the sight was more than they could bear; and the spectators, with heaving breasts and streaming eyes, cried 'Cruel!' and 'Pitiless!' and taking sweetmeats and cakes from the bosoms of their dresses threw them to the children. At noon precisely Sōgorō and his wife were bound to the crosses, which were then set upright and fixed in the ground. When this had been done, their eldest son Gennosuké was led forward to the scaffold, in front of the two parents. Then Sōgorō cried out:

'Oh! cruel, cruel! what crime has this poor child committed that he is treated thus? As for me, it matters not what becomes of me.' And the tears trickled down his face.

The spectators prayed aloud, and shut their eyes; and the executioner himself, standing behind the boy, and saying that it was a pitiless thing that the child should suffer for the father's fault, prayed silently. Then Gennosuké, who had remained with his eyes closed, said to his parents:

'Oh! my father and mother, I am going before you to paradise, that happy country, to wait for you. My little brothers and I will be on the banks of the river Sandzu,[7] and stretch out our hands and help you across. Farewell, all you who have come to see us die; and now please cut off my head at once.'

With this he stretched out his neck, murmuring a last prayer; and not only Sōgorō and his wife, but even the executioner and the spectators could not repress their tears; but the headsman, unnerved as he was, and touched to the very heart, was forced, on account of his office, to cut off the child's head, and a piteous wail arose from the parents and the spectators.

Then the younger child Sōhei said to the headsman, 'Sir, I have a sore on my right shoulder: please, cut my head off from the left shoulder, lest you should hurt me. Alas! I know not how to die, nor what I should do.'

When the headsman and the officers present heard the child's artless speech, they wept again for very pity; but there was no help for it, and the head fell off more swiftly than water is drunk up by sand. Then little Kihachi, the third son, who, on account of his tender years, should have been spared, was butchered as he was in his simplicity eating the sweetmeats which had been thrown to him by the spectators.

When the execution of the children was over, the priests of Tōkōji took their corpses, and, having placed them in their coffins, carried them away, amidst the lamentations of the bystanders, and buried them with great solemnity.

Then Shigayémon, one of the servants of Danzayémon, the chief of the Etas, who had been engaged for the purpose, was just about to thrust his spear, when O Man, Sōgorō's wife, raising her voice, said:

'Remember, my husband, that from the first you had made up your mind to this fate. What though our bodies be disgracefully exposed on these crosses? We have the promises of the gods before us; therefore, mourn not. Let us fix our minds upon death: we are drawing near to paradise, and shall soon be with the saints.

Be calm, my husband. Let us cheerfully lay down our single lives for the good of many. Man lives but for one generation; his name, for many. A good name is more to be prized than life.'

So she spoke; and Sōgorō on the cross, laughing gaily, answered:

'Well said, wife! What though we are punished for the many? Our petition was successful, and there is nothing left to wish for. Now I am happy, for I have attained my heart's desire. The changes and chances of life are manifold. But if I had five hundred lives, and could five hundred times assume this shape of mine, I would die five hundred times to avenge this iniquity. For myself I care not; but that my wife and children should be punished also is too much. Pitiless and cruel! Let my lord fence himself in with iron walls, yet shall my spirit burst through them and crush his bones, as a return for this deed.'

And as he spoke, his eyes became vermilion red, and flashed like the sun or the moon, and he looked like the demon Razetsu.[8]

'Come,' shouted he, make haste and pierce me with the spear.'

'Your wishes shall be obeyed,' said the Eta, Shigayémon, and thrust in a spear at his right side until it came out at his left shoulder, and the blood streamed out like a fountain. Then he pierced the wife from the left side; and she, opening her eyes, said in a dying voice:

'Farewell, all you who are present. May harm keep far from you. Farewell! farewell!'

and as her voice waxed faint, the second spear was thrust in from her right side, and she breathed out her spirit. Sōgorō, the colour of his face not even changing, showed no sign of fear, but opening his eyes wide, said:

'Listen, my masters! all you who have come to see this sight. Recollect that I shall pay my thanks to my lord Kōtsuké no Suké for this day's work. You shall see it for yourselves, so that it shall be talked of for generations to come. As a sign, when I am dead, my head shall turn and face towards the castle. When you see this, doubt not that my words shall come true.'

When he had spoken thus, the officer directing the execution gave a sign to the Eta, Shigayémon, and ordered him to finish the execution, so that Sōgorō should speak no more. So Shigayémon pierced him twelve or thirteen times, until he died. And when he was dead, his head turned and faced the castle. When the two councillors beheld this miracle, they came down from their raised platform, and knelt down before Sōgorō's dead body and said:

'Although you were but a peasant on this estate, you conceived a noble plan to succour the other farmers in their distress. You bruised your bones, and crushed your heart, for their sakes. Still, in that you appealed to the Shogun in person, you committed a grievous crime, and made light of your superiors; and for this it was impossible not to punish you. Still we admit that to include your wife and children in your crime, and kill them before your eyes, was a cruel deed. What is done, is done, and regret is of no avail. However, honours shall be paid to your spirit: you shall be canonized as the Saint Daimiyō, and you shall be placed among the tutelar deities of my lord's family.'

With these words the two councillors made repeated reverences before the corpse; and in this they showed their faithfulness to their lord. But he, when the matter was reported to him, only laughed scornfully at the idea that the hatred of a peasant could affect his feudal lord; and said that a vassal who had dared to hatch a plot which, had it not been for his high office, would have been sufficient to ruin him, had only met with his deserts. As for causing him to be canonized, let him be as he was. Seeing their lord's anger, his councillors could only obey. But it was not long before he had cause to know that, though Sōgorō was dead, his vengeance was yet alive.

The relations of Sōgorō and the elders of the villages having been summoned to the Court-house, the following document was issued:

'Although the property of Sōgorō, the elder of the village of Iwahashi, is confiscated, his household furniture shall be made over to his two married daughters; and the village officials will look to it that these few poor things be not stolen by lawless and unprincipled men.

'His rice-fields and corn-fields, his mountain land and forest land, will be sold by auction. His house and grounds will be given over to the elder of the village. The price fetched by his property will be paid over to the lord of the estate.

'The above decree will be published, in full, to the peasants of the village; and it is strictly forbidden to find fault with this decision.

'The 12th day of the 2nd month, of the 2nd year of the period Shōhō.'

The peasants, having heard this degree with all humility, left the Court-house. Then the following punishments were awarded to the officers of the castle, who, by rejecting the petition of the peasants in the first instance, had brought trouble upon their lord:

> Dismissed from their office, the resident councillors at Yedo and at the castle town.
>
> Banished from the province, four district governors, and three bailiffs, and nineteen petty officers.
>
> Dismissed from office, three metsukés, or censors, and seven magistrates.
>
> Condemned to hara-kiri, one district governor and one Yedo bailiff.
>
> The severity of this sentence is owing to the injustice of the officials in raising new and unprecedented taxes, and bringing affliction upon the people, and in refusing to receive the petitions of the peasants, without consulting their lord, thus driving them to appeal to the Shogun in person. In their avarice they looked not to the future, but laid too heavy a burden on the peasants, so that they made an appeal to a higher power, endangering the honour of their lord's house. For this bad government the various officials are to be punished as above.

In this wise was justice carried out at the palace at Yedo and at the Court-house at home. But in the history of the world, from the dark ages down to the present time, there are few instances of one man laying down his life for the many, as Sōgorō did: noble and peasant praise him alike.

As month after month passed away, towards the fourth year of the period Shōhō, the wife of my lord Kōtsuké no Suké, being with child, was seized with violent pains; and retainers were sent to all the different temples and shrines to pray by proxy, but all to no purpose: she continued to suffer as before. Towards the end of the seventh month of the year, there appeared, every night, a preternatural light above the lady's chamber; this was accompanied by hideous sounds as of many people laughing fiendishly, and sometimes by piteous wailings, as though myriads of persons were lamenting. The profound distress caused by this added to her sufferings; so her own privy councillor, an old man, took his place in the adjoining chamber, and kept watch. All of a sudden, he heard a noise as if a number of people were walking on the boards of the roof of my lady's room; then there was a sound of men and women weeping; and when, thunderstruck, the councillor was wondering what it could all be, there came a wild burst of laughter, and all was silent. Early the following morning, the old women who had charge of my lady's household presented themselves before my lord Kōtsuké no Suké, and said:

'Since the middle of last month, the waiting-women have been complaining to us of the ghostly noises by which my lady is nightly disturbed, and they say that they cannot continue to serve her. We have tried to soothe them, by saying that the devils should be exorcised at once, and that there was nothing to be afraid of. Still we feel that their fears are not without reason, and that they really cannot do their work; so we beg that your lordship will take the matter into your consideration.'

'This is a passing strange story of yours; however, I will go myself tonight to my lady's apartments and keep watch. You can come with me.'

Accordingly, that night my lord Kōtsuké no Suké sat up in person. At the hour of the rat (midnight) a fearful noise of voices was heard, and Sōgorō and his wife, bound to the fatal crosses, suddenly appeared; and the ghosts, seizing the lady by the hand, said:

'We have come to meet you. The pains you are suffering are terrible, but they are nothing in comparison with those of the hell to which we are about to lead you.'

At these words, Kōtsuké no Suké, seizing his sword, tried to sweep the ghosts away with a terrific cut; but a loud peal of laughter was heard, and the visions faded away.

Kōtsuké no Suké, terrified, sent his retainers to the temples and shrines to pray that the demons might be cast out; but the noises were heard nightly, as before. When the eleventh month of the year came round, the apparitions of human forms in my lady's apartments became more and more frequent and terrible, all the spirits railing at her, and howling out that they had come to fetch her. The women would all scream and faint; and then the ghosts would disappear amid yells of laughter. Night after night this happened, and

even in the daytime the visions would manifest themselves; and my lady's sickness grew worse daily, until in
the last month of the year she died, of grief and terror.
Then the ghost of Sōgorō and his wife crucified would
appear day and night in the chamber of Kōtsuké no
Suké, floating round the room, and glaring at him
with red and flaming eyes. The hair of the attendants would stand
on end with terror; and if they tried to cut at the spirits, their limbs
would be cramped, and their feet and hands would not obey their
bidding. Kōtsuké no Suké would draw the sword that lay by his
bedside; but, as often as he did so, the ghosts faded away, only to
appear again in a more hideous shape than before, until at last,
having exhausted his strength and spirits, even he became terror-
stricken. The whole household was thrown into confusion, and
day after day mystic rites and incantations were performed by the
priests over braziers of charcoal, while prayers were recited without
ceasing; but the visions only became more frequent, and there was
no sign of their ceasing. After the 5th year of Shōhō, the style of
the years was changed to Keian; and during the 1st year of Keian
the spirits continued to haunt the palace; and now they appeared in the chamber of Kōtsuké no Suké's eldest son, surrounding themselves with even more terrors than before; and
when Kōtsuké no Suké was about to go to the Shogun's castle,
they were seen howling out their cries of vengeance in the
porch of the house. At last the relations of the family
and the members of the household took
counsel together, and told Kōtsuké no
Suké that without doubt no ordinary
means would suffice to lay the ghosts; a
shrine must be erected to Sōgorō, and
divine honours paid to him, after which the

apparitions would assuredly cease. Kōtsuké no Suké having carefully considered the matter and given his consent, Sōgorō was canonized under the name of Sōgo Daimiyō, and a shrine was erected in his honour. After divine honours had been paid to him, the awful visions were no more seen, and the ghost of Sōgorō was laid for ever.

In the 2nd year of the period Keian, on the 11th day of the 10th month, on the occasion of the festival of first lighting the fire on the hearth, the various Daimios and Hatamotos of distinction went to the castle of the Shogun, at Yedo, to offer their congratulations on this occasion. During the ceremonies, my lord Hotta Kōtsuké no Suké and Sakai Iwami no Kami, lord of the castle of Matsumoto, in the province of Shinshiu, had a quarrel, the origin of which was not made public; and Sakai Iwami no Kami, although he came of a brave and noble family, received so severe a wound that he died on the following day, at the age of forty-three; and in consequence of this, his family was ruined and disgraced.[9] My lord Kōtsuké no

The ghost of Sakura

Suké, by great good fortune, contrived to escape from the castle, and took refuge in his own house, whence, mounting a famous horse called Hira-Abumi,[10] he fled to his castle of Sakura, in Shimōsa, accomplishing the distance, which is about sixty miles, in six hours. When he arrived in front of the castle, he called out in a loud voice to the guard within to open the gate, answering, in reply to their challenge, that he was Kōtsuké no Suké, the lord of the castle. The guard, not believing their ears, sent word to the councillor in charge of the castle, who rushed out to see if the person demanding admittance were really their lord. When he saw Kōtsuké no Suké, he caused the gates to be opened, and, thinking it more than strange, said:

'Is this indeed you, my lord? What strange chance brings your lordship hither thus late at night, on horseback and alone, without a single follower?'

With these words he ushered in Kōtsuké no Suké, who, in reply to the anxious inquiries of his people as to the cause of his sudden appearance, said:

'You may well be astonished. I had a quarrel today in the castle at Yedo, with Sakai Iwami no Kami, the lord of the castle of Matsumoto, and I cut him down. I shall soon be pursued; so we must strengthen the fortress, and prepare for an attack.'

The household, hearing this, were greatly alarmed, and the whole castle was thrown into confusion. In the meanwhile the people of Kōtsuké no Suké's palace at Yedo, not knowing whether their lord had fled, were in the greatest anxiety, until a messenger came from Sakura, and reported his arrival there.

When the quarrel inside the castle of Yedo and Kōtsuké no Suké's flight had been taken cognizance of, he was attainted of treason, and soldiers were sent to seize him, dead or alive. Midzuno Setsu no Kami and Gotō Yamato no Kami were charged with the execution of the order, and sallied forth, on the 13th day of the 10th month, to carry it out. When they arrived at the town of Sasai, they sent a herald with the following message:

'Whereas Kōtsuké no Suké killed Sakai Iwami no Kami inside the castle of Yedo, and has fled to his own castle without leave, he is attainted of treason; and we, being connected with him by ties of blood and of friendship, have been charged to seize him.'

The herald delivered this message to the councillor of Kōtsuké no Suké, who, pleading as an excuse that his lord was mad, begged the two nobles to intercede for him. Gotō Yamato no Kami upon this called the councillor to him, and spoke privately to him, after which the latter took his leave and returned to the castle of Sakura.

In the meanwhile, after consultation at Yedo, it was decided that, as Gotō Yamato no Kami and Midzuno Setsu no Kami were related to Kōtsuké no Suké, and might meet with difficulties for that very reason, two other nobles, Ogasawara Iki no Kami and Nagai Hida no Kami, should be sent to assist them, with orders that should any trouble arise they should send a report immediately to Yedo. In consequence of this order, the two nobles, with five thousand men, were about to march for Sakura, on the 15th of the month, when a messenger arrived from that place bearing the following despatch for the Gorōjiu, from the two nobles who had preceded them:

In obedience to the orders of His Highness the Shogun, we proceeded, on the 13th day of this month, to the castle of Sakura, and conducted a thorough investigation of the affair. It is true that Kōtsuké no Suké has been guilty of treason, but he is out of his mind; his retainers have called in physicians, and he is undergoing treatment by which his senses are being gradually restored, and his mind is being awakened from its sleep. At the time when he slew Sakai Iwami no Kami he was not accountable for his actions, and will be sincerely penitent when he is aware of his crime. We have taken him prisoner, and have the honour to await your instructions; in the meanwhile, we beg by these present to let you know what we have done.

(Signed) GOTŌ YAMATO NO KAMI

(Signed) MIDZUNO SETSU NO KAMI

To the Gorōjiu, 2nd year of Keian, 2nd month, 14th day

This despatch reached Yedo on the 16th of the month, and was read by the Gorōjiu after they had left the castle; and in consequence of the report of Kōtsuké no Suké's madness, the second expedition was put a stop to, and the following instructions were sent to Gotō Yamato no Kami and Midzuno Setsu no Kami:

With reference to the affair of Hotta Kōtsuké no Suké, lord of the castle of Sakura, in Shimōsa, whose quarrel with Sakai Iwami no Kami within the castle of Yedo ended in bloodshed. For this heinous crime and

*disregard of the sanctity of the castle, it is ordered that
Kōtsuké no Suké be brought as a prisoner to Yedo, in
a litter covered with nets, that his case may be judged.*
2nd year of Keian, 2nd month
(Signed by the Gorōjiu)   INABA MINO NO KAMI
INOUYE KAWACHI NO KAMI
KATŌ ECCHIU NO KAMI

Upon the receipt of this despatch, Hotta Kōtsuké nō Suké
was immediately placed in a litter covered with a net of green
silk, and conveyed to Yedo, strictly guarded by the retainers of
the two nobles; and, having arrived at the capital, was handed
over to the charge of Akimoto Tajima no Kami. All his retainers were quietly dispersed; and his empty castle was ordered to
be thrown open, and given in charge to Midzuno Iki no Kami.

At last Kōtsuké no Suké began to feel that the death of his
wife and his own present misfortunes were a just retribution
for the death of Sōgorō and his wife and children, and he was
as one awakened from a dream. Then night and morning,
in his repentance, he offered up prayers to the sainted spirit
of the dead farmer, and acknowledged and
bewailed his crime, vowing that, if his family
were spared from ruin and re-established,
intercession should be made at the court of
the Mikado,[11] at Kiyōto, on behalf of the spirit of
Sōgorō, so that, being worshipped with even greater
honours than before, his name should be handed
down to all generations.

In consequence of this it happened that the
spirit of Sōgorō having relaxed in its vindictiveness, and
having ceased to persecute the house of Hotta, in the 1st

month of the 4th year of Keian, Kōtsuké no Suké received a summons from the Shogun, and, having been forgiven, was made lord of the castle of Matsuyama, in the province of Déwa, with a revenue of twenty thousand kokus. In the same year, on the 20th day of the 4th month, the Shogun, Prince Iyémitsu, was pleased to depart this life, at the age of forty-eight; and whether by the forgiving spirit of the prince, or by the divine interposition of the sainted Sōgorō, Kōtsuké no Suké was promoted to the castle of Utsu no Miya, in the province of Shimotsuké, with a revenue of eighty thousand kokus; and his name was changed to Hotta Hida no Kami. He also received again his original castle of Sakura, with a revenue of twenty thousand kokus: so that there can be no doubt that the saint was befriending him. In return for these favours, the shrine of Sōgorō was made as beautiful as a gem. It is needless to say how many of the peasants of the estate flocked to the shrine: any good luck that might befall the people was ascribed to it, and night and day the devout worshipped at it.

ere follows a copy of the petition which Sōgorō presented to the Shogun:

We, the elders of the hundred and thirty-six villages of the district of Chiba, in the province of Shimōsa, and of the district of Buji, in the province of Kadzusa, most reverently offer up this our humble petition.

When our former lord, Doi Shosho, was transferred to another castle, in the 9th year of the period Kanyé, Hotta Kaga no Kami became lord of the castle of Sakura; and in the 17th year of the same period, my lord Kōtsuké no Suké succeeded him. Since that time the taxes laid upon us have been raised in the proportion of one tō and two sho to each koku.[12]

Item—At the present time, taxes are raised on nineteen of our articles of produce; whereas our former lord only required that we should furnish him with pulse and sesamum, for which he paid in rice.

Item—Not only are we not paid now for our produce, but, if it is not given in to the day, we are driven and goaded by the officials; and if there be any further delay, we are manacled and severely reprimanded; so that if our own crops fail, we have to buy produce from other districts, and are pushed to the utmost extremity of affliction.

Item—We have over and over again prayed to be relieved from these burthens, but our petitions are not received. The people are reduced to poverty, so that it is hard for them to live under such grievous taxation. Often they have tried to sell the land which they till, but none can be found to buy; so they have sometimes given over their land to the village authorities, and fled with their wives to other provinces, and seven hundred and thirty men or more have been reduced to begging, one hundred and eighty-five houses have fallen into ruins; land producing seven thousand kokus has been given up, and remains untilled, and eleven temples have fallen into decay in consequence of the ruin of those upon whom they depended.

Besides this, the poverty-stricken farmers and women, having been obliged to take refuge in other provinces, and having no abiding-place, have been driven to evil courses and bring men to speak ill of their lord; and the village officials, being unable to keep order, are blamed and reproved. No attention has been paid to our repeated representations upon this point; so we were driven to petition the Gorōjiu Kuzé Yamato no Kami as he was on his way to the castle, but our petition was returned to us. And now, as a last resource, we tremblingly venture to approach his Highness the Shogun in person.

'The 1st year of the period Shōhō, 12th month, 20th day. The seals of the elders of the 136 villages.'

The Shogun at that time was Prince Iyémitsu, the grandson of Iyéyasu. He received the name of Dai-yu-In after his death.

The Gorōjiu at that time were Hotta Kōtsuké no Suké, Sakai Iwami no Kami, Inaba Mino no Kami, Katō Ecchiu no Kami, Inouyé Kawachi no Kami.

The Wakadoshiyōri (or 2nd council) were Torii Wakasa no Kami, Tsuchiya Dewa no Kami, and Itakura Naizen no Sho.

The belief in ghosts appears to be as universal as that in the immortality of the soul, upon which it depends. Both in China and Japan the departed spirit is invested with the power of revisiting the earth, and, in a visible form, tormenting its enemies and haunting those places where the perishable part of it mourned and suffered. Haunted houses are slow to find tenants, for ghosts almost always come with revengeful intent; indeed, the owners of such houses will almost pay men to live in them, such is the dread which they inspire, and the anxiety to blot out the stigma.

One cold winter's night at Yedo, as I was sitting, with a few Japanese friends, huddled round the imperfect heat of a brazier of charcoal, the conversation turned upon the story of Sōgorō and upon ghostly apparitions in general. Many a weird tale was told that evening, and I noted down the three or four which follow, for the truth of which the narrators vouched with the utmost confidence.

About ten years ago there lived a fishmonger, named Zenroku, in the Mikawa-street, at Kanda, in Yedo. He was a poor man, living with his wife and one little boy. His wife fell sick and died, so he engaged an old woman to look after his boy while he himself went out to sell his fish. It happened, one day, that he and the other hucksters of his guild were gambling; and this coming to the ears of the authorities, they were all thrown into prison. Although their offence was in itself a light one, still they were kept for some time in durance while the matter was being investigated; and Zenroku, owing to the damp and foul air of the prison, fell sick with fever. His little child, in the meantime, had been handed over by the authorities to the charge of the petty officers of the ward to which his father belonged, and was being well cared for; for Zenroku was known to be an honest fellow, and his fate excited much compassion. One night Zenroku, pale and emaciated, entered the house in which his boy was living; and all the people joyfully congratulated him on his escape from jail. 'Why, we heard that you were sick in prison. This is, indeed, a joyful return.' Then Zenroku thanked those who had taken care of the child, saying that he had returned secretly by the favour of his jailers that night; but that on the following day his offence would be remitted, and he should be able to take possession of his house again publicly. For that night, he must return to the prison. With this he begged those present to continue their good offices to his babe; and, with a sad and reluctant expression of countenance, he left the house. On the following day, the officers of that ward were sent for by the prison authorities. They thought that they were summoned that Zenroku might be handed back to them a free man, as he himself had said to them; but to their surprise, they were told that he had died the night before in prison, and were ordered to carry away his dead body for burial. Then they knew that they had seen Zenroku's ghost; and that when he said that he should be returned to them on the morrow, he had alluded to his corpse. So they buried him decently, and brought up his son, who is alive to this day.

The next story was told by a professor in the college at Yedo, and, although it is not of so modern a date as the last, he stated it to be well authenticated, and one of general notoriety.

About two hundred years ago there was a chief of the police, named Aoyama Shuzen, who lived in the street called Bancho, at Yedo. His duty was to detect thieves and incendiaries. He was a cruel and violent man, without heart or compassion, and thought nothing of killing or torturing a man to gratify spite or revenge. This man Shuzen had in his house a servant-maid, called O Kiku (the Chrysanthemum), who had lived in the family since her childhood, and was well acquainted with her master's temper. One day O Kiku accidentally broke one of a set of ten porcelain plates, upon which he set a high value. She knew that she would suffer for her carelessness; but she thought that if she concealed the matter her punishment would be still more severe; so she went at once to her master's wife, and, in fear and trembling, confessed what she had done. When Shuzen came home, and heard that one of his favourite plates was broken, he flew into a violent rage, and took the girl to a cupboard, where he left her bound with cords, and every day cut off one of her fingers. O Kiku, tightly bound and in agony, could not move; but at last she contrived to bite or cut the ropes asunder, and, escaping into the garden, threw herself into a well, and was drowned. From that time forth, every night a voice was heard coming from the well, counting one, two, three, and so on up to nine—the number of the plates that remained unbroken—and then, when the tenth plate should have been counted, would come a burst of lamentation. The servants of the house, terrified at this, all left their master's service, until Shuzen, not having a single retainer left, was unable to perform his public duties; and when the officers of the government heard of this, he was dismissed from his office. At this time there was a famous priest, called Mikadzuki Shōnin, of the temple Denzuin, who, having been told of the affair, came one night to the house, and, when the ghost began to count the plates, reproved the spirit, and by his prayers and admonitions caused it to cease from troubling the living.

The laying of disturbed spirits appears to form one of the regular functions of the Buddhist priests; at least, we find them playing a conspicuous part in almost every ghost-story.

About thirty years ago there stood a house at Mitsumé, in the Honjō of Yedo, which was said to be nightly visited by ghosts, so that no man dared to live in it, and it remained untenanted on that account. However, a man called Miura Takéshi, a native of the province of Oshiu, who came to Yedo to set up in business as a fencing-master, but was too poor to hire a house, hearing that there was a haunted house, for which no tenant could be found, and that the owner would let any man live in it rent free, said that he feared neither man nor devil, and obtained leave to occupy the house. So he hired a fencing-room, in which he gave his lessons by day, and after midnight returned to the haunted house. One night, his wife, who took charge of the house in his absence, was frightened by a fearful noise proceeding from a pond in the garden, and, thinking that this certainly must be the ghost that she had heard so much about, she covered her head with the bed-clothes and remained breathless with terror. When her husband came home, she told him what had happened; and on the following night he returned earlier than usual, and waited for the ghostly noise. At the same time as before, a little after midnight, the same sound was heard—as though a gun had been fired inside the pond.

Opening the shutters, he looked out, and saw something like a black cloud floating on the water, and in the cloud was the form of a bald man. Thinking that there must be some cause for this, he instituted careful inquiries, and learned that the former tenant, some ten years previously, had borrowed money from a blind shampooer,[13] and, being unable to pay the debt, had murdered his creditor, who began to press him for his money, and had thrown his head into the pond. The fencing-master accordingly collected his pupils and emptied the pond, and found a skull at the bottom of it; so he called in a priest, and buried the skull in a temple, causing prayers to be offered up for the repose of the murdered man's soul. Thus the ghost was laid, and appeared no more.

The belief in curses hanging over families for generations is as common as that in ghosts and supernatural apparitions. There is a strange story of this nature in the house of Asai, belonging to the Hatamoto class. The ancestor of the present representative, six generations ago, had a certain concubine, who was in love with a man who frequented the house, and wished in her heart to marry him; but, being a virtuous woman, she never thought of doing any evil deed. But the wife of my lord Asai was jealous of the girl, and persuaded her husband that her rival in his affections had gone astray; when he heard this he was very angry, and beat her with a candlestick so that he put out her left eye. The girl, who had indignantly protested her innocence, finding herself so cruelly handled, pronounced a curse against the house; upon which, her master, seizing the candlestick again, dashed out her brains and killed her. Shortly afterwards my lord Asai lost his left eye, and fell sick and died; and from that time forth to this day, it is said that the representatives of the house have all lost their left eyes after the age of forty, and shortly afterwards they have fallen sick and died at the same age as the cruel lord who killed his concubine.

Note:— Of the many fair scenes of Yedo, none is better worth visiting than the temple of Zōjōji, one of the two great burial-places of the Shoguns; indeed, if you wish to see the most beautiful spots of any Oriental city, ask for the cemeteries: the homes of the dead are ever the loveliest places. Standing in a park of glorious firs and pines beautifully kept, which contains quite a little town of neat, clean-looking houses, together with thirty-four temples for the use of the priests and attendants of the shrines, the main temple, with its huge red pillars supporting a heavy Chinese roof of grey tiles, is approached through a colossal open hall which leads into a stone courtyard. At one end of this courtyard is a broad flight of steps—the three or four lower ones of stone, and the upper ones of red wood. At these the visitor is warned by a notice to take off his boots, a request which Englishmen, with characteristic disregard of the feelings of others, usually neglect to comply with. The main hall of the temple is of large proportions, and the high altar is decorated with fine bronze candelabra, incense-burners, and other ornaments, and on two days of the year a very curious collection of pictures representing the five hundred gods, whose images are known to all persons who have visited Canton, is hung along the walls. The big bell outside the main hall is rather remarkable on account of the great beauty of the deep bass waves of sound which it rolls through the city than on account of its size, which is as nothing when compared with that of the big bells of Moscow and Peking; still it is not to be despised even in that respect, for it is ten feet high and five feet eight inches in diameter, while its metal is a foot thick: it was hung up in the year 1673. But the chief objects of interest in these beautiful grounds are the chapels attached to the tombs of the Shoguns.

It is said that as Prince Iyéyasu was riding into Yedo to take possession of his new castle, the Abbot of Zōjōji, an ancient temple which then stood at Hibiya, near the castle, went forth and waited before the gate to do homage to the Prince. Iyéyasu, seeing that the Abbot was no ordinary man, stopped and asked his name, and entered the temple to rest himself. The smooth-spoken monk soon found such favour with Iyéyasu, that he chose Zōjōji to be his family temple; and seeing that its grounds were narrow and inconveniently near the castle, he caused it to be removed to its present site. In the year 1610 the temple was raised, by the intercession of Iyéyasu, to the dignity of the Imperial Temples, which, until the last revolution, were presided over by princes of the blood; and to the Abbot was granted the right, on going to the castle, of sitting in his litter as far as the entrance-hall, instead of dismounting at the usual place and proceeding on foot through several gates and courtyards. Nor were the privileges of the temple confined to barren honours, for it was endowed with lands of the value of five thousand kokus of rice yearly.

When Iyéyasu died, the shrine called Antoku In was erected in his honour to the south of the main temple. Here, on the seventeenth day of the fourth month, the anniversary of his death, ceremonies are held in honour of his spirit, deified as Gongen Sama, and the place is thrown open to all who may wish to come and pray. But Iyéyasu is not buried here; his remains lie in a gorgeous shrine among the mountains some eighty miles north of Yedo, at Nikkō, a place so beautiful that the Japanese have a rhyming proverb which says, that he who has not seen Nikkō should never pronounce the word Kekkō (charming, delicious, grand, beautiful).

Hidérada, the son and successor of Iyéyasu, together with Iyénobu, Iyétsugu, Iyéshigé, Iyéyoshi, and Iyémochi, the sixth, seventh, ninth, twelfth, and fourteenth Shoguns of the Tokugawa dynasty, are buried in three shrines attached to the temple; the remainder, with the exception of Iyémitsu, the third Shogun, who lies with his grandfather at Nikkō, are buried at Uyéno.

The shrines are of exceeding beauty, lying on one side of a splendid avenue of Scotch firs, which border a broad, well-kept gravel walk. Passing through a small gateway of rare design, we come into a large stone courtyard, lined with a long array of colossal stone lanterns, the gift of the vassals of the departed Prince. A second gateway, supported by gilt pillars carved all round with figures of dragons, leads into another court, in which are a bell tower, a great cistern cut out of a single block of stone like a sarcophagus, and a smaller number of lanterns of bronze; these are given by the Go San Ké, the three princely families in which the succession to the office of Shogun was vested. Inside this is a third court, partly covered like a cloister, the approach to which is a doorway of even greater beauty and richness than the last; the ceiling is gilt, and painted with arabesques and with heavenly angels playing on musical instruments, and the panels of the walls are sculptured in high relief with admirable representations of birds and flowers, life-size, life-like, all being coloured to imitate nature. Inside this enclosure stands a shrine, before the closed door of which a priest on one side, and a retainer of the house of Tokugawa on the other, sit mounting guard, mute and immovable as though they themselves were part of the carved ornaments. Passing on one side of the shrine, we come to another court, plainer than the last, and at the back of the little temple inside it is a flight of stone steps, at the top of which, protected by a bronze door, stands a simple monumental urn of bronze on a stone pedestal. Under this is the grave itself; and it has always struck me that there is no small amount of poetical feeling in this simple ending to so much magnificence; the sermon may have been preached by design, or it may have been by accident, but the lesson is there.

There is little difference between the three shrines, all of which are decorated in the same manner. It is very difficult to do justice to their beauty in words. Writing many thousand miles away from them, I have the memory before me of a place green in winter, pleasant and cool in the hottest summer; of peaceful cloisters, of the fragrance of incense, of the subdued chant of richly robed priests, and the music of bells; of exquisite designs, harmonious colouring, rich gilding. The hum of the vast city outside is unheard here: Iyéyasu himself, in the mountains of Nikkō, has no quieter resting-place than his descendants in the heart of the city over which they ruled.

Besides the graves of the Shoguns, Zōjōji contains other lesser shrines, in which are buried the wives of the second, sixth,

and eleventh Shoguns, and the father of Iyénobu, the sixth Shogun, who succeeded to the office by adoption. There is also a holy place called the Satsuma Temple, which has a special interest; in it is a tablet in honour of Tadayoshi, the fifth son of Iyéyasu, whose title was Matsudaira Satsuma no Kami, and who died young. At his death, five of his retainers, with one Ogasasawara Kemmotsu at their head, disembowelled themselves, that they might follow their young master into the next world. They were buried in this place; and I believe that this is the last instance on record of the ancient Japanese custom of Junshi, that is to say, 'dying with the master.'

There are, during the year, several great festivals which are specially celebrated at Zōjoji; the chief of these are the Kaisanki, or founder's day, which is on the eighteenth day of the seventh month; the twenty-fifth day of the first month, the anniversary of the death of the monk Hōnen, the founder of the Jōdo sect of Buddhism (that to which the temple belongs); the anniversary of the death of Buddha, on the fifteenth of the second month; the birthday of Buddha, on the eighth day of the fourth month; and from the sixth to the fifteenth of the tenth month.

At Uyéno is the second of the burial-grounds of the Shoguns. The Temple Tō-yei-zan, which stood in the grounds of Uyéno, was built by Iyémitsu, the third of the Shoguns of the house of Tokugawa, in the year 1625, in honour of Yakushi Niōrai, the Buddhist Æsculapius. It faces the Ki-mon, or Devil's Gate, of the castle, and was erected upon the model of the temple of Hi-yei-zan, one of the most famous of the holy places of Kiyōto. Having founded the temple, the next care of Iyémitsu was to pray that Morizumi, the second son of the retired emperor, should come and reside there; and from that time until 1868, the temple was always presided over by a Miya, or member of the Mikado's family, who was specially charged with the care of the tomb of Iyéyasu at Nikkō, and whose position was that of an ecclesiastical chief or primate over the east of Japan.

The temples in Yedo are not to be compared in point of beauty with those in and about Peking; what is marble there is wood here. Still they are very handsome, and in the days of its magnificence the Temple of Uyéno was one of the finest. Alas! the main temple, the hall in honour of the sect to which it belongs, the hall of services, the bell-tower, the entrance-hall, and the residence of the prince of the blood, were all burnt down in the battle of Uyéno, in the summer of 1868, when the Shogun's men made their last stand in Yedo against the troops of the Mikado. The fate of the day was decided by two field-pieces, which the latter contrived to mount on the roof of a neighbouring tea-house; and the Shogun's men, driven out of the place, carried off the Miya in the vain hope of raising his standard in the north as that of a rival Mikado. A few of the lesser temples and tombs, and the beautiful park-like grounds, are but the remnants of the former glory of Uyéno. Among these is a temple in the form of a roofless stage, in honour of the thousand-handed Kwannon. In the middle ages, during the civil wars between the houses of Gen and Hei, one Morihisa, a captain of the house of Hei, after the destruction of his clan, went and prayed for a thousand days at the temple of the thousand-handed Kwannon at Kiyomidzu, in Kiyōto. His retreat having been discovered, he was seized and brought bound to Kamakura, the chief town of the house of Gen. Here he was condemned to die at a place called Yui, by the sea-shore; but every time that the executioner lifted his sword to strike, the blade was broken by the god Kwannon, and at the same time the wife of Yoritomo, the chief of the house of Gen, was warned in a dream to spare Morihisa's life. So Morihisa was reprieved, and rose to power in the state; and all this was by the miraculous intervention of the god Kwannon, who takes such good care of his faithful votaries. To him this temple is dedicated. A colossal bronze Buddha, twenty-two feet high, set up some two hundred years ago, and a stone lantern, twenty feet high, and twelve feet round at the top, are greatly admired by the Japanese. There are only three such lanterns in the empire; the other two being at Nanzenji—a temple in Kiyōto, and Atsura, a shrine in the province of Owari. All three were erected by the piety of one man, Sakuma Daizen no Suké, in the year AD 1631.

Iyémitsu, the founder of the temple, was buried with his grandfather, Iyéyasu, at Nikkō; but both of these princes are honoured with shrines here. The Shoguns who are interred at Uyéno are Iyétsuna, Tsunayoshi, Yoshimuné, Iyéharu, Iyénori, and Iyésada, the fourth, fifth, eighth, tenth, eleventh, and thirteenth Princes of the Line. Besides them, are buried five wives of the Shoguns, and the father of the eleventh Shogun.

Notes:
1. This last crime is, of course, now obsolete.
2. The story, which also forms the subject of a play, is published, but with altered names, in order that offence may not be given to the Hotta family The real names are preserved here. The events related took place during the rule of the Shogun Iyémitsu, in the first half of the seventeenth century.
3. A Buddhist deity.
4. Destroyed during the revolution, in the summer of 1868, by the troops of the Mikado. See note on the tombs of the Shoguns, at the end of the story.
5. The name assigned after death to Iyétsuna, the fourth of the dynasty of Tokugawa, who died on the 8th day of the 5th month of the year AD 1680.
6. Buddhist text.

7. The Buddhist Styx, which separates paradise from hell, across which the dead are ferried by an old woman, for whom a small piece of money is buried with them.

8. A Buddhist fiend.

9. In the old days, if a noble was murdered, and died outside his own house, he was disgraced, and his estates were forfeited. When the Regent of the Shogun was murdered, some years since, outside the castle of Yedo, by a legal fiction it was given out that he had died in his own palace, in order that his son might succeed to his estates.

10. Level stirrups.

11. In the days of Shogun's power, the Mikado remained the Fountain of Honour, and, as chief of the national religion and the direct descendant of the gods, dispensed divine honours. So recently as last year, a decree of Mikado appeared in the Government Gazette conferring posthumous divine honours upon an anscestor of the Prince of Choshiu.

12. 10 Sho = 1 Tō.
    10ō = 1 Koku.

13. The apparently poor shaven-pated and blind shampooers of Japan drive a thriving trade as money-lenders. They give out small sums at an interest of 20 per cent per month—240 per cent per annum—and woe betide the luckless wight who falls into their clutches.

How Tajima Shumé Was Tormented by a Devil of His Own Creation

Once upon a time, a certain Rōnin, Tajima Shumé by name, an able and well-read man, being on his travels to see the world, went up to Kiyōto by the Tōkaidō.[1] One day, in the neighbourhood of Nagoya, in the province of Owari, he fell in with a wandering priest, with whom he entered into conversation. Finding that they were bound for the same place, they agreed to travel together, beguiling their weary way by pleasant talk on divers matters; and so by degrees, as they became more intimate, they began to speak without restraint about their private affairs; and the priest, trusting thoroughly in the honour of his companion, told him the object of his journey.

'For some time past,' said he, 'I have nourished a wish that has engrossed all my thoughts; for I am bent on setting up a molten image in honour of Buddha; with this object I have wandered through various provinces collecting alms and (who knows by what weary toil?) we have succeeded in amassing two hundred ounces of silver—enough, I trust, to erect a handsome bronze figure.'

What says the proverb? 'He who bears a jewel in his bosom bears poison.' Hardly had the Rōnin heard these words of the priest than an evil heart arose within him, and he thought to himself, 'Man's life, from the womb to the grave, is made up of good and of ill luck. Here am I, nearly forty years old, a wanderer, without a calling, or even a hope of advancement in the world. To be sure, it seems a shame; yet if I could steal the money this priest is boasting about, I could live at ease for the rest of my days;' and so he began casting about how best he might compass his purpose. But the priest, far from guessing the drift of his comrade's thoughts, journeyed cheerfully on, till they reached the town of Kuana. Here there is an arm of the sea, which is crossed in ferry-boats, that start as soon as some twenty or thirty passengers are gathered together; and in one of these boats the two travellers embarked. About half-way across, the priest was taken with a sudden necessity to go to the side of the boat; and the Rōnin, following him, tripped him up whilst no one was looking, and flung him into the sea. When the boatmen and passengers heard the splash, and saw the priest struggling in the water, they were afraid, and made every effort to save him; but the wind was fair, and the boat running swiftly under the bellying sails, so they were soon a few hundred yards off from the drowning man, who sank before the boat could be turned to rescue him.

When he saw this, the Rōnin feigned the utmost grief and dismay, and said to his fellow-passengers, 'This priest, whom we have just lost, was my cousin: he was going to Kiyōto, to visit the shrine of his patron; and as I happened to have business there as well, we settled to travel together. Now, alas! by this misfortune, my cousin is dead, and I am left alone.'

He spoke so feelingly, and wept so freely, that the passengers believed his story, and pitied and tried to comfort him. Then the Rōnin said to the boatmen:

'We ought, by rights, to report this matter to the authorities; but as I am pressed for time, and the business might bring trouble on yourselves as well, perhaps we had better hush it up for the present; and I will at once go on to Kiyōto and tell my cousin's patron, besides writing home about it. What think you, gentlemen?' added he, turning to the other travellers.

They, of course, were only too glad to avoid any hindrance to their onward journey, and all with one

voice agreed to what the Rōnin had proposed; and so the matter was settled. When, at length, they reached the shore, they
left the boat, and every man went his way; but the Rōnin,
overjoyed in his heart, took the wandering priest's luggage,
and, putting it with his own, pursued his journey to Kiyōto.

On reaching the capital, the Rōnin changed his name
from Shumé to Tokubei, and, giving up his position as a
Samurai, turned merchant, and traded with the dead man's
money. Fortune favouring his speculations, he began to amass
great wealth, and lived at his ease, denying himself nothing;
and in course of time he married a wife, who bore him a child.

Thus the days and months wore on, till one fine summer's night, some three years after the priest's death, Tokubei
stepped out on to the verandah of his house to enjoy the cool
air and the beauty of the moonlight. Feeling dull and lonely,
he began musing over all kinds of things, when on a sudden the deed of murder and theft, done so long ago, vividly
recurred to his memory, and he thought to himself, 'Here
am I, grown rich and fat on the money I wantonly stole.
Since then, all has gone well with me; yet, had I not been
poor, I had never turned assassin nor thief. Woe betide me!
what a pity it was!' and as he was revolving the matter in his
mind, a feeling of remorse came over him, in spite of all he
could do. While his conscience thus smote him, he suddenly,
to his utter amazement, beheld the faint outline of a man
standing near a fir-tree in the garden: on looking more attentively, he perceived that the man's whole body was thin and
worn and the eyes sunken and dim; and in the poor ghost
that was before him he recognised the very priest whom
he had thrown into the sea at Kuana. Chilled with
horror, he looked again, and saw that the priest

was smiling in scorn. He would have fled into the house, but the ghost stretched forth its withered arm, and, clutching the back of his neck, scowled at him with a vindictive glare, and a hideous ghastliness of mien, so unspeakably awful that any ordinary man would have swooned with fear. But Tokubei, tradesman though he was, had once been a soldier, and was not easily matched for daring; so he shook off the ghost, and, leaping into the room for his dirk, laid about him boldly enough; but, strike as he would, the spirit, fading into the air, eluded his blows, and suddenly reappeared only to vanish again: and from that time forth Tokubei knew no rest, and was haunted night and day.

At length, undone by such ceaseless vexation, Tokubei fell ill, and kept muttering, 'Oh, misery! misery!—the wandering priest is coming to torture me!' Hearing his moans and the disturbance he made, the people in the house fancied he was mad, and called in a physician, who prescribed for him. But neither pill nor potion could cure Tokubei, whose strange frenzy soon became the talk of the whole neighbourhood.

Now it chanced that the story reached the cars of a certain wandering priest who lodged in the next street. When he heard the particulars, this priest gravely shook his head, as though he knew all about it, and sent a friend to Tokubei's house to say that a wandering priest, dwelling hard by, had heard of his illness, and, were it never so grievous, would undertake to heal it by means of his prayers; and Tokubei's wife, driven half wild by her husband's sickness, lost not a moment in sending for the priest, and taking him into the sick man's room.

But no sooner did Tokubei see the priest than he yelled out, 'Help! help! Here is the wandering priest come to torment me again. Forgive! forgive!' and hiding his head under the coverlet, he lay quivering all over. Then the priest turned all present out of the room, put his mouth to the affrighted man's ear, and whispered:

'Three years ago, at the Kuana ferry, you flung me into the water; and well you remember it.'

But Tokubei was speechless, and could only quake with fear.

'Happily,' continued the priest, 'I had learned to swim and to dive as a boy; so I reached the shore, and, after wandering through many provinces, succeeded in setting up a bronze figure to Buddha, thus fulfilling the wish of my heart. On my journey homewards, I took a lodging in the next street, and there heard of your marvellous ailment. Thinking I could divine its cause, I came to see you, and am glad to find I was not mistaken. You have done a hateful deed; but am I not a priest, and have I not forsaken the things of this world? And would it not ill become me to bear malice? Repent, therefore, and abandon your evil ways. To see you do so I should esteem the height of happiness. Be of good cheer, now, and look me in the face, and you will see that I am really a living man, and no vengeful goblin come to torment you.'

Seeing he had no ghost to deal with, and overwhelmed by the priest's kindness, Tokubei burst into tears, and answered, 'Indeed, indeed, I don't know what to say. In a fit of madness I was tempted to kill and rob you. Fortune befriended me ever after; but the richer I grew, the more keenly I felt how wicked I had been, and the more I foresaw that my victim's vengeance

would some day overtake me. Haunted by this thought, I lost my nerve, till one night I beheld your spirit, and from that time forth fell ill. But how you managed to escape, and are still alive, is more than I can understand.'

'A guilty man,' said the priest, with a smile, 'shudders at the rustling of the wind or the chattering of a stork's beak: a murderer's conscience preys upon his mind till he sees what is not. Poverty drives a man to crimes which he repents of in his wealth. How true is the doctrine of Mōshi,[2] that the heart of man, pure by nature, is corrupted by circumstances.'

Thus he held forth; and Tokubei, who had long since repented of his crime, implored forgiveness, and gave him a large sum of money, saying, 'Half of this is the amount I stole from you three years since; the other half I entreat you to accept as interest, or as a gift.'

The priest at first refused the money; but Tokubei insisted on his accepting it, and did all he could to detain him, but in vain; for the priest went his way, and bestowed the money on the poor and needy. As for Tokubei himself, he soon shook off his disorder, and thenceforward lived at peace with all men, revered both at home and abroad, and ever intent on good and charitable deeds.

Notes:

1. The road of the Eastern Sea, the famous high-road leading from Kiyōto to Yedo. The name is also used to indicate the provinces through which it runs.

2. Mencius.

Concerning Certain Superstitions

Concerning Certain Superstitions

Cats, foxes, and badgers are regarded with superstitious awe by the Japanese, who attribute to them the power of assuming the human shape in order to bewitch mankind. Like the fairies of our Western tales, however, they work for good as well as for evil ends. To do them a good turn is to secure powerful allies; but woe betide him who injures them! He and his will assuredly suffer for it. Cats and foxes seem to have been looked upon as uncanny beasts all the world over; but it is new to me that badgers should have a place in fairy-land. The island of Shikoku, the southernmost of the great Japanese islands, appears to be the part of the country in which the badger is regarded with the greatest veneration. Among the many tricks which he plays upon the human race is one, of which I have a clever representation carved in ivory. Lying in wait in lonely places after dusk, the badger watches for benighted wayfarers: should one appear, the beast, drawing a long breath, distends his belly and drums delicately upon it with his clenched fist, producing such entrancing tones, that the traveller cannot resist turning aside to follow the sound, which, Will-o'-the-wisp-like, recedes as he advances, until it lures him on to his destruction. Love is, however, the most powerful engine which the cat, the fox, and the badger alike put forth for the ruin of man. No German poet ever imagined a more captivating water-nymph than the fair virgins by whom the knight of Japanese romance is assailed: the true hero recognises and slays the beast; the weaker mortal yields and perishes.

The Japanese story-books abound with tales about the pranks of these creatures, which, like ghosts, even play a part in the histories of ancient and noble families. I have collected a few of these, and now beg a hearing for a distinguished and two-tailed[1] connection of Puss in Boots and the Chatte Blanche.

The Vampire Cat of Nabéshima

There is a tradition in the Nabéshima[2] family that, many years ago, the Prince of Hizen was bewitched and cursed by a cat that had been kept by one of his retainers. This prince had in his house a lady of rare beauty, called O Toyo: amongst all his ladies she was the favourite, and there was none who could rival her charms and accomplishments. One day the Prince went out into the garden with O Toyo, and remained enjoying the fragrance of the flowers until sunset, when they returned to the palace, never noticing that they were being followed by a large cat. Having parted with her lord, O Toyo retired to her own room and went to bed. At midnight she awoke with a start, and became aware of a huge cat that crouched watching her; and when she cried out, the beast sprang on her, and, fixing its cruel teeth in her delicate throat, throttled her to death. What a piteous end for so

The cat of Nabéshima

fair a dame, the darling of her prince's heart, to die suddenly, bitten to death by a cat! Then the cat, having scratched out a grave under the verandah, buried the corpse of O Toyo, and assuming her form, began to bewitch the Prince.

But my lord the Prince knew nothing of all this, and little thought that the beautiful creature who caressed and fondled him was an impish and foul beast that had slain his mistress and assumed her shape in order to drain out his life's blood. Day by day, as time went on, the Prince's strength dwindled away; the colour of his face was changed, and became pale and livid; and he was as a man suffering from a deadly sickness. Seeing this, his councillors and his wife became greatly alarmed; so they summoned the physicians, who prescribed various remedies for him; but the more medicine he took, the more serious did his illness appear, and no treatment was of any avail. But most of all did he suffer in the night-time, when his sleep would be troubled and disturbed by hideous dreams. In consequence of this, his councillors nightly appointed a hundred of his retainers to sit up and watch over him; but, strange to say, towards ten o'clock on the very first night that the watch was set, the guard were seized with a sudden and unaccountable drowsiness, which they could not resist, until one by one every man had fallen asleep. Then the false O Toyo came in and harassed the Prince until morning. The following night the same thing occurred, and the Prince was subjected to the imp's tyranny, while his guards slept helplessly around him. Night after night this was repeated, until at last three of the Prince's councillors determined themselves to sit up on guard, and see whether they could overcome this mysterious drowsiness; but they fared no better than the others, and by ten o'clock were fast asleep. The next day the three councillors held a solemn conclave, and their chief, one Isahaya Buzen, said:

'This is a marvellous thing, that a guard of a hundred men should thus be overcome by sleep. Of a surety, the spell that is upon my lord and upon his guard must be the work of witchcraft. Now, as all our efforts are of no avail, let us seek out Ruiten, the chief priest of the temple called Miyō In, and beseech him to put up prayers for the recovery of my lord.'

And the other councillors approving what Isahaya Buzen had said, they went to the priest Ruiten and engaged him to recite litanies that the Prince might be restored to health.

So it came to pass that Ruiten, the chief priest of Miyō In, offered up prayers nightly for the Prince. One night, at the ninth hour (midnight), when he had finished his religious exercises and was preparing to lie down to sleep, he fancied that he heard a noise outside in the garden, as if some one were washing himself at the well. Deeming this passing strange, he looked down from the window; and there in the moonlight he saw a handsome young soldier, some twenty-four years of age, washing himself, who, when he had finished cleaning himself and had put on his clothes, stood before the figure of Buddha and prayed fervently for the recovery of my lord the Prince. Ruiten looked on with admiration; and the young man, when he had made an end of his prayer, was going away; but the priest stopped him, calling out to him:

'Sir, I pray you to tarry a little: I have something to say to you.'

'At your reverence's service. What may you please to want?'

'Pray be so good as to step up here, and have a little talk.'

'By your reverence's leave;' and with this he went upstairs.

Then Ruiten said:

'Sir, I cannot conceal my admiration that you, being so young a man, should have so loyal a spirit. I am Ruiten, the chief priest of this temple, who am engaged in praying for the recovery of my lord. Pray what is your name?'

'My name, sir, is Itō Sōda, and I am serving in the infantry of Nabéshima. Since my lord has been sick, my one desire has been to assist in nursing him; but, being only a simple soldier, I am not of sufficient rank to come into his presence, so I have no resource but to pray to the gods of the country and to Buddha that my lord may regain his health.'

When Ruiten heard this, he shed tears in admiration of the fidelity of Itō Sōda, and said:

'Your purpose is, indeed, a good one; but what a strange sickness this is that my lord is afflicted with! Every night he suffers from horrible dreams; and the retainers who sit up with him are all seized with a mysterious sleep, so that not one can keep awake. It is very wonderful.'

'Yes,' replied Sōda, after a moment's reflection, 'this certainly must be witchcraft. If I could but obtain leave to sit up one night with the Prince, I would fain see whether I could not resist this drowsiness and detect the goblin.'

At last the priest said, 'I am in relations of friendship with Isahaya Buzen, the chief councillor of the Prince. I will speak to him of you and of your loyalty, and will intercede with him that you may attain your wish.'

'Indeed, sir, I am most thankful. I am not prompted by any vain thought of self-advancement, should I succeed: all I wish for is the recovery of my lord. I commend myself to your kind favour.'

'Well, then, tomorrow night I will take you with me to the councillor's house.'

'Thank you, sir, and farewell.' And so they parted.

On the following evening Itō Sōda returned to the temple Miyō In, and having found Ruiten, accompanied him to the house of Isahaya Buzen: then the priest, leaving Sōda outside, went in to converse with the councillor, and inquire after the Prince's health.

'And pray, sir, how is my lord? Is he in any better condition since I have been offering up prayers for him?'

'Indeed, no; his illness is very severe. We are certain that he must be the victim of some foul sorcery; but as there are no means of keeping a guard awake after ten o'clock, we cannot catch a sight of the goblin, so we are in the greatest trouble.'

'I feel deeply for you: it must be most distressing. However, I have something to tell you. I think that I have found a man who will detect the goblin; and I have brought him with me.'

'Indeed! who is the man?'

'Well, he is one of my lord's foot-soldiers, named Itō Sōda, a faithful fellow, and I trust that you will grant his request to be permitted to sit up with my lord.'

'Certainly, it is wonderful to find so much loyalty and zeal in a common soldier,' replied Isahaya Buzen, after a moment's reflection; 'still it is impossible to allow a man of such low rank to perform the office of watching over my lord.'

'It is true that he is but a common soldier,' urged the priest; 'but why not raise his rank in consideration of his fidelity, and then let him mount guard?'

'It would be time enough to promote him after my lord's recovery. But come, let me see this Itō Sōda, that I may know what manner of man he is: if he pleases me, I will consult with the other councillors, and perhaps we may grant his request.'

'I will bring him in forthwith,' replied Ruiten, who thereupon went out to fetch the young man.

When he returned, the priest presented Itō Sōda to the councillor, who looked at him attentively, and, being pleased with his comely and gentle appearance, said:

'So I hear that you are anxious to be permitted to mount guard in my lord's room at night. Well, I must consult with the other councillors, and we will see what can be done for you.'

When the young soldier heard this he was greatly elated, and took his leave, after warmly thanking Buiten, who had helped him to gain his object. The next day the councillors held a meeting, and sent for Itō Sōda, and told him that he might keep watch with the other retainers that very night. So he went his way in high spirits, and at nightfall, having made all his preparations, took his place among the hundred gentlemen who were on duty in the prince's bed-room.

Now the Prince slept in the centre of the room, and the hundred guards around him sat keeping themselves awake with entertaining conversation and pleasant conceits. But, as ten o'clock approached, they began to doze off as they sat; and in spite of all their endeavours to keep one another awake, by degrees they all fell asleep. Itō Sōda all this while felt an irresistible desire to sleep creeping over him, and, though he tried by all sorts of ways to rouse himself, he saw that there was no help for it, but by resorting to an extreme measure, for which he had already made his preparations. Drawing out a piece of oil paper which he had brought with him, and spreading it over the mats, he sat down upon it; then he took the small knife which he carried in the sheath of his dirk, and stuck it into his own thigh. For awhile the pain of the wound kept him awake; but as the slumber by which he was assailed was the work of sorcery, little bylittle he became drowsy again. Then he twisted the knife round and round in his thigh, so that the pain becoming very violent, he was proof against the feeling of sleepiness, and kept a faithful watch. Now the oil paper which he had spread under his legs was in order to prevent the blood, which might spurt from his wound, from defiling the mats.

So Itō Sōda remained awake, but the rest of the guard slept; and as he watched, suddenly the sliding-doors of the Prince's room were drawn open, and he saw a figure coming in stealthily, and, as it drew nearer, the form was that of a marvellously beautiful woman some twenty-three years of age. Cautiously she looked around her; and when she saw that all the guard were asleep, she smiled an ominous smile, and was going up to the Prince's bedside, when she perceived that in one corner of the room there was a man yet awake. This seemed to startle her, but she went up to Sōda and said:

'I am not used to seeing you here. Who are you?'

'My name is Itō Sōda, and this is the first night that I have been on guard.'

'A troublesome office, truly! Why, here are all the rest of the guard asleep. How is it that you alone are awake? You are a trusty watchman.'

'There is nothing to boast about. I'm asleep myself, fast and sound.'

'What is that wound on your knee? It is all red with blood.'

'Oh! I felt very sleepy; so I stuck my knife into my thigh, and the pain of it has kept me awake.'

'What wondrous loyalty!' said the lady.

'Is it not the duty of a retainer to lay down his life for his master? Is such a scratch as this worth thinking about?'

Then the lady went up to the sleeping prince and said, 'How fares it with my lord tonight?' But the Prince, worn out with sickness, made no reply. But Sōda was watching her eagerly, and guessed that it was O Toyo, and made up his mind that if she attempted to harass the Prince he would kill her on the spot. The goblin, however, which in the form of O Toyo had been tormenting the Prince every night, and had come again that night for no other purpose, was defeated by the watchfulness of Ito Sōda; for whenever she drew near to the sick man, thinking to put her spells upon him, she would turn and look behind her, and there she saw Itō Sōda glaring at her; so she had no help for it but to go away again, and leave the Prince undisturbed.

At last the day broke, and the other officers, when they awoke and opened their eyes, saw that Itō Sōda had kept awake by stabbing himself in the thigh; and they were greatly ashamed, and went home crestfallen.

That morning Itō Sōda went to the house of Isahaya Buzen, and told him all that had occurred the previous night. The councillors were all loud in their praises of Itō Sōda's behaviour, and ordered him to keep watch again that night. At the same hour, the false O Toyo came and looked all round the room, and all the guard were asleep, excepting Itō Sōda, who was wide awake; and so, being again frustrated, she returned to her own apartments.

Now as since Sōda had been on guard the Prince had passed quiet nights, his sickness began to get better, and there was great joy in the palace, and Sōda was promoted and rewarded with an estate. In the meanwhile O Toyo, seeing that her nightly visits bore no fruits, kept away; and from that time forth the night-guard were no longer subject to fits of drowsiness. This coincidence struck Sōda as very strange, so he went to Isahaya Buzen and told him that of a certainty this O Toyo was no other than a goblin. Isahaya Buzen reflected for a while, and said:

'Well, then, how shall we kill the foul thing?'

'I will go to the creature's room, as if nothing were the matter, and try to kill her; but in case she should try to escape, I will beg you to order eight men to stop outside and lie in wait for her.'

Having agreed upon this plan, Sōda went at nightfall to O Toyo's apartment, pretending to have been sent with a message from the Prince. When she saw him arrive, she said:

'What message have you brought me from my lord?'

'Oh! nothing in particular. Be so look as to look at this letter;' and as he spoke, he drew near to her, and suddenly drawing his dirk cut at her; but the goblin, springing back, seized a halberd, and glaring fiercely at Sōda, said:

'How dare you behave like this to one of your lord's ladies? I will have you dismissed;' and she tried to strike Sōda with the halberd. But Sōda fought desperately with his dirk; and the goblin, seeing that she was no match for him, threw away the halberd, and from a beautiful woman became suddenly transformed into a cat, which, springing up the sides of the room, jumped on to the roof. Isahaya Buzen and his eight men who were watching outside shot at the cat, but missed it, and the beast made good its escape.

So the cat fled to the mountains, and did much mis-chief among the surrounding people, until at last the Prince of Hizen ordered a great hunt, and the beast was killed.

But the Prince recovered from his sickness; and Itō Sōda was richly rewarded.

The Story of the Faithful Cat

About sixty years ago, in the summer-time, a man went to pay a visit at a certain house at Osaka, and, in the course of conversation, said:

'I have eaten some very extraordinary cakes today,' and on being asked what he meant, he told the following story:

'I received the cakes from the relatives of a family who were celebrating the hundredth anniversary of the death of a cat that had belonged to their an-cestors. When I asked the history of the af-fair, I was told that, in former days, a young girl of the family, when she was about sixteen years old, used always to be followed about by a tom-cat, who was reared in the house, so much so that the two were never separated for an instant. When her father perceived this, he was very angry, thinking that the tom-cat, forgetting the kindness with which he had been treated for years in the house, had fallen in love with his daughter, and intended to cast a spell upon her; so he determined that he must kill the beast. As he was planning this in secret, the cat overheard him, and that night went to his pillow, and, assuming a human voice, said to him:

'"You suspect me of being in love with your daughter; and although you might well be justified in so think-ing, your suspicions are groundless. The fact is this: There is a very large old rat who has been living for many years in your granary. Now it is this old rat who is in love with my young mistress, and this is why I dare not leave her side for a moment, for fear the old rat should carry her off. Therefore I pray you to dispel your suspicions. But as I, by myself, am no match for the rat, there is a famous cat, named Buchi, at the house of Mr. So-and-so, at Ajikawa: if you will borrow that cat, we will soon make an end of the old rat."

'When the father awoke from his dream, he thought it so wonderful, that he told the household of it; and the following day he got up very early and went off to Ajikawa, to inquire for the house which the cat had indicated, and had no difficulty in finding it; so he called upon the master of the house, and told him what his own cat had said, and how he wished to borrow the cat Buchi for a little while.

'That's a very easy matter to settle,' said the other: 'pray take him with you at once;' and accordingly the father went home with the cat Buchi in charge. That night he put the two cats into the granary; and after a little while, a frightful clatter was heard, and then all was still again; so the people of the house opened the door, and crowded out to see what had happened; and there they beheld the two cats and the rat all locked together, and panting for breath; so they cut the throat of the rat, which was as big as either of the cats: then they attended to the two cats; but, although they gave them ginseng[3] and other restoratives, they both got weaker and weaker, until at last they died. So the rat was thrown into the river; but the two cats were buried with all honours in a neighbouring temple.'

How a Man was Bewitched and Had His Head Shaved by the Foxes

In the village of Iwahara, in the province of Shinshiu, there dwelt a family which had acquired considerable wealth in the wine trade. On some auspicious occasion it happened that a number of guests were gathered together at their house, feasting on wine and fish; and as the wine-cup went round, the conversation turned upon foxes. Among the guests was a certain carpenter, Tokutarō by name, a man about thirty years of age, of a stubborn and obstinate turn, who said:

'Well, sirs, you've been talking for some time of men being bewitched by foxes; surely you must be under their influence yourselves, to say such things. How on earth can foxes have such power over men? At any rate, men must be great fools to be so deluded. Let's have no more of this nonsense.'

Upon this a man who was sitting by him answered:

'Tokutarō little knows what goes on in the world, or he would not speak so. How many myriads of men are there who have been bewitched by foxes? Why, there have been at least twenty or thirty men tricked by the brutes on the Maki Moor alone. It's hard to disprove facts that have happened before our eyes.'

'You're no better than a pack of born idiots,' said Tokutarō. 'I will engage to go out to the Maki Moor this very night and prove it. There is not a fox in all Japan that can make a fool of Tokutarō.'

'Thus he spoke in his pride; but the others were all angry with him for boasting, and said:

'If you return without anything having happened, we will pay for five measures of wine and a thousand copper cash worth of fish; and if you are bewitched, you shall do as much for us.'

Tokutarō took the bet, and at nightfall set forth for the Maki Moor by himself. As he neared the moor, he saw before him a small bamboo grove, into which a fox ran; and it instantly occurred to him that the foxes of the moor would try to bewitch him. As he was yet looking, he suddenly saw the daughter of the headman of the village of Upper Horikané, who was married to the headman of the village of Maki.

'Pray, where are you going to, Master Tokutarō?' said she.

'I am going to the village hard by.'

'Then, as you will have to pass my native place, if you will allow me, I will accompany you so far.'

Tokutarō thought this very odd, and made up his mind that it was a fox trying to make a fool of him; he accordingly determined to turn the tables on the fox, and answered:

'It is a long time since I have had the pleasure of seeing you; and as it seems that your house is on my road, I shall be glad to escort you so far.'

With this he walked behind her, thinking he should certainly see the end of a fox's tail peeping out; but, look as he might, there was nothing to be seen. At last they came to the village of Upper Horikané; and when they reached the cottage of the girl's father, the family all came out, surprised to see her.

'Oh dear! oh dear! here is our daughter come: I hope there is nothing the matter.'

And so they went on, for some time, asking a string of questions.

In the meanwhile, Tokutarō went round to the kitchen door, at the back of the house, and, beckoning out the master of the house, said:

'The girl who has come with me is not really your daughter. As I was going to the Maki Moor, when I arrived at the bamboo grove, a fox jumped up in front of me, and when it had dashed into the grove it immediately took the shape of your daughter, and offered to accompany me to the village; so I pretended to be taken in by the brute, and came with it so far.'

On hearing this, the master of the house put his head on one side, and mused a while; then, calling his wife, he repeated the story to her, in a whisper.

But she flew into a great rage with Tokutarō, and said:

'This is a pretty way of insulting people's daughters. The girl is our daughter, and there's no mistake about it. How dare you invent such lies?'

'Well,' said Tokutarō, 'you are quite right to say so; but still there is no doubt that this is a case of witchcraft.'

Seeing how obstinately he held to his opinion, the old folks were sorely perplexed, and said:

'What do you think of doing?'

'Pray leave the matter to me: I'll soon strip the false skin off, and show the beast to you in its true colours. Do you two go into the store-closet, and wait there.'

With this he went into the kitchen, and, seizing the girl by the back of the neck, forced her down by the hearth.

'Oh! Master Tokutarō, what means this brutal violence? Mother! father! help!'

So the girl cried and screamed; but Tokutarō only laughed, and said:

'So you thought to bewitch me, did you? From the moment you jumped into the wood, I was on the look-out for you to play me some trick. I'll soon make you show what you really are;' and as he said this, he twisted her two hands behind her back, and trod upon her, and tortured her; but she only wept, and cried:

'Oh! it hurts, it hurts!'

'If this is not enough to make you show your true form, I'll roast you to death;' and he piled firewood on the hearth, and, tucking up her dress, scorched her severely.

'Oh! oh! this is more than I can bear;' and with this she expired.

The two old people then came running in from the rear of the house, and, pushing aside Tokutarō, folded their daughter in their arms, and put their hands to her mouth to feel whether she still breathed; but life was extinct, and not the sign of a fox's tail was to be seen about her. Then they seized Tokutarō by the collar, and cried:

'On pretence that our true daughter was a fox, you have roasted her to death. Murderer! Here, you there, bring ropes and cords, and secure this Tokutarō!'

So the servants obeyed, and several of them seized Tokutarō and bound him to a pillar. Then the master of the house, turning to Tokutarō, said:

'You have murdered our daughter before our very eyes. I shall report the matter to the lord of the manor, and you will assuredly pay for this with your head. Be prepared for the worst.'

And as he said this, glaring fiercely at Tokutarō, they carried the corpse of his daughter into the store-closet. As they were sending to make the matter known in the village of Maki, and taking other measures, who should come up but the priest of the temple called Anrakuji, in the village of Iwahara, with an acolyte and a servant, who called out in a loud voice from the front door:

'Is all well with the honourable master of this house? I have been to say prayers today in a neighbouring village, and on my way back I could not pass the door without at least inquiring after your welfare. If you are at home, I would fain pay my respects to you.'

As he spoke thus in a loud voice, he was heard from the back of the house; and the master got up and went out, and, after the usual compliments on meeting had been exchanged, said:

'I ought to have the honour of inviting you to step inside this evening; but really we are all in the greatest trouble, and I must beg you to excuse my impoliteness.'

'Indeed! Pray, what may be the matter?' replied the priest. And when the master of the house had told the whole story, from beginning to end, he was thunderstruck, and said:

'Truly, this must be a terrible distress to you.' Then the priest looked on one side,  and saw Tokutarō bound, and exclaimed, 'Is not that Tokutarō that I see there?'

'Oh, your reverence,' replied Tokutarō, piteously, 'it was this, that, and the other: and I took it into my head that the young lady was a fox, and so I killed her. But I pray your reverence to intercede for me, and save my life;' and as he spoke, the tears started from his eyes.

'To be sure,' said the priest, 'you may well bewail yourself; however, if I save your life, will you consent to become my disciple, and enter the priesthood?'

'Only save my life, and I'll become your disciple with all my heart.'

When the priest heard this, he called out the parents, and said to them:

'It would seem that, though I am but a foolish old priest, my coming here today has been unusually well timed. I have a request to make of you. Your putting Tokutarō to death won't bring your daughter to life again. I have heard his story, and there certainly was no malice prepense on his part to kill your daughter. What he did, he did thinking to do a service to your family; and it would surely be better to hush the matter up. He wishes, moreover, to give himself over to me, and to become my disciple.'

'It is as you say,' replied the father and mother, speaking together. 'Revenge will not recall our daughter. Please dispel our grief, by shaving his head and making a priest of him on the spot.'

'I'll shave him at once, before your eyes,' answered the priest, who immediately caused the cords which bound Tokutarō to be untied, and, putting on his priest's scarf, made him join his hands together in a posture of prayer. Then the reverend man stood up behind him, razor in hand, and, intoning a hymn, gave two or three strokes of the razor, which he then handed to his acolyte, who made a clean shave of Tokutarō's hair. When the latter had finished his obeisance to the priest, and the ceremony was over, there was a loud burst of laughter; and at the same moment the day broke, and Tokutarō found himself alone, in the middle of a large moor. At first, in his surprise, he thought that it was all a dream, and was much annoyed at having been tricked by the foxes. He then passed his hand over his head, and found that he was shaved quite bald. There was nothing for it but to get up, wrap a handkerchief round his head, and go back to the place where his friends were assembled.

'Hallo, Tokutarō! so you've come back. Well, how about the foxes?'

'Really, gentlemen,' replied he, bowing, 'I am quite ashamed to appear before you.'

Then he told them the whole story, and, when he had finished, pulled off the kerchief, and showed his bald pate.

'What a capital joke!' shouted his listeners, and amid roars of laughter, claimed the bet of fish, and wine. It was duly paid; but Tokutarō never allowed his hair to grow again, and renounced the world, and became a priest under the name of Sainen.

There are a great many stories told of men being shaved by the foxes; but this story came under the personal observation of Mr. Shōminsai, a teacher of the city of Yedo, during a holiday trip which he took to the country where the event occurred; and I[4] have recorded it in the very selfsame words in which he told it to me.

The Grateful Foxes

One fine spring day, two friends went out to a moor to gather fern, attended by a boy with a bottle of wine and a box of provisions. As they were straying about, they saw at the foot of a hill a fox that had brought out its cub to play; and whilst they looked on, struck by the strangeness of the sight, three children came up from a neighbouring village with baskets in their hands, on the same errand as themselves. As soon as the children saw the foxes, they picked up a bamboo stick and took the creatures stealthily in the rear; and when the old foxes took to flight, they surrounded them and beat them with the stick, so that they ran away as fast as their legs could carry them; but two of the boys held down the cub, and, seizing it by the scruff of the neck, went off in high glee.

The two friends were looking on all the while, and one of them, raising hi s voice, shouted out, 'Hallo! you boys! what are you doing with that fox?'

The eldest of the boys replied, 'We're going to take him home and sell him to a young man in our village. He'll buy him, and then he'll boil him in a pot and eat him.'

'Well,' replied the other, after considering the matter attentively, 'I suppose it's all the same to you whom you sell him to. You'd better let me have him.'

'Oh, but the young man from our village promised us a good round sum if we could find a fox, and got us to come out to the hills and catch one; and so we can't sell him to you at any price.'

'Well, I suppose it cannot be helped, then; but how much would the young man give you for the cub?'

'Oh, he'll give us three hundred cash at least.'

'Then I'll give you half a bu;⁵ and so you'll gain five hundred cash by the transaction.'

'Oh, we'll sell him for that, sir. How shall we hand him over to you?'

'Just tie him up here,' said the other; and so he made fast the cub round the neck with the string of the napkin in which the luncheon-box was wrapped, and gave half a bu to the three boys, who ran away delighted.

The man's friend, upon this, said to him, 'Well, certainly you have got queer tastes. What on earth are you going to keep the fox for?'

'How very unkind of you to speak of my tastes like that. If we had not interfered just now, the fox's cub would have lost its life. If we had not seen the affair, there would have been no help for it. How could I stand by and see life taken? It was but a little I spent—only half a bu—to save the cub, but had it cost a fortune I should not have grudged it. I thought you were intimate enough with me to know my heart; but today you have accused me of being eccentric, and I see how mistaken I have been in you. However, our friendship shall cease from this day forth.'

And when he had said this with a great deal of firmness, the other, retiring backwards and bowing with his hands on his knees, replied:

'Indeed, indeed, I am filled with admiration at the goodness of your heart. When I hear you speak thus, I feel more than ever how great is the love I bear you. I thought that you might wish to use the cub as a sort of decoy to lead the old ones to you, that you might pray them to bring prosperity and virtue to your house. When I called you eccentric just now, I was but trying your heart, because I had some suspicions of you; and now I am truly ashamed of myself.'

And as he spoke, still bowing, the other replied, 'Really! was that indeed your thought? Then I pray you to forgive me for my violent language.'

When the two friends had thus become reconciled, they examined the cub, and saw that it had a slight wound in its foot, and could not walk; and while they were thinking what they should do, they spied out the herb called 'Doctor's Nakasé,' which was just sprouting; so they rolled up a little of it in their fingers and applied it to the part. Then they pulled out some boiled rice from their luncheon-box and offered it to the cub, but it showed no sign of wanting to eat; so they stroked it gently on the back, and petted it; and as the pain of the wound seemed to have subsided, they were admiring the properties of the herb, when, opposite to them, they saw the old foxes sitting watching them by the side of some stacks of rice straw.

'Look there! the old foxes have come back, out of fear for their cub's safety. Come, we will set it free!' And with these words they untied the string round the cub's neck, and turned its head towards the spot where the old foxes sat; and as the wounded foot was no longer painful, with one bound it dashed to its parents' side and licked them all over for joy, while they seemed to bow their thanks, looking towards the two friends. So, with peace in their hearts, the latter went off to another place, and, choosing a pretty spot, produced the wine bottle and ate their noon-day meal; and after a pleasant day, they returned to their homes, and became firmer friends than ever.

Now the man who had rescued the fox's cub was a tradesman in good circumstances: he had three or four agents and two maid-servants, besides men-servants; and altogether he lived in a liberal manner. He was married, and this union had brought him one son, who had reached his tenth year, but had been attacked by a strange disease which defied all the physician's skill and drugs. At last a famous physician prescribed the liver taken from a live fox, which, as he said, would certainly effect a cure. If that were not forthcoming, the most expensive medicine in the world would not restore the boy to health. When the parents heard this, they were at their wits' end. However, they told the state of the case to a man who lived on the mountains. 'Even though our child should die for it,' they said, 'we will not ourselves deprive other creatures of their lives; but you, who live among the hills, are sure to hear when your neighbours go out fox-hunting. We don't care what price we might have to pay for a fox's liver; pray, buy one for us at any expense.' So they pressed him to exert himself on their behalf; and he, having promised faithfully to execute the commission, went his way.

In the night of the following day there came a messenger, who announced himself as coming from the person who had undertaken to procure the fox's liver; so the master of the house went out to see him.

'I have come from Mr. So-and-so. Last night the fox's liver that you required fell into his hands; so he sent me to bring it to you.' With these words the messenger produced a small jar, adding, 'In a few days he will let you know the price.'

When he had delivered his message, the master of the house was greatly pleased, and said, 'Indeed, I am deeply grateful for this kindness, which will save my son's life.'

Then the goodwife came out, and received the jar with every mark of politeness.

'We must make a present to the messenger.'

'Indeed, sir, I've already been paid for my trouble.'

'Well, at any rate, you must stop the night here.'

'Thank you, sir: I've a relation in the next village whom I have not seen for a long while, and I will pass the night with him;' and so he took his leave, and went away.

The parents lost no time in sending to let the physician know that they had procured the fox's liver. The next day the doctor came and compounded a medicine for the patient, which at once produced a good effect, and there was no little joy in the household. As luck would have it, three days after this the man whom they had commissioned to buy the fox's liver came to the house; so the goodwife hurried out to meet him and welcome him.

'How quickly you fulfilled our wishes, and how kind of you to send at once! The doctor prepared the medicine, and now our boy can get up and walk about the room; and it's all owing to your goodness.'

'Wait a bit!' cried the guest, who did not know what to make of the joy of the two parents. 'The commission with which you entrusted me about the fox's liver turned out to be a matter of impossibility, so I came today to make my excuses; and now I really can't understand what you are so grateful to me for.'

'We are thanking you, sir,' replied the master of the house, bowing with his hands on the ground, 'for the fox's liver which we asked you to procure for us.'

'I really am perfectly unaware of having sent you a fox's liver: there must be some mistake here. Pray inquire carefully into the matter.'

'Well, this is very strange. Four nights ago, a man of some five or six and thirty years of age came with a verbal message from you, to the effect that you had sent him with a fox's liver, which you had just procured, and said that he would come and tell us the price another day. When we asked him to spend the night here, he answered that he would lodge with a relation in the next village, and went away.'

The visitor was more and more lost in amazement, and; leaning his head on one side in deep thought, confessed that he could make nothing of it. As for the husband and wife, they felt quite out of countenance at having thanked a man so warmly for favours of which he denied all knowledge; and so the visitor took his leave, and went home.

That night there appeared at the pillow of the master of the house a woman of about one or two and thirty years of age, who said, 'I am the fox that lives at such-and-such a mountain. Last spring, when I was taking out my cub to play, it was carried off by some boys, and only saved by your goodness. The desire to requite this kindness pierced me to the quick. At last, when calamity attacked your house, I thought that I might be of use to you. Your son's illness could not be cured without a liver taken from a live fox, so to repay your kindness I killed my cub and took out its liver; then its sire, disguising himself as a messenger, brought it to your house.'

And as she spoke, the fox shed tears; and the master of the house, wishing to thank her, moved in bed, upon which his wife awoke and asked him what was the matter; but he too, to her great astonishment, was biting the pillow and weeping bitterly.

'Why are you weeping thus?' asked she.

At last he sat up in bed, and said, 'Last spring, when I was out on a pleasure excursion, I was the means of saving the life of a fox's cub, as I told you at the time. The other day I told Mr. So-and-so that, although my son were to die before my eyes, I would not be the means of killing a fox on purpose; but asked him, in case he heard of any hunter killing a fox, to buy it for me. How the foxes came to hear of this I don't know; but the foxes to whom I had shown kindness killed their own cub and took out the liver; and the old dog-fox, disguising himself as a messenger from the person to whom we had confided the commission, came here with it. His mate has just been at my pillow-side and told me all about it; hence it was that, in spite of myself, I was moved to tears.'

When she heard this, the goodwife likewise was blinded by her tears, and for a while they lay lost in thought; but at last,

The feast of Inari Sama

coming to themselves, they lighted the lamp on the shelf on which the family idol stood, and spent the night in reciting prayers and praises, and the next day they published the matter to the household and to their relations and friends. Now, although there are instances of men killing their own children to requite a favour, there is no other example of foxes having done such a thing; so the story became the talk of the whole country.

Now, the boy who had recovered through the efficacy of this medicine selected the prettiest spot on the premises to erect a shrine to Inari Sama,[6] the Fox God, and offered sacrifice to the two old foxes, for whom he purchased the highest rank at the court of the Mikado.

The passage in the tale which speaks of rank being purchased for the foxes at the court of the Mikado is, of course, a piece of nonsense. 'The saints who are worshipped in Japan,' writes a native authority, 'are men who, in the remote ages, when the country was developing itself, were sages, and by their great and virtuous deeds having earned the gratitude of future generations, received divine honours after their death. How can the Son of Heaven, who is the father and mother of his people, turn dealer in ranks and honours? If rank were a matter of barter, it would cease to be a reward to the virtuous.'

All matters connected with the shrines of the Shintō, or indigenous religion, are confided to the superintendence of the families of Yoshida and Fushimi, Kugés or nobles of the Mikado's court at Kiyōto. The affairs of the Buddhist or imported religion are under the care of the family of Kanjuji. As it is necessary that those who as priests perform the honourable office of serving the gods should be persons of some standing, a certain small rank is procured for them through the intervention of the representatives of the above noble families, who, on the issuing of the required patent, receive as their perquisite a fee, which, although insignificant in itself, is yet of importance to the poor Kugés, whose penniless condition forms a great contrast to the wealth of their inferiors in rank, the Daimios. I believe that this is the only case in which rank can be bought or sold in Japan. In China, on the contrary, in spite of what has been written by Meadows and other admirers of the examination system, a man can be what he pleases by paying for it; and the coveted button, which is nominally the reward of learning and ability, is more often the prize of wealthy ignorance.

The saints who are alluded to above are the saints of the whole country, as distinct from those who for special deeds are locally worshipped. To this innumerable class frequent allusion is made in these Tales.

Touching the remedy of the fox's liver, prescribed in the tale, I may add that there would be nothing strange in this to a person acquainted with the Chinese pharmacopoeia, which the Japanese long exclusively followed, although they are now successfully studying the art of healing as practised in the West. When I was at Peking, I saw a Chinese physician prescribe a decoction of three scorpions for a child struck down with fever; and on another occasion a groom of mine, suffering from dysentery, was treated with acupuncture of the tongue. The art of medicine would appear to be at the present time in China much

a

in the state in which it existed in Europe in the sixteenth century, when the excretions and secretions of all manner of animals, saurians, and venomous snakes and insects, and even live bugs, were administered to patients. 'Some physicians,' says Matthiolus, 'use the ashes of scorpions, burnt alive, for retention caused by either renal or vesical calculi. But I have myself thoroughly experienced the utility of an oil I make myself, whereof scorpions form a very large portion of the ingredients. If only the region of the heart and all the pulses of the body be anointed with it, it will free the patients from the effects of all kinds of poisons taken by the mummies were much commended, and often prescribed with due academical solemnity; and the bones of the human skull, pulverized and administered with oil, were used as a specific in cases of renal calculus. (See Petri, *Andreae Matthioli Opera*, 1574.)

These remarks were made to me by a medical gentleman to whom I mentioned the Chinese doctor's prescription of corpion tea, and they seem to me so curious that I insert them for comparison's sake.

The Prince and the Badger

In days of yore there lived a forefather of the Prince of Tosa who went by the name of Yamanouchi Kadzutoyo. At the age of fourteen this prince was amazingly fond of fishing, and would often go down to the river for sport. And it came to pass one day that he had gone thither with but one retainer, and had made a great haul, that a violent shower suddenly came on. Now, the prince had no rain-coat with him, and was in so sorry a plight that he took shelter under a willow-tree and waited for the weather to clear; but the storm showed no sign of abating, and there was no help for it, so he turned to the retainer and said:

'This rain is not likely to stop for some time, so we had better hurry home.'

As they trudged homeward, night fell, and it grew very dark; and their road lay over a long bank, by the side of which they found a girl, about sixteen years old, weeping bitterly. Struck with wonder, they looked steadfastly at her, and perceived that she was exceedingly comely. While Kadzutoyo stood doubting what so strange a sight could portend, his retainer, smitten with the girl's charms, stepped up to her and said:

'Little sister, tell us whose daughter you are, and how it comes that you are out by yourself at night in such a storm of rain. Surely it is passing strange.'

'Sir,' replied she, looking up through her tears, 'I am the daughter of a poor man in the castle town. My mother died when I was seven years old, and my father has now wedded a shrew, who loathes and ill-uses me; and in the midst of my grief he is gone far away on his business, so I was left alone with my stepmother; and this very night she spited and beat me till I could bear it no longer, and was on my way to my aunt's, who dwells in yonder village, when the shower came on; but as I lay waiting for the rain to stop, I was seized with a spasm, to which I am subject, and was in great pain, when I had the good luck to fall in with your worships.'

As she spoke, the retainer fell deeply in love with her matchless beauty, whilst his lord Kadzutoyo, who from the outset had not uttered a word, but stood brooding over the matter, straightway drew his sword and cut off her head. But the retainer stood aghast, and cried out:

'Oh! my young lord, what wicked deed is this that you've done? The murder of a man's daughter will bring trouble upon us, for you may rely on the business not ending here.'

'You don't know what you're talking about,' answered Kadzutoyo: 'only don't tell any one about it, that is all I ask;' and so they went home in silence.

As Kadzutoyo was very tired, he went to bed, and slept undisturbed by any sense of guilt; for he was brave and fearless. But the retainer grew very uneasy, and went to his young lord's parents and said:

'I had the honour of attending my young lord out fishing today, and we were driven home by the rain. And as we came back by the bank, we descried a girl with a spasm in her stomach, and her my young lord straightway slew; and although he has bidden me tell it to no one, I cannot conceal it from my lord and my lady.'

Kadzutoyo's parents were sore amazed, bewailing their son's wickedness, and went at once to his room and woke him; his father shed tears and said:

'Oh! dastardly cut-throat that you are! how dare you kill another man's daughter without provocation? Such unspeakable villany is unworthy a Samurai's son. Know, that the duty of every Samurai is to keep watch over the country, and to protect the people; and such is his daily task. For sword and dirk are given to men that they may slay rebels, and faithfully serve their prince, and not that they may go about committing sin and killing the daughters of innocent men. Whoever is fool enough not to understand this will repeat his misdeed, and will assuredly bring shame on his kindred. Grieved as I am that I should take away the life which I gave you, I cannot suffer you to bring dishonour on our house; so prepare to meet your fate!'

With these words he drew his sword; but Kadzutoyo, without a sign of fear, said to his father:

'Your anger, sir, is most just; but remember that I have studied the classics and understand the laws of right and wrong, and be sure I would never kill another man without good cause. The girl whom I slew was certainly no human being, but some foul goblin: feeling certain of this, I cut her down. Tomorrow I beg you will send your retainers to look for the corpse; and if it really be that of a human being, I shall give you no further trouble, but shall disembowel myself.'

Upon this the father sheathed his sword, and awaited daybreak. When the morning came, the old prince, in sad distress, bade his retainers lead him to the bank; and there he saw a huge badger, with his head cut off, lying dead by the roadside; and the prince was lost in wonder at his son's shrewdness. But the retainer did not know what to make of it, and still had his doubts. The prince, however, returned home, and sending for his son, said to him:

'It's very strange that the creature which appeared to your retainer to be a girl, should have seemed to you to be a badger.'

'My lord's wonder is just,' replied Kadzutoyo, smiling: 'she appeared as a girl to me as well. But here was a young girl, at night, far from any inhabited place. Stranger still was her wondrous beauty; and strangest of all that, though it was pouring with rain, there was not a sign of wet on her clothes; and when my retainer asked how long she had been there, she said she had been on the bank in pain for some time; so I had no further doubt but that she was a goblin, and I killed her.'

'But what made you think she must be a goblin because her clothes were dry?'

'The beast evidently thought that, if she could bewitch us with her beauty, she might get at the fish my retainer was carrying; but she forgot that, as it was raining, it would not do for her clothes not to be wet; so I detected and killed her.'

When the old prince heard his son speak thus, he was filled with admiration for the youth's sagacity; so, conceiving that Kadzutoyo had given reliable proof of wisdom and prudence, he resolved to abdicate;[7] and Kadzutoyo was proclaimed Prince of Tosa in his stead.

Notes:

1. Cats are found in Japan, as in the Isle of Man, with stumps, where they should have tails. Sometimes this is the result of art, sometimes of a natural shortcoming. The cats of Yedo are of bad repute as mousers, their energies being relaxed by much petting at the hands of ladies. The Cat of Nabéshima, so says tradition, was a monster with two tails.

2. The family of the Prince of Hizen, one of the eighteen chief Daimios of Japan.

3. A restorative in high repute. The best sorts are brought from Korea.

4. The author of the 'Kanzen-Yawa,' the book from which the story is taken.

5. *Bu.* This coin is generally called by foreigners 'ichibu', which means 'one bu'. To talk of '*a hundred ichibus*' is as though a Japanese were to say '*a hundred one shillings*'. Four bus make a *riyo*, or ounce; and any sum above three bus is spoken of as so many riyos and bus ao 101 riyos and three bus equal 407 bus. The bu is worth about 1*s.* 4*d.* [1876] [1*s.* 4*d.* is equivalent to about 7p]

6. Inari Sama is the title under which was deified a certain mythical personage, called Uga, to whom tradition attributes the honour of having first discovered and cultivated the rice-plant. He is represented carrying a few ears of rice, and is symbolised by a snake guarding a bale of rice grain. The foxes wait upon him, and do his bidding. Inasmuch as rice is the most important and necessary product of Japan, the honours which Inari Sama receives are extraordinary. Almost every house in the country contains somewhere about the grounds a pretty little shrine in his honour; and on a certain day of the second month of the year his feast is celebrated with much beating of drums and other noises,

in which the children take a special delight. 'On this day,' says the Ó-Satsuyō, a Japanese cyclopædia, 'at Yedo, where there are myriads upon myriads of shrines to Inari Sama, there are all sorts of ceremonies. Long banners with inscriptions are erected, lamps and lanterns are hung up, and the houses are decked with various dolls and figures; the sound of flutes and drums is heard, the people dance and make holiday according to their fancy. In short, it is the most bustling festival of the Yedo year.'

7. *Inkiyō*, abdication. The custom of abdication is common among all classes, from the Emperor down to his meanest subject. The Emperor abdicates after consultation with his ministers: the Shogun has to obtain the permission of the Emperor; the Daimios, that of the Shogun. The abdication of the Emperor was called *Sentō*; that of the Shogun, *Ogoshō*; in all other ranks it is called *Inkiyō*. It must be remembered that the princes of Japan, in becoming Inkiyō, resign the semblance and the name, but not the reality of power. Both in their own provinces and in the country at large they play a most important part. The ex-Princes of Tosa, Uwajima and Owari, are far more notable men in Japan than the actual holders of the titles.

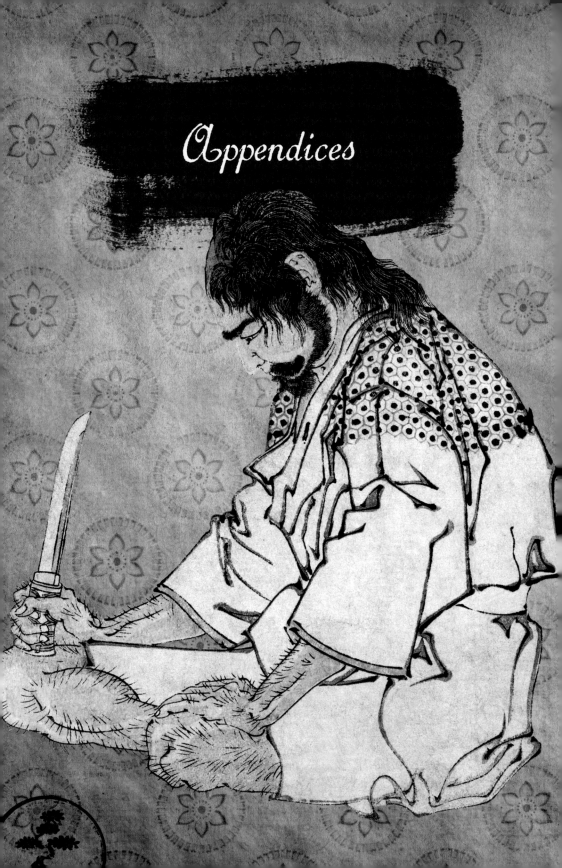

Appendices

AN ACCOUNT OF THE HARA-KIRI
(From a rare Japanese manuscript)

Seppuku (*hara-kiri*) is the mode of suicide adopted amongst Samurai when they have no alternative but to die. Some there are who thus commit suicide of their own free will; others there are who, having committed some crime which does not put them outside the pale of the privileges of the Samurai class, are ordered by their superiors to put an end to their own lives. It is needless to say that it is absolutely necessary that the principal, the witnesses, and the seconds who take part in the affair should be acquainted with all the ceremonies to be observed. A long time ago, a certain Daimio invited a number of persons, versed in the various ceremonies, to call upon him to explain the different forms to be observed by the official witnesses who inspect and verify the head, etc., and then to instruct him in the ceremonies to be observed in the act of suicide; then he showed all these rites to his son and to all his retainers. Another person has said that, as the ceremonies to be gone through by principal, witnesses, and seconds are all very important matters, men should familiarise themselves with a thing which is so terrible, in order that, should the time come for them to take part in it, they may not be taken by surprise.

The witnesses go to see and certify the suicide. For seconds, men are wanted who have distinguished themselves in the military arts. In old days, men used to bear these things in mind; but nowadays the fashion is to be ignorant of such ceremonies, and if upon rare occasions a criminal is handed over to a Daimio's charge, that he may perform *hara-kiri*, it often happens, at the time of execution, that there is no one among all the prince's retainers who is competent to act as second, in which case a man has to be engaged in a hurry from some other quarter to cut off the head of the criminal, and for that day he changes his name and becomes a retainer of the prince, either of the middle or lowest class, and the affair is entrusted to him, and so the difficulty is got over: nor is this considered to be a disgrace. It is a great breach of decorum if the second, who is a most important officer, commits any mistake (such as not striking off the head at a blow) in the presence of the witnesses sent by the Government. On this account a skilful person must be employed; and, to hide the unmanliness of his own people, a prince must perform the ceremony in this imperfect manner. Every Samurai should be able to cut off a man's head: therefore, to have to employ a stranger to act as second is to incur the charge of ignorance of the arts of war, and is a bitter mortification. However, young men, trusting to their youthful ardour, are apt to be careless, and are certain to make a mistake. Some people there are who, not lacking in skill on ordinary occasions, lose their presence of mind in public, and cannot do themselves justice. It is all the more important, therefore, as the act occurs but rarely, that men who are liable to be called upon to be either principals or seconds or witnesses in the *hara-kiri* should constantly be examined in their skill as swordsmen, and should be familiar with all the rites, in order that when the time comes they may not lose their presence of mind.

According to one authority, capital punishment may be divided into two kinds—beheading and strangulation. The ceremony of *hara-kiri* was added afterwards in the case of persons belonging to the military class being condemned to death. This was first instituted in the days of the Ashikaga[1] dynasty. At that time the country was in a state of utter confusion; and there were men who, although fighting, were neither guilty of high treason nor of infidelity to their feudal lords, but who by the chances of war were taken prisoners. To drag out such men as these, bound as criminals, and cut their heads off, was intolerably cruel; accordingly, men hit upon a ceremonious mode of suicide by disembowelling, in order to comfort the departed spirit. Even at present, where it becomes necessary to put to death a man who has been guilty of some act not unworthy of a Samurai, at the time of the execution witnesses are sent to the house; and the criminal, having bathed and put on new clothes, in obedience to the commands of his superiors, puts an end to himself, but does not on that account forfeit his rank as a Samurai. This is a law for which, in all truth, men should be grateful.

On the Preparation of the Place of Execution

In old days the ceremony of *hara-kiri* used to be performed in a temple. In the third year of the period called Kan-yei (AD 1626), a certain person, having been guilty of treason, was ordered to disembowel himself, on the fourteenth day of the first month, in the temple of Kichijōji, at Komagomé, in Yedo. Eighteen years later, the retainer of a certain Daimio, having had a dispute with a sailor belonging to an Osaka coasting-ship, killed the sailor; and, an investigation having been made into the matter by the Governor of Osaka, the retainer was ordered to perform *hara-kiri*, on the twentieth day of the sixth month, in the temple called Sokusanji, in Osaka. During the period Shōhō (middle of seventeenth century), a certain man, having been guilty of heinous mis-conduct, performed *hara-kiri* in the temple called Shimpukuji, in the Kōji-street of Yedo. On the fourth day of the fifth month of the second year of the period Meiréki (AD 1656), a certain man, for having avenged the death of his cousin's husband at a place called Shimidzudani, in the Kōji-street, disembowelled himself in the temple called Honseiji. On the twenty-sixth day of the sixth month of the eighth year of the period Yempō (AD 1680), at the funeral ceremonies in honour of the anniversary of the death of Genyuin Sama, a former Shogun, Naitō Idzumi no Kami, having a cause of hatred against Nagai Shinano no Kami, killed him at one blow with a short sword, in the main hall of the temple called Zōjōji (the burial-place of the Shoguns in Yedo). Idzumi no Kami was arrested by the officers present, and on the following day performed *hara-kiri* at Kiridōshi, in the temple called Seiriuji.

In modern times the ceremony has taken place at night, either in the palace or in the garden of a Daimio, to whom the condemned man has been given in charge. Whether it takes place in the palace or in the garden depends upon the rank of the individual. Daimios and Hatamotos, as a matter of course, and the higher retainers of the Shogun, disembowel themselves in the palace: retainers of lower rank should do so in the garden. In the case of vassals of feudatories, according to the rank of their families, those who, being above the grade of captains, carry the bâton,[2] should perform *hara-kiri* in the palace; all others in the garden. If, when the time comes, the persons engaged in the ceremony are in any doubt as to the proper rules to be followed, they should inquire of competent persons, and settle the question. At the beginning of the eighteenth century, during the period Genroku, when Asano Takumi no Kami[3] disembowelled himself in the palace of a Daimio called Tamura, as the whole thing was sudden and unexpected, the garden was covered with matting, and on the top of this thick mats were laid and a carpet, and the affair was concluded so; but there are people who say that it was wrong to treat a Daimio thus, as if he had been an ordinary Samurai. But it is said that in old times it was the custom that the ceremony should take place upon a leather carpet spread in the garden; and further, that the proper place is inside a picket fence tied together in the garden: so it is wrong for persons who are only acquainted with one form of the ceremony to accuse Tamura of having acted improperly. If, however, the object was to save the house from the pollution of blood, then the accusation of ill-will may well be brought; for the preparation of the place is of great importance.

Formerly it was the custom that, for personages of importance, the enclosure within the picket fence should be of thirty-six feet square. An entrance was made to the south, and another to the north: the door to the south was called *Shugiyōmon* ('the door of the practice of virtue'); that to the north was called *Umbanmon* ('the door of the warm basin'[4]). Two mats, with white binding, were arranged in the shape of a hammer, the one at right angles to the other; six feet of white silk, four feet broad, were stretched on the mat, which was placed lengthwise; at the four corners were erected four posts for curtains. In front of the two mats was erected a portal, eight feet high by six feet broad, in the shape of the portals in front of temples, made of a fine sort of bamboo wrapped in white[5] silk. White curtains, four feet broad, were hung at the four corners, and four flags, six feet long, on which should be inscribed four quotations from the sacred books. These flags, it is said, were immediately after the ceremony carried away to the grave. At night two lights were placed, one upon either side of the two mats. The candles were placed in saucers upon stands of bamboo, four feet high, wrapped in white silk. The person who was to disembowel himself, entering the picket fence by the north entrance, took his place upon the white silk upon the mat facing the north. Some there were, however, who said that he should sit facing the west: in that case the whole place must be prepared accordingly. The seconds enter the enclosure by the south entrance, at the same time as the principal enters by the north, and take their places on the mat that is placed crosswise.

Nowadays, when the *hara-kiri* is performed inside the palace, a temporary place is made on purpose, either in the garden or in some unoccupied spot; but if the criminal is to die on the day on which he is given in charge, or on the next day, the ceremony, having to take place so quickly, is performed in the reception-room. Still, even if there is a lapse of time between the period of giving the prisoner in charge and the execution, it is better that the ceremony should take place in a decent room in the house than in a place made on purpose. If it is heard that, for fear of dirtying his house, a man has made a place expressly, he will be blamed for it. It surely can be no disgrace to the house of a soldier that he was ordered to perform the last offices towards a Samurai who died by *hara-kiri*. To slay his enemy against whom he has cause of hatred, and then to kill himself, is the part of a noble Samurai; and it is sheer nonsense to look upon the place where he has disembowelled himself as polluted. In the beginning of the eighteenth century, seventeen of the retainers of Asano Takumi no Kami performed *hara-kiri* in the garden of a palace at Shirokané, in Yedo. When it was over, the people of the palace called upon the priests of a sect named Shugenja to come and purify the place; but when the lord of the palace heard this, he ordered the place to be left as it was; for what need was there to purify a place where faithful Samurai had died by their own hand? But in other palaces to which the remainder of the retainers of Takumi no Kami were entrusted, it is said that the places of execution were purified. But the people of that day praised Kumamoto Ko (the Prince of Higo), to whom the palace at Shirokané belonged. It is a currish thing to look upon death in battle or by *hara-kiri* as a pollution: this is a thing to bear in mind. In modern times the place of *hara-kiri* is eighteen feet square in all cases; in the centre is a place to sit upon, and the condemned man is made to sit facing the witnesses; at other times he is placed with his side to the witnesses: this is according to the nature of the spot. In some cases the seconds turn their backs to the witnesses. It is open to question, however, whether this is not a breach of etiquette. The witnesses should be consulted upon these arrangements. If the witnesses have no objection, the condemned man should be placed directly opposite to them. The place where the witnesses are seated should be removed more than twelve or eighteen feet from the condemned man. The place from which the sentence is read should also be close by. The writer has been furnished with a plan of the *hara-kiri* as it is performed at present. Although the ceremony is gone through in other ways also, still it is more convenient to follow the manner indicated.

If the execution takes place in a room, a kerchief of five breadths of white cotton cloth or a quilt should be laid down, and it is also said that two mats should be prepared; however, as there are already mats in the room, there is no need for special mats: two red rugs should be spread over all, sewed together, one on the top of the other; for if the white cotton cloth be used alone, the blood will soak through on to the mats;

therefore it is right the rugs should be spread. On the twenty-third day of the eighth month of the fourth year of the period Yenkiyō (AD 1740), at the *hara-kiri* of a certain person there were laid down a white cloth, eight feet square, and on that a quilt of light green cotton, six feet square, and on that a cloth of white hemp, six feet square, and on that two rugs. On the third day of the ninth month of the ninth year of the period Tempō (AD 1838), at the *hara-kiri* of a certain person it is said that there were spread a large double cloth of white cotton, and on that two rugs. But, of these two occasions, the first must be commended for its careful preparation. If the execution be at night, candlesticks of white wood should be placed at each of the four corners, lest the seconds be hindered in their work. In the place where the witnesses are to sit, ordinary candlesticks should be placed, according to etiquette; but an excessive illumination is not decorous. Two screens covered with white paper should be set up, behind the shadow of which are concealed the dirk upon a tray, a bucket to hold the head after it has been cut off, an incense-burner, a pail of water, and a basin. The above rules apply equally to the ceremonies observed when the *hara-kiri* takes place in a garden. In the latter case the place is hung round with a white curtain, which need not be new for the occasion. Two mats, a white cloth, and a rug are spread. If the execution is at night, lanterns of white paper are placed on bamboo poles at the four corners. The sentence having been read inside the house, the persons engaged in the ceremony proceed to the place of execution; but, according to circumstances, the sentence may be read at the place itself. In the case of Asano Takumi no Kami, the sentence was read out in the house, and he afterwards performed *hara-kiri* in the garden. On the third day of the fourth month of the fourth year of the period Tenmei

(AD 1784), a Hatamoto named Sano, having received his sentence in the supreme court-house, disembowelled himself in the garden in front of the prison. When the ceremony takes place in the garden, matting must be spread all the way to the place, so that sandals need not be worn. The reason for this is that some men in that position suffer from a rush of blood to the head, from nervousness, so their sandals might slip off their feet without their being aware of their loss; and as this would have a very bad appearance, it is better to spread matting. Care must be taken lest, in spreading the matting, a place be left where two mats join, against which the foot might trip. The white screens and other things are prepared as has been directed above. If any curtailment is made, it must be done as well as circumstances will permit. According to the crime of which a man who is handed over to any Daimio's charge is guilty, it is known whether he will have to perform *hara-kiri*; and the preparations should be made accordingly. Asano Takumi no Kami was taken to the palace of Tamura Sama at the hour of the monkey (between three and five in the afternoon), took off his dress of ceremony, partook of a bowl of soup and five dishes, and drank two cups of warm water, and at the hour of the cock (between five and seven in the evening) disembowelled himself. A case of this kind requires much attention; for great care should be taken that the preparations be carried on without the knowledge of the principal. If a temporary room has been built expressly for the occasion, to avoid pollution to the house, it should be kept a secret. It once happened that a criminal was received in charge at the palace of a certain nobleman, and when his people were about to erect a temporary building for the ceremony, they wrote to consult some of the parties concerned; the letter ran as follows:

'The house in which we live is very small and inconvenient in all respects. We have ordered the guard to treat our prisoner with all respect; but our retainers who are placed on guard are much inconvenienced for want of space; besides, in the event of fire breaking out or any extraordinary event taking place, the place is so small that it would be difficult to get out. We are thinking, therefore, of adding an apartment to the original building, so that the guard may be able at all times to go in and out freely, and that if, in case of fire or otherwise, we should have to leave the house, we may do so easily. We beg to consult you upon this point.'

When a Samurai has to perform *hara-kiri* by the command of his own feudal lord, the ceremony should take place in one of the lesser palaces of the clan. Once upon a time, a certain prince of the Inouyé clan, having a just cause of offence against his steward, who was called Ishikawa Tōzayémon, and wishing to punish him, caused him to be killed in his principal palace at Kandabashi, in Yedo. When this matter was reported to the Shogun, having been convicted of disrespect of the privileges of the city, he was ordered to remove to his lesser palace at Asakusa. Now, although the *hara-kiri* cannot be called properly an execution, still, as it only differs from an ordinary execution in that by it the honour of the Samurai is not affected, it is only a question of degree; it is a matter of ceremonial. If the principal palace[6] is a long distance from the Shogun's castle, then the *hara-kiri* may take place there; but there can be no objection whatever to its taking place in a minor palace. Nowadays, when a man is condemned to *hara-kiri* by a Daimio, the ceremony usually takes place in one of the lesser palaces; the place commonly selected is an open space near the horse-exercising ground, and the preparations which I have described above are often shortened according to circumstances.

When a retainer is suddenly ordered to perform *hara-kiri* during a journey, a temple or shrine should be hired for the occasion. On these hurried occasions, coarse mats, faced with finer matting or common mats, may be used. If the criminal is of rank to have an armour-bearer, a carpet of skin should be spread, should one be easily procurable. The straps of the skin (which are at the head) should, according to old custom, be to the front, so that the fur may point backwards. In old days, when the ceremony took place in a garden, a carpet of skin was spread. To hire a temple for the purpose of causing a man to perform *hara-kiri* was of frequent occurrence: it is doubtful whether it may be done at the present time. This sort of question should be referred beforehand to some competent person, that the course to be adopted may be clearly understood.

In the period Kambun (AD 1661–1673) a Prince Sakai, travelling through the Bishiu territory, hired a temple or shrine for one of his retainers to disembowel himself in; and so the affair was concluded.

On the Ceremonies Observed at the Hara-Kiri of a Person Given in Charge to a Daimio

When a man has been ordered by the Government to disembowel himself, the public censors, who have been appointed to act as witnesses, write to the prince who has the criminal in charge, to inform them that they will go to his palace on public business. This message is written directly to the chief, and is sent by an assistant censor; and a suitable answer is returned to it. Before the ceremony, the witnesses send an assistant censor to see the place, and look at a plan of the house, and to take a list of the names of the persons who are to be present; he also has an interview with the *kaishaku*, or seconds, and examines them upon the way of performing the ceremonies. When all the preparations have been made, he goes to fetch the censors; and they all proceed together to the place of execution, dressed in their hempen-cloth dress of ceremony. The retainers of the palace are collected to do obeisance in the entrance-yard; and the lord, to whom the criminal has been entrusted, goes as far as the front porch to meet the censors, and conducts them to the front reception-room. The chief censor then announces to the lord of the palace that he has come to read out the sentence of such an one who has been condemned to perform *hara-kiri*, and that the second censor has come to witness the execution of the sentence. The lord of the palace then inquires whether he is expected to attend the execution in person, and, if any of the relations or family of the criminal should beg to receive his remains, whether their request should be complied with; after this he announces that he will order everything to be made ready, and leaves the room. Tea, a fire-box for smoking, and sweetmeats are set before the censors; but they decline to accept any hospitality until their business shall have been concluded. The minor officials follow the same rule. If the censors express a wish to see the place of execution, the retainers of the palace show the way, and their lord accompanies them; in this, however, he may be replaced by one of his *karō* or councillors. They then return, and take their seats in the reception-room. After this, when all the preparations have been made, the master of the house leads the censors to the place where the sentence is to be read; and it is etiquette that they should wear both sword and dirk.[7] The lord of the palace takes his place on one side; the inferior censors sit on either side in a lower place. The councillors and other officers of the palace also take their places. One of the councillors present, addressing the censors without moving from his place, asks whether he shall bring forth the prisoner.

Previously to this, the retainers of the palace, going to the room where the prisoner is confined, inform him that, as the censors have arrived, he should change his dress, and the attendants bring out a change of clothes upon a large tray: it is when he has finished his toilet that the witnesses go forth and take their places in the appointed order, and the principal is then introduced. He is preceded by one man, who should be of the rank of *Mono-gashira* (retainer of the fourth rank), who wears a dirk, but no sword. Six men act as attendants; they should be of the fifth or sixth rank; they walk on either side of the principal. They are followed by one man who should be of the rank of *Yōnin* (councillor of the second class). When they reach the place, the leading man draws on one side and sits down, and the six attendants sit down on either side of the principal. The officer who follows him sits down behind him, and the chief censor reads the sentence.

When the reading of the sentence is finished, the principal leaves the room and again changes his clothes, and the chief censor immediately leaves the palace; but the lord of the palace does not conduct him to the door. The second censor returns to the reception-room until the principal has changed his clothes. When the principal has taken his seat at the place of execution, the councillors of the palace announce to the second censor that all is ready; he then proceeds to the place, wearing his sword and dirk. The lord of the palace, also wearing his sword and dirk, takes his seat on one side. The inferior censors and councillors sit in front of the censor: they wear the dirk only. The assistant second brings a dirk upon a tray, and, having placed it in front of the principal, withdraws on one side: when the principal leans his head forward, his chief second strikes off his head, which is immediately shown to the censor, who identifies it, and tells the master of the palace that he is satisfied, and thanks him for all his trouble. The corpse, as it lies, is hidden by a white screen which is set up around it, and incense is brought out. The witnesses leave the place. The lord of the palace accompanies them as far as the porch, and the retainers prostrate themselves in the yard as before. The retainers who should be present at the place of execution are one or two councillors (*Karō*), two or three second councillors (*Yōnin*), two or three *Monogashira*, one chief of the palace (*Rusui*), six attendants, one chief second, two assistant seconds, one man to carry incense, who need not be a person of rank—any Samurai will do. They attend to the setting up of the white screen.

The duty of burying the corpse and of setting the place in order again devolves upon four men; these are selected from Samurai of the middle or lower class; during the performance of their duties, they hitch up their trousers and wear neither sword nor dirk. Their names are previously sent in to the censor, who acts as witness; and to the junior censors, should they desire it. Before the arrival of the chief censor, the requisite utensils for extinguishing a fire are prepared, firemen are engaged,[8] and officers constantly go the rounds to watch against fire. From the time when the chief censor comes into the house until he leaves it, no one is allowed to enter the premises. The servants on guard at the entrance porch should wear their hempen dresses of ceremony. Everything in the palace should be conducted with decorum, and the strictest attention paid in all things.

When any one is condemned to *hara-kiri*, it would be well that people should go to the palace of the Prince of Higo, and learn what transpired at the execution of the Rōnins of Asano Takumi no Kami. A curtain was hung round the garden in front of the reception-room; three mats were laid down, and upon these was placed a white cloth. The condemned men were kept in the reception-room, and summoned, one by one; two men, one on each side, accompanied them; the second, followed behind; and they proceeded together to the place of execution. When the execution was concluded in each case, the corpse was hidden from the sight of the chief witness by a white screen, folded up in white cloth, placed on a mat, and carried off to the rear by two foot-soldiers; it was then placed in a coffin. The blood-stained ground was sprinkled with sand, and swept clean; fresh mats were laid down, and the place prepared anew; after which the next man was summoned to come forth.

On Certain Things to be Borne in Mind by the Witnesses

When a clansman is ordered by his feudal lord to perform *hara-kiri*, the sentence must be read out by the censor of the clan, who also acts as witness. He should take his place in front of the criminal, at a distance of twelve feet; according to some books, the distance should be eighteen feet, and he should sit obliquely, not facing the criminal; he should lay his sword down by his side, but, if he pleases, he may wear it in his girdle; he must read out the sentence distinctly. If the sentence be a long document, to begin reading in a very loud voice and afterwards drop into a whisper has an appearance of faint-heartedness; but to read it throughout in a low voice is worse still: it should be delivered clearly from beginning to end. It is the duty of the chief witness to set an example of fortitude to the other persons who are to take part in the execution. When the second has finished his work, he carries the head to the chief witness, who, after inspecting it, must declare that he has identified it; he then should take his sword, and leave his place. It is sufficient, however, that the head should be struck off without being carried to the chief witness; in that case, the second receives his instructions beforehand. On rising, the chief witness should step out with his left foot and turn to the left. If the ceremony takes place out of doors, the chief witness, wearing his sword and dirk, should sit upon a box; he must wear his hempen dress of ceremony; he may hitch his trousers up slightly; according to his rank, he may wear his full dress—that is, wings over his full dress. It is the part of the chief witness to instruct the seconds and others in the duties which they have to perform, and also to preconcert measures in the event of any mishap occurring.

If whilst the various persons to be engaged in the ceremony are rubbing up their military lore, and preparing themselves for the event, any other person should come in, they should immediately turn the conversation. Persons of the rank of Samurai should be familiar with all the details of the *hara-kiri*; and to be seen discussing what should be done in case anything went wrong, and so forth, would have an appearance of ignorance. If, however, an intimate friend should go to the place, rather than have any painful concealment, he may be consulted upon the whole affair.

When the sentence has been read, it is probable that the condemned man will have some last words to say to the chief witness. It must depend on the nature of what he has to say whether it will be received or not. If he speaks in a confused or bewildered manner, no attention is paid to it: his second should lead him away, of his own accord or at a sign from the chief witness.

If the condemned man be a person who has been given in charge to a prince by the Government, the prince after the reading of the sentence should send his retainers to the prisoner with a message to say that the decrees of the Government are not to be eluded, but that if he has any last wishes to express, they are ordered by their lord to receive them. If the prisoner is a man of high rank, the lord of the palace should go in person to hear his last wishes.

The condemned man should answer in the following way:

'Sir, I thank you for your careful consideration, but I have nothing that I wish to say. I am greatly indebted to you for the great kindness which I have received since I have been under your charge. I beg you to take my respects to your lord and to the gentlemen of your clan who have treated me so well.' Or he may say, 'Sirs, I have nothing to say; yet, since you are so kind as to think of me, I should be obliged if you would deliver such and such a message to such an one.' This is the proper and becoming sort of speech for the occasion. If the prisoner entrusts them with any message, the retainers should receive it in such a manner as to set his mind at rest. Should he ask for writing materials in order to write a letter, as this is forbidden by the law, they should tell him so, and not grant his request. Still they must feel that it is painful to refuse the request of a dying man, and must do their best to assist him. They must exhaust every available kindness and civility, as was done in the period Genroku, in the case of the Rōnins of Asano Takumi no Kami. The Prince of Higo, after the sentence had been read, caused paper and writing materials to be taken to their room. If the prisoner is light-headed from excitement, it is no use furnishing him with writing-materials. It must depend upon circumstances; but when a man has murdered another, having made up his mind to abide by the consequences, then that man's execution should be carried through with all honour. When a man kills another on the spot, in a fit of ungovernable passion, and then is bewildered and dazed by his own act, the same pains need not be taken to conduct matters punctiliously. If the prisoner be a careful man, he will take an early opportunity after he has been given in charge to express his wishes. To carry kindness so far as to supply writing materials and the like is not obligatory. If any doubt exists upon the point, the chief witness may be consulted.

After the Rōnins of Asano Takumi no Kami had heard their sentence in the palace of Matsudaira Oki no Kami, that Daimio in person went and took leave of them, and calling Oishi Chikara,[9] the son of their chief, to him, said, 'I have heard that your mother is at home in your own country; how she will grieve when she hears of your death and that of your father, I can well imagine. If you have any message that you wish to leave for her, tell me, without standing upon ceremony, and I will transmit it without delay.' For a while Chikara kept his head bent down towards the ground; at last he drew back a little, and, lifting his head, said, 'I humbly thank your lordship for what you have been pleased to say. My father warned me from the first that our crime was so great that, even were we to be pardoned by a gracious judgment upon one count, I must not forget that there would be a hundred million counts against us for which we must commit suicide: and that if I disregarded his words his hatred would pursue me after death. My father impressed this upon me at the temple called Sengakuji, and again when I was separated from him to be taken to the palace of Prince Sengoku. Now my father and myself have been condemned to perform *hara kiri*, according to the wish of our hearts. Still I cannot forget to think of my mother. When we parted at Kiyōto, she told me that our separation would be for long, and she bade me not to play the coward when I thought of her. As I took a long leave of her then, I have no message to send to her now.' When he spoke thus, Oki no Kami and all his retainers, who were drawn up around him, were moved to tears in admiration of his heroism.

Although it is right that the condemned man should bathe and partake of wine and food, these details should be curtailed. Even should he desire these favours, it must depend upon his conduct whether they be granted or refused. He should be caused to die as quickly as possible. Should he wish for some water to drink, it should be given to him. If in his talk he should express himself like a noble Samurai, all pains should be exhausted in carrying out his execution. Yet however careful a man he may be, as he nears his death his usual demeanour will undergo a change. If the execution is delayed, in all probability it will cause the prisoner's courage to fail him; therefore, as soon as the sentence shall have been passed, the execution should be brought to a conclusion. This, again, is a point for the chief witness to remember.

Concerning Seconds (*Kaishaku*)

When the condemned man is one who has been given in charge for execution, six attendants are employed; when the execution is within the clan, then two or three attendants will suffice; the number, however, must depend upon the rank of the principal. Men of great nerve and strength must be selected for the office; they must wear their hempen dress of ceremony, and tuck up their trousers; they must on no account wear either sword or dirk, but have a small poniard hidden in their bosom: these are the officers who attend upon the condemned man when he changes his dress, and who sit by him on the right hand and on the left hand to guard him whilst the sentence is being read. In the event of any mistake occurring (such as the prisoner attempting to escape), they knock him down; and should he be unable to stand or to walk, they help to support him. The attendants accompanying the principal to the place of execution, if they are six in number, four of them take their seats some way off and mount guard, while the other two should sit close behind the principal. They must understand that should there be any mistake they must throw the condemned man, and, holding him down, cut off his head with their poniard, or stab him to death. If the second bungles in cutting off the head and the principal attempts to rise, it is the duty of the attendants to kill him. They must help him to take off his upper garments and bare his body. In recent times, however, there have been cases where the upper garments have not been removed: this depends upon circumstances. The setting up of the white screen, and the laying the corpse in the coffin, are duties which, although they may be performed by other officers, originally devolved upon the six attendants. When a common man is executed, he is bound with cords, and so made to take his place; but a Samurai wears his dress of ceremony, is presented with a dagger, and dies thus. There ought to be no anxiety lest such a man should attempt to escape; still, as there is no knowing what these six attendants may be called upon to do, men should be selected who thoroughly understand their business.

The seconds are three in number—the chief second, the assistant second, and the inferior second. When the execution is carried out with proper solemnity, three men are employed; still a second and assistant second are sufficient. If three men serve as seconds, their several duties are as follows: The chief second strikes off the head; that is his duty: he is the most important officer in the execution by *hara-kiri*. The assistant second brings forward the tray, on which is placed the dirk; that is his duty: he must perform his part in such a manner that the principal second is not hindered in his work. The assistant second is the officer of second importance in the execution. The third or inferior second carries the head to the chief witness for identification; and in the event of something suddenly occurring to hinder either of the other two seconds, he should bear in mind that he must be ready to act as his substitute: his is an office of great importance, and a proper person must be selected to fill it.

Although there can be no such thing as a *kaishaku* (second) in any case except in one of *hara-kiri*, still in old times guardians and persons who assisted others were also called *kaishaku*: the reason for this is because the *kaishaku*, or second, comes to the assistance of the principal. If the principal were to make any mistake at the fatal moment, it would be a disgrace to his dead body: it is in order to prevent such mistakes that the *kaishaku*, or second, is employed. It is the duty of the *kaishaku* to consider this as his first duty.

When a man is appointed to act as second to another, what shall be said of him if he accepts the office with a smiling face? Yet must he not put on a face of distress. It is as well to attempt to excuse oneself from performing the duty. There is no heroism in cutting a man's head off well, and it is a disgrace to do it in a bungling manner; yet must not a man allege lack of skill as a pretext for evading the office, for it is an unworthy thing that a Samurai should want the skill required to behead a man. If there are any that advocate employing young men as seconds, it should rather be said that their hands are inexpert. To play the coward and yield up the office to another man is out of the question. When a man is called upon to perform the office, he should express his readiness to use his sword (the dirk may be employed, but the sword is the proper weapon). As regards the sword, the second should borrow that of the principal: if there is any objection to this, he should receive a sword from his lord; he should not use his own sword. When the assistant seconds have been appointed, the three should take counsel together about the details of the place of execution, when they have been carefully instructed by their superiors in all the ceremonies; and having made careful inquiry, should there be anything wrong, they should appeal to their superiors for instruction. The seconds wear their dresses of ceremony when the criminal is a man given in charge by the Government: when he is one of their own clan, they need only wear the trousers of the Samurai. In old days it is said that they were dressed in the same way as the principal; and some authorities assert that at the *hara-kiri* of a nobleman of high rank the seconds should wear white clothes, and that the handle of the sword should be wrapped in white silk. If the execution takes place in the house, they should partially tuck up their trousers; if in the garden, they should tuck them up entirely.

The seconds should address the principal, and say, 'Sir, we have been appointed to act as your seconds; we pray you to set your mind at rest,' and so forth; but this must depend upon the rank of the criminal. At this time, too, if the principal has any last wish to express, the second should receive it, and should treat him with every consideration in order to relieve his anxiety. If the second has been selected by the principal on account of old friendship between them, or if the latter, during the time that he has been in charge, has begged some special retainer of the palace to act as his second in the event of his being condemned to death, the person so selected should thank the principal for choosing so unworthy a person, and promise to beg his lord to allow him to act as second: so he should answer, and comfort him, and having reported the matter to his lord, should act as second. He should take that opportunity to borrow his principal's sword in some such terms as the following: 'As I am to have the honour of being your second, I would fain borrow your sword for the occasion. It may be a consolation to you to perish by your own sword, with which you are familiar.' If, however, the principal declines, and prefers to be executed with the second's sword, his wish must be complied with. If the second should make an awkward cut with his own sword, it is a disgrace to him; therefore he should borrow some one else's sword, so that the blame may rest with the sword, and not with the swordsman. Although this is the rule, and although every Samurai should wear a sword fit to cut off a man's head, still if the principal has begged to be executed with the second's own sword, it must be done as he desires.

It is probable that the condemned man will inquire of his second about the arrangements which have been made: he must attend therefore to rendering himself capable of answering all such questions. Once upon a time, when the condemned man inquired of his second whether his head would be cut off at the moment when he received the tray with the dirk upon it, 'No,' replied the second; 'at the moment when you stab yourself with the dirk your head will be cut off.' At the execution of one Sanō, he told his second that, when he had stabbed himself in the belly, he would utter a cry; and begged him to be cool when he cut off his head. The second replied that he would do as he wished, but begged him in the mean-time to take the tray with the dirk, according to proper form. When Sanō reached out his hand to take the tray, the second cut off his head immediately. Now, although this was not exactly right, still as the second acted so in order to save a Samurai from the disgrace of performing the *hara-kiri* improp-erly (by crying out), it can never be wrong for a second to act kindly, If the principal urgently requests to be allowed really to disembowel himself, his wish may, according to circum-stances, be granted; but in this case care must be taken that no time be lost in striking off the head. The custom of striking off the head, the prisoner only going through the semblance of disembowelling himself, dates from the period Yempo (about 190 years ago). [about 1678]

When the principal has taken his place, the second strips his right shoulder of the dress of ceremony, which he allows to fall behind his sleeve, and, drawing his sword, lays down the scabbard, taking care that his weapon is not seen by the princi-pal; then he takes his place on the left of the principal and close behind him. The principal should sit facing the west, and the second facing the north, and in that position should he strike the blow. When the second perceives the assistant second bring out the tray on which is laid the dirk, he must brace up his nerves and settle his heart beneath his navel: when the tray is laid down, he must put himself in position to strike the blow. He should step out first with the left foot, and then change so as to bring his right foot forward: this is the position which he should assume to strike; he may, however, reverse the position of his feet. When the principal removes his upper garments, the second must poise his sword: when the principal reaches out his hand to draw the tray towards him, as he leans his head forward a little, is the exact moment for the second to strike. There are all sorts of traditions about this. Some say that the principal should take the tray and raise it respectfully to his head, and set it down; and that this is the moment to strike. There are three rules for the time of cutting off the head: the first is when the dirk is laid on the tray; the second is when the principal looks at the left side of his belly before inserting the dirk; the third is when he inserts the dirk. If these three moments are allowed to pass, it becomes a difficult matter to cut off the head: so says tradition. However, four moments for cutting are also recorded: first, when the assistant second retires after having laid down the stand on which is the dirk; second, when the principal draws the stand towards him; third, when he takes the dirk in his hand; fourth, when he makes the incision into the belly. Although all four ways are approved, still the first is too soon; the last three are right and proper. In short, the blow should be struck without delay. If he has struck off the head at a blow without failure, the second, taking care not to raise his sword, but holding it point downwards, should retire backward a little and wipe his weapon kneeling; he should have plenty of white paper ready in his girdle or in his ·bosom to wipe away the blood and rub up his sword; having replaced his sword in its scabbard, he should readjust his upper garments and take his seat to the rear. When the head has fallen, the junior second should enter, and, taking up the head, present it to the witness for inspection. When he has identified it, the ceremony is concluded. If there is no assistant or junior second, the second, as soon as he has cut off the head, carrying his sword reversed in his left hand, should take the head in his right hand, holding it by the topknot of hair, should advance towards the witness, passing on the right side of the corpse, and show the right profile of the head to the witness, resting the chin of the head upon the hilt of his sword, and kneeling on his left knee; then returning again round by the left of the corpse, kneeling on his left knee, and carrying the head in his left hand and resting it on the edge of his sword, he should again show the left profile to the witness. It is also laid down as another rule, that the second, laying down his sword, should take out paper from the bosom of his dress, and placing the head in the palm of his left hand, and taking the top-knot of hair in his right hand, should lay the head upon the paper, and so submit it for inspection. Either way may be said to be right.

Note:—To lay down thick paper, and place the head on it, shows a disposition to pay respect to the head; to place it on the edge of the sword is insulting: the course pursued must depend upon the rank of the person. If the ceremony is to be curtailed, it may end with the cutting off of the head: that must be settled beforehand, in consultation with the witness. In the event of the second making a false cut, so as not to strike off the head at a blow, the second must take the head by the top-knot, and, pressing it down, cut it off. Should he take bad aim and cut the shoulder by mistake, and should the principal rise and cry out, before he has time to writhe, he should hold him down and stab him to death, and then cut off his head, or the assistant seconds, who are sitting behind, should come forward and hold him down, while the chief second cuts off his head. It may be necessary for the second, after he has cut off the head, to push down the body, and then take up the head for inspection. If the body does not fall at once, which is said to be sometimes the case, the second should pull the feet to make it fall.

There are some who say that the perfect way for the second to cut off the head is not to cut right through the neck at a blow, but to leave a little uncut, and, as the head hangs by the skin, to seize the top-knot and slice it off, and then submit it for inspection. The reason of this is, lest, the head being struck off at a blow, the ceremony should be confounded with an ordinary execution. According to the old authorities, this is the proper and respectful manner. After the head is cut off, the eyes are apt to blink, and the mouth to move, and to bite the pebbles and sand. This being hateful to see, at what amongst Samurai is so important an occasion, and being a shameful thing, it is held to be best not to let the head fall, but to hold back a little in delivering the blow. Perhaps this may be right; yet it is a very difficult matter to cut so as to leave the head hanging by a little flesh, and there is the danger of missing the cut; and as any mistake in the cut is most horrible to see, it is better to strike a fair blow at once. Others say that, even when the head is struck off at a blow, the semblance of slicing it off should be gone through afterwards; yet be it borne in mind that; this is unnecessary.

hree methods of carrying the sword are recognised amongst those skilled in swordsmanship. If the rank of the principal be high, the sword is raised aloft; if the principal and second are of equal rank, the sword is carried at the centre of the body; if the principal be of inferior rank, the sword is allowed to hang downwards. The proper position for the second to strike from is kneeling on one knee, but there is no harm in his standing up: others say that, if the execution takes place inside the house, the second should kneel; if in the garden, he should stand. These are not points upon which to insist obstinately: a man should strike in whatever position is most convenient to him.

The chief duty for the assistant second to bear in mind is the bringing in of the tray with the dirk, which should be produced very quietly when the principal takes his place: it should be placed so that the condemned man may have to stretch his hand well out in order to reach it.[10] The assistant second then returns to his own place; but if the condemned man shows any signs of agitation, the assistant second must lend his assistance, so that the head may be properly cut off. It once happened that the condemned man, having received the tray from the assistant second, held it up for a long time without putting it down, until those near him had over and over again urged him to set it down. It also happens that after the tray has been set down, and the assistant second has retired, the condemned man does not put out his hand to take it; then must the assistant second press him to take it. Also the principal may ask that the tray be placed a little nearer to him, in which case his wish must be granted. The tray may also be placed in such a way that the assistant second, holding it in his left hand, may reach the dirk to the condemned man, who leans forward to take it. Which is the best of all these ways is uncertain. The object to aim at is, that the condemned man should lean forward to receive the blow. Whether the assistant second retires, or not, must depend upon the attitude assumed by the condemned man.

If the prisoner be an unruly, violent man, a fan, instead of a dirk, should be placed upon the tray; and should he object to this, he should be told, in answer, that the substitution of the fan is an ancient custom. This may occur sometimes. It is said that once upon a time, in one of the palaces of the Daimios, a certain brave matron murdered a man, and having been allowed to die with all the honours of the *hara-kiri*, a fan was placed upon the tray, and her head was cut off. This may be considered right and proper. If the condemned man appears inclined to be turbulent, the seconds, without showing any sign of alarm, should hurry to his side, and, urging him to get ready, quickly cause him to make all his preparations with speed, and to sit down in his place; the chief second, then drawing his sword, should get ready to strike, and, ordering him to proceed as fast as possible with the ceremony of receiving the tray, should perform his duty without appearing to be afraid.

A certain Prince Katō, having condemned one of his councillors to death, assisted at the ceremony behind a curtain of slips of bamboo. The councillor, whose name was Katayama, was bound, and during that time glared fiercely at the curtain, and showed no signs of fear. The chief second was a man named Jihei, who had always been used to treat Katayama with great respect. So Jihei, sword in hand, said to Katayama, 'Sir, your last moment has arrived: be so good as to turn your cheek so that your head may be straight.' When Katayama heard this, he replied, 'Fellow, you are insolent;' and as he was looking round, Jihei struck the fatal blow. The lord Katō afterwards inquired of Jihei what was the reason of this; and he replied that, as he saw that the prisoner was meditating treason, he determined to kill him at once, and put a stop to this rebellious spirit. This is a pattern for other seconds to bear in mind.

When the head has been struck off, it becomes the duty of the junior second to take it up by the top-knot, and, placing it upon some thick paper laid over the palm of his hand, to carry it for inspection by the witness. This ceremony has been explained above. If the head be bald, he should pierce the left ear with the stiletto carried in the scabbard of his dirk, and so carry it to be identified. He must carry thick paper in the bosom of his dress. Inside the paper he shall place a bag with rice bran and ashes, in order that he may carry the head without being sullied by the blood. When the identification of the head is concluded, the junior second's duty is to place it in a bucket.

If anything should occur to hinder the chief second, the assistant second must take his place. It happened on one occasion that before the execution took place the chief second lost his nerve, yet he cut off the head without any difficulty; but when it came to taking up the head for inspection, his nervousness so far got the better of him as to be extremely inconvenient. This is a thing against which persons acting as seconds have to guard.

As a corollary to the above elaborate statement of the ceremonies proper to be observed at the *hara-kiri*, I may here describe an instance of such an execution which I was sent officially to witness. The condemned man was

Taki Zenzaburō, an officer of the Prince of Bizen, who gave the order to fire upon the foreign settlement at Hiogo in the month of February 1868—an attack to which I have alluded in the preamble to the story of the Eta Maiden and the Hatamoto. Up to that time no foreigner had witnessed such an execution, which was rather looked upon as a traveller's fable.

The ceremony, which was ordered by the Mikado himself, took place at 10:30 at night in the temple of Seifukuji, the head-quarters of the Satsuma troops at Hiogo. A witness was sent from each of the foreign legations. We were seven foreigners in all.

We were conducted to the temple by officers of the Princes of Satsuma and Choshiu. Although the ceremony was to be conducted in the most private manner, the casual remarks which we overheard in the streets, and a crowd lining the principal entrance to the temple, showed that it was a matter of no little interest to the public. The courtyard of the temple presented a most picturesque sight; it was crowded with soldiers standing about in knots round large fires, which threw a dim flickering light over the heavy eaves and quaint gable-ends of the sacred buildings. We were shown into an inner room, where we were to wait until the preparation for the ceremony was completed: in the next room to us were the high Japanese officers. After a long interval, which seemed doubly long from the silence which prevailed, Itō Shunské, the provisional Governor of Hiogo, came and took down our names, and informed us that seven *kenshi*, sheriffs or witnesses, would attend on the part of the Japanese. He and another officer represented the Mikado; two captains of Satsuma's infantry, and two of Choshiu's, with a representative of the Prince of Bizen, the clan of the condemned man, completed the number, which was probably arranged in order to tally with that of the foreigners. Itō Shunské further inquired whether we wished to put any questions to the prisoner. We replied in the negative.

A further delay then ensued, after which we were invited to follow the Japanese witnesses into the *hondo* or main hall of the temple, where the ceremony was to be performed. It was an imposing scene. A large hall with a high roof supported by dark pillars of wood. From the ceiling hung a profusion of those huge gilt lamps and ornaments peculiar to Buddhist temples. In front of the high altar, where the floor, covered with beautiful white mats, is raised some three or four inches from the ground, was laid a rug of scarlet felt. Tall candles placed at regular intervals gave out a dim mysterious light, just sufficient to let all the proceedings be seen. The seven Japanese took their places on the left of the raised floor, the seven foreigners on the right. No other person was present.

After an interval of a few minutes of anxious suspense, Taki Zenzaburō, a stalwart man, thirty-two years of age, with a noble air, walked into the hall attired in his dress of ceremony, with the peculiar hempen-cloth wings which are worn on great occasions. He was accompanied by a *kaishaku* and three officers, who wore the *jimbaori* or war surcoat with gold-tissue facings. The word *kaishaku*, it should be observed, is one to which our word *executioner* is no equivalent term. The office is that of a gentleman: in many cases it is performed by a kinsman or friend of the condemned, and the relation between them is rather that of principal and second than that of victim and executioner. In this instance the *kaishaku* was a pupil of Taki Zenzaburō, and was selected by the friends of the latter from among their own number for his skill in swordsmanship.

With the *kaishaku* on his left hand, Taki Zenzaburō advanced slowly towards the Japanese witnesses, and the two bowed before them, then drawing near to the foreigners they saluted us in the same way, perhaps even with more deference: in each case the salutation was ceremoniously returned. Slowly, and with great dignity, the condemned man mounted on to the raised floor, prostrated himself before the high altar twice, and seated[11] himself on the felt carpet with his back to the high altar, the *kaishaku* crouching on his left-hand side. One of the three attendant officers then came forward, bearing a stand of the kind used in temples for offerings, on which, wrapped in paper, lay the *wakizashi*, the short sword or dirk of the Japanese, nine inches and a half in length, with a point and an edge as sharp as a razor's. This he handed, prostrating himself, to the condemned man, who received it reverently, raising it to his head with both hands, and placed it in front of himself.

After another profound obeisance, Taki Zenzaburō, in a voice which betrayed just so much emotion and hesitation as might be expected from a man who is making a painful confession, but with no sign of either in his face or manner, spoke as follows:

'I, and I alone, unwarrantably gave the order to fire on the foreigners at Kōbé, and again as they tried to escape. For this crime I disembowel myself, and I beg you who are present to do me the honour of witnessing the act.'

Bowing once more, the speaker allowed his upper garments to slip down to his girdle, and remained naked to the waist. Carefully, according to custom, he tucked his sleeves under his knees to prevent himself from falling backwards; for a noble Japanese gentleman should die falling forwards. Deliberately, with a steady hand, he took the dirk that lay before him;

he looked at it wistfully, almost affectionately; for a moment he seemed to collect his thoughts for the last time, and then stabbing himself deeply below the waist on the left-hand side, he drew the dirk slowly across to the right side, and, turning it in the wound, gave a slight cut upwards. During this sickeningly painful operation he never moved a muscle of his face. When he drew out the dirk, he leaned forward and stretched out his neck; an expression of pain for the first time crossed his face, but he uttered no sound. At that moment the *kaishaku*, who, still crouching by his side, had been keenly watching his every movement, sprang to his feet, poised his sword for a second in the air; there was a flash, a heavy, ugly thud, a crashing fall; with one blow the head had been severed from the body.

A dead silence followed, broken only by the hideous noise of the blood throbbing out of the inert heap before us, which but a moment before had been a brave and chivalrous man. It was horrible.

The *kaishaku* made a low bow, wiped his sword with a piece of paper which he had ready for the purpose, and retired from the raised floor; and the stained dirk was solemnly borne away, a bloody proof of the execution.

The two representatives of the Mikado then left their places, and, crossing over to where the foreign witnesses sat, called us to witness that the sentence of death upon Taki Zenzaburō had been faithfully carried out. The ceremony being at an end, we left the temple.

The ceremony, to which the place and the hour gave an additional solemnity, was characterized throughout by that extreme dignity and punctiliousness which are the distinctive marks of the proceedings of Japanese gentlemen of rank; and it is important to note this fact, because it carries with it the conviction that the dead man was indeed the officer who had committed the crime, and no substitute. While profoundly impressed by the terrible scene it was impossible at the same time not to be filled with admiration of the firm and manly bearing of the sufferer, and of the nerve with which the *kaishaku* performed his last duty to his master. Nothing could more strongly show the force of education. The Samurai, or gentle-man of the military class, from his earliest years learns to look upon the *hara-kiri* as a ceremony in which some day he may be called upon to play a part as principal or second. In old-fash-ioned families, which hold to the traditions of ancient chivalry, the child is instructed in the rite and familiarized with the idea as an honourable expiation of crime or blotting out of disgrace. If the hour comes, he is prepared for it, and gravely faces an ordeal which early training has robbed of half its horrors. In what other country in the world does a man learn that the last tribute of affection which he may have to pay to his best friend may be to act as his executioner?

Since I wrote the above, we have heard that, before his entry into the fatal hall, Taki Zenzaburō called round him all those of his own clan who were present, many of whom had carried out his order to fire, and, addressing them in a short speech, acknowledged the heinousness of his crime and the justice of his sentence, and warned them solemnly to avoid any repetition of attacks upon foreigners. They were also ad-dressed by the officers of the Mikado, who urged them to bear no ill-will against us on account of the fate of their fellow-clansman. They declared that they entertained no such feeling.

The opinion has been expressed that it would have been politic for the foreign representatives at the last moment to have interceded for the life of Taki Zenzaburō. The question is believed to have been debated among the representatives themselves. My own belief is that mercy, although it might have produced the desired effect among the more civilised clans, would have been mistaken for weakness and fear by those wilder people who have not yet a personal knowledge of foreigners. The offence—an attack upon the flags and subjects of all the Treaty Powers, which lack of skill, not of will, alone prevented from ending in a universal massacre—was the gravest that has been committed upon foreigners since their residence in Japan. Death was undoubtedly deserved, and the form chosen was in Japanese eyes merciful and yet judicial. The crime might have involved a war and cost hundreds of lives; it was wiped out by one death. I believe that, in the interest of Japan as well as in our own, the course pursued was wise, and it was very satisfactory to me to find that one of the ablest Japanese ministers, with whom I had a discussion upon the subject, was quite of my opinion.

The ceremonies observed at the *hara-kiri* appear to vary slightly in detail in different parts of Japan; but the following memorandum upon the subject of the rite, as it used to be practised at Yedo during the rule of the Tycoon, clearly establishes its judicial character. I translated it from a paper drawn up for me by a Japanese who was able to speak of what he had seen himself. Three different ceremonies are described:

1st. *Ceremonies observed at the 'hara-kiri' of a Hatamoto (petty noble of the Tycoon's court) in prison.*—This is conducted with great secrecy. Six mats are spread in a large courtyard of the prison; an *ometsuké* (officer whose duties appear to consist in the surveillance of other officers), assisted by two other *ometsukés* of the second and third class, acts as *kenshi* (sheriff or witness), and sits in front of the mats. The condemned man, attired in his dress of ceremony, and wearing his wings of hempen cloth, sits in the centre of the mats. At each of the four corners of the mats sits a prison official. Two officers of the Governor of the city act as *kaishaku* (executioners or seconds), and take their place, one on the right hand and the other on the left hand of the condemned. The *kaishaku* on the left side, announcing his name and surname, says, bowing, 'I have the honour to act as *kaishaku* to you; have you any last wishes to confide to mc?' The condemned man thanks him and accepts the offer or not, as the case may be. He then bows to the sheriff, and a wooden dirk nine and a half inches long is placed before him at a distance of three feet, wrapped in paper, and lying on a stand such as is used for offerings in temples. As he reaches forward to take the wooden sword, and stretches out his neck, the *kaishaku* on his left-hand side draws his sword and strikes off his head. The *kaishaku* on the right-hand side takes up the head and shows it to the sheriff. The body is given to the relations of the deceased for burial. His property is confiscated.

2nd. *The ceremonies observed at the 'hara-kiri' of a Daimio's retainer.*—When the retainer of a Daimio is condemned to perform the *hara-kiri*, four mats are placed in the yard of the *yashiki* or palace. The condemned man, dressed in his robes of ceremony and wearing his wings of hempen cloth, sits in the centre. An officer acts as chief witness, with a second witness under him. Two officers, who act as *kaishaku*, are on the right and left of the condemned man; four officers are placed at the corners of the mats. The *kaishaku*, as in the former case, offers to execute the last wishes of the condemned. A dirk nine and a half inches long is placed before him on a stand. In this case the dirk is a real dirk, which the man takes and stabs himself with on the left side, below the navel, drawing it across to the right side. At this moment, when he leans forward in pain, the *kaishaku* on the left-hand side cuts off the head. The *kaishaku* on the right-hand side takes up the head, and shows it to the sheriff. The body is given to the relations for burial. In most cases the property of the deceased is confiscated.

3rd. *Self-immolation of a Daimio on account of disgrace.*—When a Daimio had been guilty of treason or offended against the Tycoon, inasmuch as the family was disgraced, and an apology could neither be offered nor accepted, the offending Daimio was condemned to *hara-kiri.* Calling his councillors around him, he confided to them his last will and testament for transmission to the Tycoon. Then, clothing himself in his court dress, he disembowelled himself, and cut his own throat. His councillors then reported the matter to the Government, and a coroner was sent to investigate it. To him the retainers handed the last will and testament of their lord, and be took it to the Gorōjiu (first council), who transmitted it to the Tycoon. If the offence was heinous, such as would involve the ruin of the whole family, by the clemency of the Tycoon, half the property might be confiscated, and half returned to the heir; if the offence was trivial, the property was inherited intact by the heir, and the family did not suffer.

In all cases where the criminal disembowels himself of his own accord without condemnation and without investigation, inasmuch as he is no longer able to defend himself, the offence is considered as non-proven, and the property is not confiscated. In the year 1869 a motion was brought forward in the Japanese parliament by one Ono Seigorō, clerk of the house, advocating the abolition of the practice of *hara-kiri*. Two hundred members out of a house of 209 voted against the motion, which was supported by only three speakers, six members not voting on either side. In this debate the *seppuku*, or *hara-kiri*, was called 'the very shrine of the Japanese national spirit, and the embodiment in practice of devotion to principle,' 'a great ornament to the empire,' 'a pillar of the constitution,' 'a valuable institution, tending to the honour of the nobles, and based on a compassionate feeling towards the official caste,' 'a pillar of religion and a spur to virtue.' The whole debate (which is well worth reading, and an able translation of which by Mr. Aston has appeared in a recent Blue Book) shows the affection with which the Japanese cling to the traditions of a chivalrous past. It is worthy of notice that the proposer, Ono Seigorō, who on more than one occasion rendered himself conspicuous by introducing motions based upon an admiration of our Western civilization, was murdered not long after this debate took place.

There are many stories on record of extraordinary heroism being displayed in the hara-kiri. The case of a young fellow, only twenty years old, of the Choshiu clan, which was told me the other day by an eye-witness, deserves mention as a marvellous instance of determination. Not content with giving himself the one necessary cut, he slashed himself thrice horizontally and twice vertically. Then he stabbed himself in the throat until the dirk protruded on the other side, with its sharp edge to the front; setting his teeth in one supreme effort, he drove the knife forward with both hands through his throat, and fell dead.

One more story and I have done. During the revolution, when the Tycoon, beaten on every side, fled ignominiously to Yedo, he is said to have determined to fight no more, but to yield everything. A member of his second council went to him and said, 'Sir, the only way for you now to retrieve the honour of the family of Tokugawa is to disembowel yourself; and to prove to you that I am sincere and disinterested in what I say, I am here ready to disembowel myself with you.' The Tycoon flew into a great rage, saying that he would listen to no such nonsense, and left the room. His faithful retainer, to prove his honesty, retired to another part of the castle, and solemnly performed the *hara-kiri*

Notes:
1. Ashikaga, third dynasty of Shoguns, flourished from AD 1336 to 1568. The practice of suicide by disembowelling is of great antiquity. This is the time when the ceremonies attending it were invented.

2. A bâton with a tassel of paper strips, used for giving directions in wartime.

3. See the story of the Forty-seven Rōnin.

4. No Japanese authority that I have been able to consult gives any explanation of this singular name.

5. White, in China and Japan, is the colour of mourning.

6. The principal yashikis (palaces) of the nobles are for the most part immediately round the Shogun's castle, in the enclosure known as the official quarter. Their proximity to the palace forbids their being made the scenes of executions.

7. A Japanese removes his sword on entering a house, retaining only his dirk.

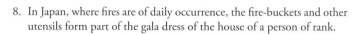

8. In Japan, where fires are of daily occurrence, the fire-buckets and other utensils form part of the gala dress of the house of a person of rank.

9. Oishi Chikara was separated from his father, who was one of the seventeen delivered over to the charge of the Prince of Higo.

10. It should be placed about three feet away from him.

11. Seated himself—that is, in the Japanese fashion, his knees and toes touching the ground, and his body resting resting on his heels. In this position, which is one of respect, he remained until his death.

FUNERAL RITES
(From the 'Sho-Rei Hikki')

On the death of a parent, the mourning clothes worn are made of coarse hempen cloth, and during the whole period of mourning these must be worn night and day. As the burial of his parents is the most important ceremony which a man has to go through during his whole life, when the occasion comes, in order that there be no confusion, he must employ some person to teach him the usual and proper rites. Above all things to be reprehended is the burning of the dead: they should be interred without burning.[1]

The ceremonies to be observed at a funeral should by rights have been learned before there is occasion to put them in practice. If a man have no father or mother, he is sure to have to bury other relations; and so he should not disregard this study. There are some authorities who select lucky days and hours and lucky places for burying the dead, but this is wrong; and when they talk about curses being brought upon posterity by not observing these auspicious seasons and places, they make a great mistake. It is a matter of course that an auspicious day must be chosen so far as avoiding wind and rain is concerned, that men may bury their dead without their minds being distracted; and it is important to choose a fitting cemetery, lest in after-days the tomb should be damaged by rain, or by men walking over it, or by the place being turned into a field, or built upon. When invited to a friend's or neighbour's funeral, a man should avoid putting on smart clothes and dresses of ceremony; and when he follows the coffin, he should not speak in a loud voice to the person next him, for that is very rude; and even should he have occasion to do so, he should avoid entering wine-shops or tea-houses on his return from the funeral.

The list of persons present at a funeral should be written on slips of paper, and firmly bound together. It may be written as any other list, only it must not be written beginning at the right hand, as is usually the case, but from the left hand (as is the case in European books).

On the day of burial, during the funeral service, incense is burned in the temple before the tablet on which is inscribed the name under which the dead person enters salvation.[2] The incense-burners, having washed their hands, one by one, enter the room where the tablet is exposed, and advance half-way up to the tablet, facing it; producing incense wrapped in paper from their bosoms, they hold it in their left hands, and, taking a pinch with the right hand, they place the packet in their left sleeve. If the table on which the tablet is placed be high, the person offering incense half raises himself from his crouching position; if the table be low, he remains crouching to burn the incense, after which he takes three steps backwards, with bows and reverences, and retires six feet, when he again crouches down to watch the incense-burning, and bows to the priests who are sitting in a row with their chief at their head, after which he rises and leaves the room. Up to the time of burning the incense no notice is taken of the priest. At the ceremony of burning incense before the grave, the priests are not saluted. The packet of incense is made of fine paper folded in three, both ways.

Note—The reason why the author of the 'Sho-rei Hikki' has treated so briefly of the funeral ceremonies is probably that these rites, being invariably entrusted to the Buddhist priesthood, vary according to the sect of the latter; and, as there are no less than fifteen sects of Buddhism in Japan, it would be a long matter to enter into the ceremonies practised by each. Should Buddhism be swept out of Japan, as seems likely to be the case, men will probably return to the old rites which obtained before its introduction in the sixth century of our era. What those rites were I have been unable to learn.

Notes:

1. On the subject of burning the dead, see a note to the story of Chōbei of Bandzuin.

2. After death, a person receives a new name. For instance, the famous Prince Tokugawa Iyéyasu entered salvation as Gongen Sama. This name is called *okurina*, or the accompanying name.

Illustration Credits

LIBRARY OF CONGRESS

1 (bottom), 6–7, 11, 14–15 (leaves, man), 16 (top, coins), 18–19 (coins), 23, 26 (top), 27 (right), 28, 29, 33 (hat), 34, 35 (bottom), 38, 39, 40, 42, 43 (top, bottom right), 44, 45, 48, 49, 54 (bottom), 55, 56–57, 58 (coins), 65 (bottom), 66, 68–69 (leaves, birds), 70, 70–71, 71, 74–75 (coins, rice), 76–77, 82 (coins), 83, 84–85, 87, 88 (right), 89 (top, bottom left), 90–91, 92, 95, 96, 96–97, 97 (paper), 99 (left), 102 (top, bottom), 103 (right), 104, 104–105, 111, 112–113, 114, 114–115, 118, 119, 123, 124 (coins), 125, 126, 127, 128, 129, 130–131 (coins), 132, 133, 134–135 (leaves), 137, 138, 139, 140–141 (coins), 142, 145, 148, 152, 154–155, 156–157, 158, 159, 160–161 (coins), 162–163, 164–165, 166, 166–167, 168, 171, 172–173, 183 (top), 184, 188 (bottom), 189, 190, 190, 190–191, 193, 197, 199, 200, 201, 202, 203, 204, 206, 207 (bottle), 208, 209, 210, 210–211, 212, 219, 221, 222 (left), 224, 226–227, 235, 266, 269, 270–271, book case image.

TALES OF OLD JAPAN, MACMILLAN AND CO., 1876

18, 26 (bottom), 35 (top), 41 (bottom), 52, 59, 63, 86, 98 (top), 102 (middle), 110, 113, 116 (bottom), 124, 136, 153, 188 (top), 214

All other graphics and design elements sourced from Depositphotos, Dover Publications, iStockphoto.com, a Private Collection, and the Scott Russo Archive

久盈

大多家の臣として知葉田辰家が旗下の将となり賊軍の急戦を宅間盛盈が軍勢を引揚させんと波良長彦次郎と諸共ふ踏止て殿の戦ふ上方勢の鏑浪打て追来と支戦ふ其有様万夫も更に敵すべうもなしり雄一上方勢五人の久盈が為ふ進薦て見るこゝに上冠者の振舞ふるを鏑閃で突くる碁を石門見返てよっ合て互ふ竜虎の勢の挑ーーーー数刻の戦ふ労果かと合郷八今朝より手に争堪べき竞ふ討死鏑法斯ふ乱小処を石松いろって操出を

鏑ふ胸技と串れ強勇無双の久盈のーー重なーーーけ

一家畧傳史
柳下亭種員記

一勇齋
國丂万画